Dan Glaubke

1003

Out of the Loop

This story is a mix of memoir, fantasy and fiction. It reflects life on the northwest side of Chicago in the forties. World War II is ending, another is just down the road. It takes you out of the Loop, away from the Magnificent Mile, to a typical middle class neighborhood. A place where some boys are in the awkward stage that puberty presents and mirrors life and death happenings along the way to manhood.

This book is a work of fiction.

Actual names and characters are used fictitiously and any resemblance to actual characters is entirely coincidental. Many of the places and locals represented in this book still exist. Quite a few do not. And as a present resident of the northwest side (of Ecuadorian descent) told the author recently, " Neighborhood changing!"

Six Corners Publishing
13447 Wildwood Lane
Huntley, Illinois 60142

Copyright © 2007 by Daniel D. Glaubke
ISBN 0-9789403-0-X
ISBN 978- 0-9789403-0-0
First Six Corners Publishing paperback printing: July, 2007

Printed in the United States of America.

Dedication

For Madeline, Rose, Doc and Elmer,
Bonnadeen,
Marion, Elizabeth,
Dana, Dirk, Drew.
Joe, Kathleen, Jackie,
Kristen, Daniel, Allison, Rebecca, David, Eric
... for all you have blessed me with!

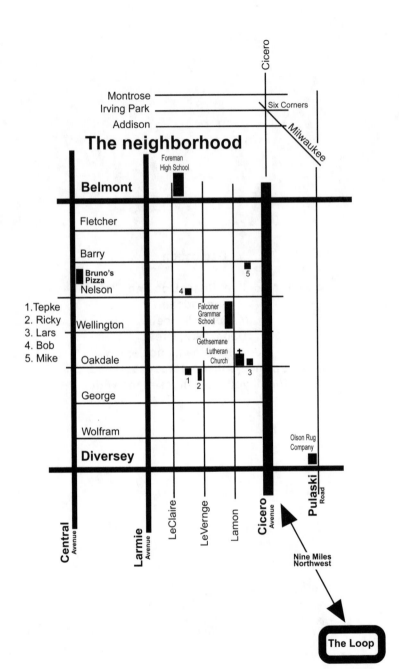

One

Chicago, June 1945

Nine miles northwest of the Loop rain is falling as the big red streetcar rolls down the tracks. There's a slow moving junk truck on the tracks ahead of it. The truck shouldn't be there. So the streetcar's motorman keeps stomping on the clangor, trying to get the truck to move out of his way.

Then it happens.

The old truck's brake lights have flared to a bright, alarming red. The motorman reacts fast, pulls hard on his brake lever, but not soon enough. As "big red" slides, coming to a screeching halt, it bumps the rickety truck and spills some junk on the tracks.

Dan Glaubke

Bob, Lars, Mike, and I have raced out of the George Street prairie on the west side of Cicero and are heading east. We have crossed Cicero Avenue, dodging the streetcar and a number of cars and trucks, as we head for the alley up ahead.

I'm Ben Tepke and at the moment I'm more than a few yards behind the other guys. I came close, real close, to gettin clipped by the junk truck. Didn't stop. Not for a fraction of a second. Just kept on running, laughing, weaving and waving at the truck driver and motorman who are swearing a blue streak.

I caught up to the other guys lickity-split as we headed down the alley behind the Cicero Avenue store fronts, running toward Belmont Avenue and the bank. Been planning this for a week. When the rain came, it seemed like the perfect time to pull it off. Bob, he's the oldest, fifteen, solidly built, stands about five-ten. He has bright blue eyes, blonde hair and is the most serious guy among us. This bank job is his idea and he knows what has to be done. Rain begins to pour now. Thunder roars, lighting flashes and the rain, mixed with the horseshit sittin in the alley, smells like the horses left just minutes ago. Rain does that to horseshit. Renews the stink. We keep on running. When we reach the bank, we spend a couple of minutes catching our breath, looking it over. The tricky part of this caper will be busting out the alley window on the second floor, without drawing anyone's attention. Belmont's a busy street and anyone walking by the alley as we hustle up the telephone pole will know we're up to no good.

It's time. Bob says, "Ben, you stand guard on Belmont and watch for anyone walking. Let us know. Lars and Mike will be right behind me. When we get inside, you follow along. Understand?"

Out of the Loop

I say, "Sure," as I trot to the corner and take a look.

"It's okay guys. Not a soul walkin on either side of the street."

"Let's go!" Bob says as he climbs the fence, grabs the climbing spike on the telephone pole, then pulls himself up for a foothold as he moves up to the window.

Then he takes out his flashlight and breaks the window pane where the latch is located. He yanks the window open. It takes some effort, for the window hasn't been opened in a while. Then in a minute's time all three guys are inside.

I have to wait a couple of minutes. A guy walking his dog in the rain turns the corner on Cicero and is heading my way down Belmont. The dog takes a leak on a fireplug and then, for some unknown reason, the guy turns around and heads the other way. So I hop up the fence, jump on the pole leading to the window and I'm in.

"Ben what took you so long?" says Mike. Mike Bell is fourteen, five-eight, has a slight build, dirty blonde hair, green eyes and is the best looking guy of the bunch. The best athlete, too. Agile.

"Guy with a dog. Dog took a leak. Looked like they was coming my way. Then the guy changed his mind."

Enough light is coming through the window to figure out I'm in a woman's washroom. No urinals. Never been in a women's toilet before. First time for everything, I guess. First and last bank job, that's for sure. Don't think I'll ever be in many women's powder rooms either.

Bob says, "Ben you hang close to Mike, he's got a flash-light, too. Lars you come with me!"

Lars Swanson is fourteen. He isn't short or tall, skinny or fat. Like the rest of us he's still growing, He has curly brown hair, blue eyes and an eagle beak for a nose -- but he's not

3

ugly by any means.

Bob said we couldn't get into too much trouble if we was caught, the bank folded during the crash in 1929. Sounded like fun and, since school is out, what could be more exciting than pulling a bank job?

We ain't hoodlums, don't have a gang, We're just guys. We do crazy things at times, but we're not destructive. Busting into the bank is crazy, breaking the window is destructive but it's just one small pane. We've stalked out of the washroom. We're on a balcony with doors that lead to a number of other rooms and there's a railing that lets you see the whole first floor of the bank below. Not much doing up here so we head for the stairs. We smell like a combination of rain, sweat and wet clothes. When you're livin dangerously, you're supposed to smell a bit rancid. Read that in a book somewhere. On the first floor are counters, teller windows, and stacks of paper piled up in places. The bank must have been beautiful before it crashed. The wood all around is mahogany, dried out now, dull, but I'll bet it was beautiful. My Grampa was a furniture finisher for Marshall Fields before he retired and I'll bet he could make this wood shine again in no time. Not that I'll tell him I was here. He'd shit. And Dad would warm my behind so I couldn't sit if he found out. The teller windows have fancy brass bars. Under a layer of grime, brass glints from an assortment of knobs and fittings. Everything in the place is coated with dust. Our wet duds are picking up dust every time we brush against something.

Mike looks at me and says, "Come on, Ben, let's look for some dough."

He tells me that as he heads for the teller windows.

"You think they left money lying around when they

closed the doors?"

"Who knows? Let's give a look."

"You're nuts!"

As we open the third teller drawer, sure enough Mike finds money. A dime. A mercury dime with a 1921 date. It was in a crack, standing on end. When the bank closed, the dime was probably wedged too tight to get it out. Now sixteen years later the wood has shrunk and the dime is there for the taking.

"How we gonna divvy up the dime, Mike?"

Mike says, "I'm not dividing nothing! Find your own dime, smart ass. It was my idea to look for dough and you thought I was nuts."

"Well, don't spend it all in one place."

We give the bank the once over. Go into the basement where the vault was located. It's open. Fancy. A lot of glass, gears, dials and do-dads. No one wants to go in it. If the door closed you'd die of suffocation in a few minutes. Don't know that for sure, but I'll bet you wouldn't last long. You can see where the deposit boxes should be and they aren't there. Nothing in the vault but dust now.

All-in-all we have spent close to an hour wandering around, shuffling papers, looking in all the nooks and crannies. All the "somethings of value" are long gone, but this does nothing to dull the excitement of being in a place we don't belong.

It's time to get going. The rain is coming down harder than before, and we decide to leave in reverse order. Bob finds some cardboard and with his jackknife cuts a piece to fit the broken window pane. As I climb down the pole, the going is slower than before because the wind is whistling and the rain is coming down in sheets. As I come off the fence a hand grabs me by my collar and pulls me down in the dirt. Then a foot is planted in my back and a gruff voice says, "Stay down there, shut your mouth and don't move."

As Lars comes off the fence, the foot comes off my back, and Lars winds up lying next to me, the foot now resting on his back. Then Mike and Bob are put down the same way.

A cop. One cop. His "black and white" is parked at the head of the alley, but we couldn't see it from the bank window through the downpour.

He says, "You guys stay down and don't move." Then he walks back to his patrol car, pulls out his radio phone and says he needs a paddy wagon. As he starts to answer the question about where to send it, Lars whispers, "He can't chase four of us. Let's get out of here now!"

At that instant, four scared rabbits leap up and start running for their lives. The cop yells, "Stop! Stop or I'll shoot!" But he has nothing to shoot at. Before the words leave his mouth all four of us have turned a corner. I leap through the first fence gate that's open, legs movin like they never moved before, and Lars is right behind me. Bob and Mike race through the parking lot of the hamburger joint next to the bank, heading for the west side of Cicero as fast as they can. Heading for the used car lots there and points west.

Once through the first gangway, Lars goes his way and I go mine. I cut through so many gangways, yards, streets and alleys that I lose count. I wind up on the railroad tracks behind the huge Hall Printing Company. I run all the way down the tracks to Diversey Avenue where I think I'm having a heart attack and will never be able to catch my breath again. After a minute or two, I continue to sprint west, cross Cicero, cut

Out of the Loop

through the Rasmussen gas station and into the alley behind it. Can't run anymore. Got a pain in my side. Walk on, trying to be as inconspicuous as possible. I'm soaked, shivering, feeling like what it must feel like to be buck naked sittin on an iceberg.

Home at last, wondering how the other guys made out, I walk up the back porch steps and open the kitchen door. Mom's at the sink, doing dishes. When she turns her head and sees me she screams, "Stop! Stop right there! What on earth happened to you? Don't you move another step!"

Can't imagine what I look like ... yes I can... and I'm dripping dirty water on the floor. "We was playing games, Mom, and I got dirty, that's all."

"That's all! You're a mess, making a mess of my kitchen! Get out! Get out and go down to the basement door and wait. I'll be down as soon as I wipe up after you! Get out! Now!"

Must have taken Mom a half hour to finally let me in. Seemed like it. I'm still shivering something awful. Before I can say a word she says, "You take every stitch of those dirty clothes off that dirty body of yours right now! Do you hear me?"

I've only taken one step through the basement door, and she's as mad as I've ever seen her. I say, "I'm not gonna get undressed and stand here naked. What are you talking about?"

"Yes, you are young man. You're going to take everything off and put it in the wash tub. Then you're going to march upstairs and take a shower. Then after we have supper, you're going to come down here and get the mud off of those shoes and clean them up. Understand?"

Dan Glaubke

"Awww, Mom, I ..."

"Don't you *Awww Mom me*, get those clothes off now and go!"

Peelin everything off is no easy task, I'll tell you. Stuff is wet, stinks, and Mom's standing there, taking everything from me and tossing it the wash tub. I don't think she's seen me naked in years and I'm trying my best to cover myself as I drop the shorts. *Geez.* Then when I turn to go, she slaps a good one on my backside and says, "Just wait till your father gets home."

The hot shower feels wonderful. As I warm up I wonder how Bob, Mike and Lars are doing. Wonder what lies they are tellin their folks. I've been under that shower a half hour or more when Gramps pounds on the bathroom door and tells me to hurry up.

At supper I don't have a tough time. Dad is working and not home. Mom has calmed down. Gramps is after me. I just keep tellin him we were having a ball in the rain, playing Reliveio and Baby-in-the-Hole. You just get dirty playing those games, and in the rain you get real dirty. No big deal. Gramps knows something is fishy. He always seems to know when I'm not tellin things the way they really happened. Got to clue the other guys about what I said because they'll be comin over. The Tepke bungalow is a regular meeting place for all the guys.

My Dad, Alfred Tepke, saved a long time before he could afford this house. For eight years we lived in the Swanson's two-flat down the street. That's how Lars and I became buddies. We don't have a car so my dad takes a trolley bus and a streetcar to get to work and most of the time he is on his way to work long before I'm awake. He usually comes home late at night, too. He works in a dental laboratory and

8

since the war started he's been making dentures for the Navy.

My Mom was born and raised in Cincinnati, Ohio. Met my Dad on a blind date. She's a strong, no nonsense woman that cares about everything under her roof, keeps the house clean and tidy and loves to cook. I was born two years after my parents married.

Our bungalow has six rooms on the main floor. A living room, dining room, kitchen, two bedrooms and a bathroom. It isn't fancy, just warm, clean and comfortable.

When my Grandpa moved in with us, after Grandma died, Dad fixed up two bedrooms and a bathroom in the attic. That's when I got a room of my own. Before Grandpa moved in, I had to share the second bedroom with my younger sister. But only in the winter time. In the heat of summer, I used to sleep on the screened-in back porch with all six of the big windows open. Except when it was raining. When it rained and poured I'd stay awake for hours at night, looking out those windows. Watching the lighting bolts light up the clouds as they roiled and churned, listening to the thunder rumble and roar.

At that time I still had to share the bathroom with Mom, Dad and my sister Lisa. Now, Gramps and I have only each other to worry about as far as our bathroom goes. We sorta look out for each other, too.

The basement has been fixed up great. Dad did it all himself. There's tile on the concrete floor and the concrete walls are painted. My Dad has hung Currier and Ives prints on the walls. He saves the prints from calendars some salesman gives him every year. He framed the prints himself. The coal furnace area in the back of the basement is partitioned off from the fixed-up front part. My Mom's washing machine with a hand wringer and her ironing board are in the back part of the basement with a couple of wash tubs.

The coal furnace, coal bin and boiler are in the back part of the basement, too. The coal bin is really a big room, big enough to hold a half-ton of coal. My Dad has a big work bench along the wall opposite the furnace. He is really a handy guy when it comes to fixing and making things. He says he gets his handy ways from Gramps. When Grampa hears that it puffs up his chest good.

Our basement is where Bob, Mike, Lars and I hang out a lot. My Dad has made a swell baseball dart game that everyone likes, there's also a ping-pong table that gets a lot of action. On the outer walls of the coal bin there are hand prints in red on a yellow background. The yellow paint starts about waist high and runs up to the ceiling. The lower panels are painted in red. My Dad paints the hands of all invited guests red in some kind of washable paint and then presses the hand to the yellow part of the wall. Then he carefully stencils the name of the visitor under their hand print. It's neat and there are a lot hands in evidence. When I asked Dad what was going to happen when all the yellow space was used up, he told me he would ask guests to drop their pants, paint their butts yellow and back them into the lower red panels of the coal bin walls. I couldn't wait to tell everyone that story!

In a small bookcase in a corner of the basement, my Dad keeps a collection of monthly Coronet magazines. The magazines are about the same size as the Reader's Digest, but unlike the Reader's Digest they contain a photographic spread in the center of the magazine of naked women. The women are beautiful and all you can really see are their knockers, but the guys who aren't playing ping pong ain't complaining. These magazine pages are getting somewhat worn.

Out of the Loop

There is also a cold cellar in the front part of the basement filled with potatoes, onions and other stuff that needs a cool place to be stored. My Dad keeps some booze in the cold cellar, too. No one drinks in the family, the liquor is there for entertaining guests.

Bob, Mike and Lars all live close by. It's how we came to be friends. We all went to the same grammar school that's the glue that has bound us together. That and the neighborhood. Our neighborhood isn't a ghetto area; and it's not a place for the rich and ritzy. It's a blue collar neighborhood where Italians, Polish, Germans, Irish, Swedes and Greeks live together without malice or hostility. There are a lot of churches in the neighborhood. Catholic, Lutheran, Methodist, and Bible Churches.

It's a place where most people are nosy and the gossip flows whatever the occasion. These are good, hard working people that take pride in how their homes look, keep the wood trim painted, and the sidewalks swept. They care about the small lawns in front of their bungalows and plant little vegetable gardens in the back yard along with flowers. When it comes to flowers, Hollyhocks seem to be the all-time favorite and they grow like weeds along the alley fences.

No one that lives here lives on an acre of ground or even a half acre. Bungalows and two-flats are on lots that are 35 feet wide and 125 feet long. If a neighbor sneezes, you tend to say, "God Bless You" because windows are open in the hot and humid days of summer and sound doesn't have far to travel between homes.

Behind most of the bungalows you'll find a garage. Usually it's a one car garage. The garage doors open on the alley. The alleys on the northwest side of Chicago are busy places. You can find horse-drawn garbage wagons, rag-pickers, fruit and vegetable wagons, milkmen, knife sharpeners, and ice wagons moving along in the alleys on any given day. So you have to watch where you step. Alleys are where the cars are washed; where apple basket basketball hoops are nailed to telephone poles, and where kids play catch and tag, among other things.

There are few refrigerators on the northwest side. So people depend on the ice man to help keep food and milk from spoiling. Everyone with an ice box has a common sign to put up in a window at the back of the house that tells the ice man in the alley how many pounds (25, 50, 75, 100) of ice he should bring up to the box. All of us kids love the ice man. We swipe ice chips off the ice wagon all summer long.

Two

"Hi Lars, it's me."

I've waited twenty minutes for the folks on the other end of our party line to get off the telephone. Finally got through and, lucky for me, Lars answered.

"Wasn't that a ball, Ben? How long did it take you to get home? I must have run for twenty minutes before I dared crossing Cicero."

"You alone?"

"Yeah. My Ma's in the basement, washin.

"I'm not. I'll be down after I get done with chores, in about an hour or so. You gonna be home?"

"Yeah, I'll be here, bye."

Dan Glaubke

After taking the garbage out, washing the bathroom floor, bathtub, and sink I'm out the door and on my way to see Lars. Lars lives two blocks away, a five minute walk, but I'm usually running. I'm runnin today, but not even half as fast as I was moving last night on the way home. My shoes are still damp from that episode.

"I dreamed about our bank job, last night. Dreamt I was in jail with guys that murdered someone. I was covered with horseshit and they turned a hose on me. It was awful. Thought about what we did while doing chores. It was great fun 'till that cop put us down. And then runnin away. Can you believe it! If you hadn't said, 'Let's go,' we'd have wound up in jail for sure." I'm grinning and coughing up this mouthful of words as Lars and I are sitting on the stoop of his two-flat.

The rain headed east during the night and today is hot, humid, the sun shining and there's not a cloud in the sky.

"Yeah, don't know what made me say it. I was scared shitless. Thinking I was gonna die when the old man bailed me out of the clink and put his belt on my butt. Was more scared about that than a ride to jail."

"I'll bet that cop won't tell a soul that he let four kids escape. What do you think he told the guy he talked to about sending a paddy wagon?"

"Who knows? I'm just glad we got away clear."

"Have you talked to Bob or Mike?"

"Called them after I talked to you. They both went to Mike's place. Mike carries a key to his basement and they sat down there and dried off for a while before Bob went home. Mike's dad put a shower in the basement so Mike showered and then changed into some clothes from the wash hamper. Said his Gramma didn't know he came in wet and dirty so he didn't

14

have to explain anything. Bob's Mom and Dad were still working when he got home so he didn't have any explaining to do either,"

"What did you tell your folks, Lars?"

"Told 'em we were playing Reliveio in the rain and I fell. That's how I got so dirty."

Laughing, I tell him that I told Mom and Gramps the same story.

"Bob told me that we shouldn't go anywhere near that bank anytime soon. Said that cop might be sore enough to hang around, thinking we might try the same thing again."

"I ain't about to go there, that's for sure!" No sir, I had already thought about staying clear of Belmont and Cicero for awhile.

Then Lars said, "Mike's shootin pool at 20th Century Bowling Alley after lunch. Bob said we should meet there and talk about things."

20th Century Bowling Alley is a big place, on Cicero Avenue, a couple of blocks north of Belmont. As you open the doors to get inside your ears are bombarded by the rumble, rumble, rumble of granite-like balls gliding over the hard varnished floors of twenty bowling lanes. You hear erupting pins flying into padded pits and the mechanical crunch of racks parking those wooden sentinels so they can be pummeled once again. These are sounds that can't be duplicated, for the tempo and melody are as original as a complicated piece of music. In addition to the bowling lanes, racks of balls and spectator seating, there is a pool hall with sixteen tables, a bar and a sit-down counter that serves food.

There are a couple of old guys, alcoholics, that spot pins and it seems that they live here, spending their nights sleeping on the wooden benches back in the locker area. Most of the pin spotters are kids like us. The alley pays three cents a line and if you're lucky enough to get some kids, girls or ladies that don't bowl so good, well, it isn't hard work. But spotting can be dangerous if you get some strong arm "nuts" that are bent on busting the pins, in addition to knocking them down. If you catch a flying pin in the pit you can get a busted arm or leg or have your insides ruptured or maybe even die. These guys blow those pins over like setting off dynamite. Since you can't pick who you spot for, taking on the job ain't for sissies.

When we get to the pool tables, Mike is hard at work. Playing straight pool with some old guy. Looks like the guy must be twenty-five or thirty. Mike's a hustler and at fourteen can usually beat guys a lot older. Makes no difference what the game is, straight pool, eight ball, banks or billiards, he can run a table with the best. He always carries enough cash to gamble with and looks for suckers willing to take him on. Owns his own cue stick. He doesn't always win, but wins more often than not. We like to watch him. When he's not shooting, he talks to us. But his eyes never leave the table. He can talk and methodically think about all the shot possibilities lying on the felt. Mike tells us that he has taken this guy three out of four games and they agreed to play five so he'll be finished shortly. A few minutes later, when Mike banks the last ball in a side pocket, the game is over.

"How much you win?" Asks Bob.

"Won three, lost one, then he wanted to double up. Won the last one, so I made two bucks and he has to pay for the table time."

"Not bad, Mike," I say. "You increased your earnings

to $2.10 in two days."

"Haven't checked, but that dime might be worth more than ten cents."

Bob then says, "We really lucked out yesterday. It's a good thing it was raining, we couldn't have made that break if it had been a day like today. The cop would have nailed one of us."

"It's a good thing Ricky wasn't along," Lars says as he looks at me.

"What do you mean?" I've been forced to have the new kid on the block tag along lately. He's only twelve. He hadn't been invited to go along yesterday and didn't know a thing about it.

Lars answers with, "The kid's a jerk. Talks too much and can't keep a secret. If he had been with us he'd have been the one the cop nailed and he'd have squealed on all of us. For Pete's sake, don't tell him anything about it. It'll be all over the neighborhood in matter of minutes."

"Yeah, he does talk a lot. I'm not gonna tell him anything."

Bob thinks we should get our stories straight, just in case our parents happen to get together and talk about things. Lars explains that he and I told our folks that we had been playing Reliveio and Bob and Mike agree that that's what the party line will be.

*****

"You guys ever ..." Those are the warning words Bob always uses to get our attention.

"You guys ever felt like breaking into a bank?"

"You guys ever felt like biking to Tim-Buk-Tu?"

"You guys ever thought about visiting the stock yards?" Things like that.

Don't know why the rest of us never come up with great ideas like Bob does, but we don't and that's the way it is. So the day after pulling off our first bank job, sittin in the bowling alley pool parlor, Bob says, "You guys ever thought about hitchhiking to Lake Geneva? It's only 90 miles away. They have a great beach, boat rides and game parlors. Bet we could make it up there in two hours or less. Leave early in the morning come back in the afternoon. What do you say?"

"When?" The word comes puffin out of the mouths of Mike, Lars and me, all at the same instant.

"Well, whenever we feel like it. Just have to plan a day we can do it."

"How much money will it take?" Lars and I both want to know.

"I figure if we take the boat ride, eat, swim, play some games, we should be able to get by with two or three dollars. It'll be a lot of fun for a few bucks."

"Well I don't have that right now, but I think I can scrape it up," Lars says, "How about you Ben?"

"I've got some money Gramps and my aunts gave me for graduation. I can lend you a couple of bucks, Lars."

"So can I," Mike says.

"I didn't mean tomorrow," Bob laughs, "I was thinking about the Fourth of July. Maybe we could stay overnight. Sleep on the beach. And there should be a lot of traffic, make it easier to hitch a ride."

Lars comes back with, "Fine with me. That's two weeks from now."

"Fine with me, too!" Says Mike, How about you Ben?"

"Sure, I'm in. Let's do it!"

Three

I graduated from Falconer grammar school a few weeks ago. Wasn't easy, but I made it. I'll be going to Foreman High when school starts in September. Bob and Mike will be sophomores at Foreman when school begins. Lars has transferred to Lane, wants me to go there, too. But that's a streetcar and bus ride away and I can walk to Foreman. And Lane's an all boys school. I'll go to Foreman.

We've been playing softball a lot, the team's made up of a lot a guys in the neighborhood. We're pretty good. Bob gets the games lined up. We play other neighborhood teams. The tough part is getting a kid to umpire. All the guys on both teams chip in a dime a piece, we buy a new 16-inch ball and the winner keeps the ball. We usually play in the Falconer schoolyard. You can have four games going at once at Falconer, the play yard is that big. The school takes up a whole city block.

Dan Glaubke

When we started playing ball there this afternoon, we were the only game going. In the third inning, some crazy pilot in a small plane starts flying overhead, doing stunts. He's doing loops, diving and going in fancy circles. Crazy. We haven't seen a small plane flying overhead in ages. We're still at war with the Japs and planes flying over our neighborhood have been nonexistent. We thought this guy might be practicing for doing those smoke signs in the sky. You know, sky writin. Haven't seen any sky writing since the war began.

All of a sudden that plane goes into a dive. A steep one. Can't see it anymore. We've stopped the game watching it doing its tricks and now we're waiting to see it come up over the horizon once again. But it doesn't happen.

Mike suddenly says, "No! No!" Screams the words that the rest of us are thinking.

Then it comes. The crash. The boom. The explosion. The smoke in the sky off to the southeast of where we're playing. That ends the ball game. We're on our bikes now, racing away from the schoolyard, not knowing where we're going for sure, but going in the direction we saw smoke.

The plane went down somewhere on the east side of Cicero Avenue. Somewhere. Mike, Lars, Bob, Ricky and I are peddling as fast as we can down Cicero, going south. A fire truck passes us up before we hit Diversey. We aren't sittin on the bike seats anymore, we're standing, driving the pedals up and down as fast as we can, passing parked cars without worrying about those whipping past us. We're sucking in air and gasping for breath as we pass Deming, Altgelt and Montana streets and we've timed it right to make the light at Fullerton. Getting closer now. It's past Belden Avenue.

The smoke rising is thick. It's east of us on Palmer. There are fire trucks, police cars, policemen all around trying

Out of the Loop

to keep everyone away. The crowd is huge.

The plane missed hitting an apartment building by just a few feet. It could have killed a lot of people, but it hit a garage across the alley from the apartment building's parking lot. Everyone is asking the same question. What happened to the pilot? What happened is, he's dead. Flew that plane right into a garage and died.

Kaboom!

Makes you think. A short while ago he was breathing, having fun, flying and now he's dead, burned to a crisp. What was he thinking about when he hit that garage? Was it God? His mom and dad? Some girlfriend? Or was he just trying to figure someway to come out of the crash alive?

We talked about that. Bob, Lars, Mike, Ricky and me. We didn't have any answers, just talked. Watched the firemen. The cops. The people standing around. Some of the women were crying. Watched for an hour or so. What was left of the plane and garage was still smoking when we left.

When I got home from the crash I found Dad sitting at the kitchen table, reading the newspaper and having a cup of coffee.

"What are you doing home so early," I asked him.

"Having the lab painted. Sent everyone home early. The paint makes your eyes water, smells really bad. The crew said, it will smell great tomorrow and be dry enough so we can get back to work. What did you do today, Ben?"

I told him all about the plane crash, about how we saw the thing go down, then rode over to Palmer to have a look. Talked about how gruesome it was. How the firemen blocked everyone's view so you couldn't see the pilot being removed from the wreckage. What was left of him. Talked about what people were saying.

21

"Do you think he was thinking about God when he died, Dad?"

"Well, I don't know how to answer that, Ben. We don't know if he believed in God. Maybe. Maybe all he was thinking about was how not to hurt anyone. You said he missed the apartment building by just a few feet. That was probably what he was thinking about."

"Yeah. Do you think it hurt? Hittin and burning?"

"Only for a second or two, not longer than that."

"Yeah, guess you're right."

"Go get cleaned up."

"Sure. Where's Mom?"

"Downstairs washing clothes. If I were you, I wouldn't be playing those games you play in the rain anymore. Your Mom told me about the fit she had when you came home the other day. We don't need you getting sick and that's a good way to get pneumonia."

"Won't be playin in the rain anymore. Learned my lesson."

"Good. Be back down here in twenty minutes and tell Grandpa. Your Mom has made chicken soup and we want to listen to Jack Benny after we eat. Okay?"

As I walk past Grandpa's room, I find him sitting in his easy chair, looking at a magazine.

"Hi Grandpa. Soup's on. We're going to eat in twenty minutes."

When he looks up at me, he says, "Hi, Ben. Are you going to be doing anything special tomorrow?"

"The guys are going down to Lincoln Park zoo."

"Oh, I was wondering if you might like to go downtown with me."

Out of the Loop

"Hey, great. Sure. I don't have to go to the zoo."
"I was planning on leaving around 8:00. Is that okay?"
"Sure thing Grandpa, I'll be ready."

Four

Gramps fell and broke his leg a few years ago, but he still loves to walk in spite of the limp he has. He's only about five-foot-two or three, and the limp gives him a distinctive swagger. You can tell Gramps by his walk a block away and Gramps loves to walk. Loves to talk, too.

He started taking me places before I could walk or talk. Used to push me in a buggy when he and Grandma lived in Cicero. Pushed me up and down 22nd street on Saturdays and Sundays, at times when Mom and Dad had things to do. He's told me that on one Saturday he was pushing the buggy by a Cicero bank as bank robbers came flying out the door with guns in hand. He said they almost knocked the buggy over. I think that might be an exaggeration. He was probably a block or two away from that bank when the crooks came busting out, but it's

25

a good story anyway. Then there was the time when I was five. I don't remember how it happened, but he stopped at Joe Poolala's gas station on Cicero and 24th street to talk. Didn't have a car, but knew Mr. Poolala and liked talkin to him. While he's jawin and wasn't watching, I walked right up to a grease pit and fell in. Gramps says I fell six feet and he doesn't know why I wasn't killed. Wound up full of grease, crying and with a bump on my head. Mom was mad because he didn't watch me close enough, my clothes were a mess and the bump took the good part of a week to go down. Dad thought it was funny. Gramps didn't and kept saying how sorry he was. No one in the family can stay mad at him for very long. He's nice, fun to be around and me fallin in was punishment enough. It's a wonder he didn't have a stroke. That's what Dad said.

He's taken me down to the Lincoln Park Zoo a few times. It seems like he can walk forever without being tired. The last time we went to the Zoo I was seven or eight and before going home he stopped in a tavern for a beer. When he got that frosted mug in front of him he sat me up on the bar and told the bartender to give him an empty shot glass. He dipped the shot glass in the beer, gave it to me and said, "Here's to you, kid!" Of course he told me not to tell Mom or Dad, but you can bet I told everyone else.

We left for the Loop right at 8:00 AM to the minute, after Mom fixed us breakfast. We took the streetcar down to the elevated, rode the elevated to the Merchandise Mart. That's where Gramps used to work. The Marshall Field's furniture repair place is located there. Gramps went right to the employee entrance on the sixth floor and I thought he was going to punch a time card. There are only a couple of guys left that were on the job when he worked there and they were happy to see him. Said he looked good. Asked what he was doing with all his spare time. He talked long enough about what he was doing now to make them nervous. Even though they went on working they were wondering when we would be leaving. I could tell. No one was bothering us, but I sensed these guys were nervous. When we said good bye, they said "Hurry back," but I'm not sure they meant it.

****

Shortly before noon Lars, Mike and Bob get on the Diversey Parkway bus and travel to Lincoln Park. And the Zoo. The day is warm and most of the animals are lolling in the outside enclosures. The aroma of the zoo is heavy in the air. The main event for the guys, the most important thing on the trip agenda, is spending some time with Bushman. Bushman, the 550 pound gorilla sits in a huge enclosure in the gorilla house, and is the biggest attraction the zoo has.

"Look at that beast," Lars says with his mouth hanging open, elbowing his way through a bunch of smaller kids.

Mike can't stand still. He's busy making gorilla sounds in front of the cage. Hopping up and down scratching under his breast with his right hand, doing his best to imitate what he thinks might bring Bushman to attention and get him off his comfortable looking sitting position at the back of the enclosure. Bob's laughing and so are all the kids in the crowd.

Bob says, "They should let you in there to dance with him, Mike. Where did you learn to speak his language?"

Lars is shaking his head. The crowd around the cage doesn't know where to look. Heads are bobbing between Bushman and Mike, Mike and Bushman. Everyone in the place spends a good half hour waiting, and all the while Mike continues to see if he can get Bushman animated. But all the ape does is sit there, stare back at the crowd and pick his nose. So finally the boys move on.

****

"Where are we going from here, Grandpa?" I ask after we leave the Merchandise Mart.

"Down to State and Randolph, want to say hi to a friend of mine."

So we cross the river and walk down Wacker to State, then over to Randolph. There's a newspaper stand on the east side of the street, right across the street from the Marshall Field's department store. Gramps knows Tony, the guy who runs it. The guy really likes Gramps, I can tell. Even knows his name is Frank. Gramps always introduces me as his oldest grandson, Alfred's boy. He doesn't have any other grandsons. I'm it! Even though I don't join in the conversation much, I enjoy listening to Gramps and the newspaper guy. They talk about the war. The Japs. And what's going on in Washington, and if Harry Truman knows what he's doing. Talk about Roosevelt and agree that he stayed in the White House too long. Talked about what it was like on State Street when the war in Europe ended last month, when people were jumping up and down, cars honking, confetti flying.

As they talk, Tony keeps on selling newspapers, making change. He never misses a beat as his customers come and go.

State and Randolph is a wonderful place to stand and watch people, streetcars, automobiles and trucks go by. They say that State and Madison is the busiest street corner in the world, and that's two blocks away. But this is a busy corner, too. Most of the people on the street are all dressed up. There seem to be more women than men walking around. Women with shopping bags full of stuff. Some tugging kids along by the hand. Most of the men have on hats, suits and ties and are carrying briefcases. There are some pretty young women walking along State Street, too. The movie shows are all lit up even though it's daylight. When the war started they turned off all the show lights, but they're back on now. The department stores have a never-ending stream of men, women and children going through their doors. Going in and coming out. Going in and coming out. There are cops on horses clopping along as well as cops standing in the middle of the intersections directing traffic. There are guys on bicycles carrying bags of things, cruising along the gutters, trying to keep out of harm's way and trying not to hit people crossing the street as they peddle along. There must be six streetcars in a row going north and six more going south on State Street. I could stay here all day, watching.

****

When the guys leave the Zoo they begin walking south through the park and come out where the Chicago Historical Society sits. It isn't intentional. Bob says, "Any of you guys been inside this place?"

No one has, so they walk up to the entrance door and go in. It's a free day. If it wasn't, they would have passed up the opportunity.

"It's sort of boring," Lars says after passing a few exhibits. But Bob and Mike are taking things in, reading the exhibit signs, as they move along from hall to hall. Not many people in the place today, probably because the summer weather is so nice.

Dan Glaubke

After climbing the stairs to the second floor, things get a little more lively. They come to small area closed off by a half door barrier. In the room is a bed. It is the bed that Abraham Lincoln died in, or so the sign says. Well, Mike looks around, looks around again and then jumps over the half door and goes over to the bed. He lies down in it with his hands behind his head. He lies there with eyes closed, making loud snoring sounds. Bob and Lars are hysterical. Then, after getting up once again, Mike takes the time to smooth out the bed spread so the bed looks just as it did before, climbs back over the barricade looking like an angel that he isn't. And not a moment too soon. Because all of a sudden a museum guard appears from around a corner. He looks at them and asks, "What's so funny, boys?"

*****

After Gramps says so-long to the newspaper guy, we walk down to Wabash and head south under the El tracks. The Marshall Field's store windows have all kinds of stuff to look at as you walk down the street. Women's clothes, men's clothes, kids clothes, furniture, jewelry, things that cost a lot of money,

When we get about a half a block down the street, a pan handler stops us. Asks Gramps for some money. Gramps looks him up and down and in a rough voice says, "Hey dummy, get on the other side of Wabash, I'm working this side of the street!"

The bum is really startled, his mouth drops open and without another word he cuts right across the street. I try as hard as I can to keep a straight face but it doesn't last long. Gramps pinches my arm and says, "Shush up for a couple minutes." But he takes another step and then he's laughing, too. We're both laughing like crazy. The bum is really hustling, going as fast as he can, going the other way down Wabash.

"How did you think of saying that Grandpa? That was great."

"Well, I used to say it all the time when I was a bum."

That makes me laugh for more than a block, and after Gramps quits chuckling, he tells me, "Now we're going to go up the street to the Palmer House Hotel. We'll cut through their arcade, and go back to State Street. I want to head over to the Berghoff restaurant for lunch. Is that okay with you?"

"Sure, I'm starved!"

The Palmer House arcade has all kinds of fancy shops. The stuff for sale in them costs a lot. It isn't five and dime stuff like you find in Woolworth. This is a fancy hotel. Told Gramps I had to take a leak and he asked if I could hold it 'till we get to the Berghoff.

He said, "If you take a leak here it will cost you a dime or quarter to get a towel to dry your hands. They've got a guy that stands in there all day, turns the water on in the sink, then hands you a towel. You have to tip him."

"I can wait. Don't have a dime."

*****

Bob, Lars and Mike are moving. Moving away from the guard and Bob looks back over his shoulder and says, "Nothing, nothing's funny, just ... well nothing's funny," but he's said it giggling, he can't keep from giggling, thinking about

Mike lying there in that bed where Honest Abe took his last breath.

"Then why are you laughing"

At that moment all three bozos are laughing and moving down the hall quickly to the stairs and toward the exit.

"You boys be quiet and settle down." The guard says. But Bob, Mike and Lars are no longer there to hear it.

They have raced out of the museum door and are still laughing as they head for home.

*****

When Gramps and I get to the Berghoff Restaurant, we head down the stairs into the basement lunchroom and Gramps orders a root beer for me and a beer for himself. He only has a beer once in a great while and this is a good place to have one.

I'm not used to hearing Gramps speak German, but he talks to the waiter like he just got off the boat. He orders sausage and sauerkraut for us to eat. Even though we spent four years fighting the Krauts, the waiter takes a few minutes talking to gramps in German. Most of the people that eat here have a German background. They're not Nazis, they're just good old German Americans. Gramps was only five when his Mom and Dad brought him to the States and the whole family learned to speak English very fast. He told me that. But he also learned German at home so he knows two languages. My Grandma used to speak German, too. But only when she went to the German Meat Market or when she swore at Gramps when they were playing pinochle. Gramps doesn't have a whisper of an accent, neither did my Grandma.

When we finished eating we leave the restaurant and walk back to Wabash Avenue where there's a tobacco store that Gramps likes. Knows the guy behind the counter because he's been coming here for years. He buys a couple of cigars, some pipe and chewing tobacco. This place smells heavenly. Smells sweet. Not like candy or cake, it has a smell all of it's own. Just like a tavern has a smell all of its own when the beer is flowing. Can't describe how this place smells other than tell you it smells delicious. Don't understand how tobacco can smell so good but taste so terrible. Us guys have tried smokin cigarettes but smokin makes me sick. Bob's the only one that doesn't turn green. After leaving the tobacco store, Gramps and I head for home. We go home a different way, ride the Milwaukee Avenue streetcar to Diversey and transfer. Takes a little longer but there is more to see.

*****

"What made you do it Mike?"

"Couldn't resist."

"If that guard had been two seconds earlier we'd be headin for jail again." Lars says as he punches Mike's arm.

"Nah, we'd have run like hell and out the door before he could think about what to do next."

Then they laugh some more. Laugh and talk about the day, Bushman, and Lincoln's bed and things past, things to think about doing. It was a good day.

Five

Can you imagine four guys standing on the running board of a coupe? Hanging on for dear life as the guy driving is traveling down the road at sixty miles an hour, passing trucks and cars like it's a life or death matter to get somewhere? I can't, but that's what's happening. Shit and two makes eight, why did we do it?

We left home at seven thirty this morning. The four of us. Bob, Mike Lars and me. Going to Lake Geneva on the Fourth of July. We left wearing bathing suits under our pants, a towel under our arms and money in our pockets. Thinking about swimming, lying on the beach, taking a boat ride, having fun. We took the Cicero Avenue streetcar to the end of the line, started walking north and figured we would split up two and two, because hitching a ride would be easier than four guys thumbing together. But we had only walked a short way and hadn't split as yet when this guy driving a pickup stopped, asked where we were going and would we like a lift. He said he was on his way to Milwaukee. So Bob got in the cab and Mike, Lars and I climbed into the truck bed in back and off we went. When he dropped us off at Route 50 in Wisconsin, the road to Lake Geneva, Bob was in fine shape, but Mike, Lars and me were stiff and sore from bouncing around in back. There was no way to get comfortable in the back of that pickup and we rode over a mess of potholes that rattled our bones.

As we crossed the road at the drop off point, we started heading west, walking together. Before we had taken twenty steps, a coupe pulled over and stopped ahead of us. It's a guy and his girl friend. They saw us get out of the pickup and thought we might be going to Lake Geneva. They asked if we would like a ride.

Lars says, "Sure, we'd like a ride, but you don't have room for four guys."

The girl says, "Sure we do."

And her boyfriend follows with, "Toss your towels in the trunk, hop up on the boards, and hang on!"

We look at each other, thinking; four guys mulling over the situation and no one wants to be the guy that chickens out. Mike finally shrugs and says, "Sure, lets go!"

Now we're hanging on for dear life. Hangin by our fingernails. Holding on through the open windows, with hair blowing, eyes watering, trying hard to keep our rear ends puckered because we don't have a change of underwear or another pair of pants. From where we hooked up with this character, Lake Geneva is about 35 miles due west. Hair-raising miles glued to the running boards, traveling on a two lane road, wondering if the guy driving knows where his brakes are located. I hope he won't hit those brakes hard because we'll be flying the rest of the way if he does. It takes us less than thirty-five minutes to go those 35 miles. When the guy pulls into a parking place in the center of town, I get off the running board, looking for the guardian angel that got us here safely. We tell the guy "thanks" but don't say much else until he and his girl are too far away to hear.

"I don't want to do that again," I say.

"Why?" Mike and Bob ask me.

Lars says, "That was a lot of fun!"

I don't know where these guys are coming from, I think they want me to believe that it was fun but it was terrifying. With a capital "T".

"Wonder if they'd take us back to Chicago, when they're ready to go back?" Bob is smiling when he says it.

"I'll go back and ask," Lars says.

But Bob tells him, "That won't work. We'd have to plan on being here when they were ready to go and we don't want to do that."

I'm thinking it might be a good idea to take a Greyhound bus home.

It's a hot day. A hot, hot day and between baking on the beach and swimming in the wonderful cool water, we are having a great time. I don't burn. I get a tan pretty quick in the summer time, but Bob burns easily and has to take care. Mike has to be careful, too. But Lars is a lot like me. Tans easily and we're both getting a lot darker today.

Lake Geneva is huge. I've never been here before. It isn't as big as Lake Michigan, but it's big. And beautiful. And the water's clean and cool and invigorating. Mike checked out the time that the mail boat leaves. It makes a round trip, stops at a few places to drop off and pick up mail. It's a double decker and it will be the most expensive thing we do here, but I'm looking forward to it. I've never been on a boat.

There are a lot of girls on the beach. Most are older than I am. I like looking at the girls in their bathing suits. Some like to be looked at, too, you can tell. None of us have had a date as yet. We used to play games with the neighbor hood girls, but we've given that up. Too much other stuff to do, but we all like looking at girls, that's for sure.

After the wonderful boat ride, the day's fun is finished and by 5:30 we head for home. We don't have as much luck hitchhiking south as we did when we came this morning. Lars and I walked ahead of Bob and Mike when we left for home. After a few minutes, they were picked up, and passed us by with Mike making funny faces at us out of the car window, sitting in the back seat of a Buick. It took Lars and me a half hour to land our first ride, the second one was faster but they left us off just a few miles past the place they picked us up. Then it was the better part of an hour before we landed another ride. A guy in a semi with a load of furniture to take to St. Louis stops. He is traveling south and the first leg of his journey is taking him down the road to Cicero Avenue. He's a nice guy that tells us how much fun driving a truck is. Tells us how beautiful the country is. He drives all the way to California and east to New York at times. He says that sittin in the seat of a semi is the best place in the world to see the sights. You're up high and can see a lot more than when you're sittin in car.

He talks to us all the way to Oakdale Avenue and it makes the trip go by pretty fast.

Out of the Loop

Bob and Mike made it home by 8:30. Takes Lars and me until 11:30. I don't care. It's not every day you get a chance to ride in a semi. Other than the boat ride, the ride in the semi is the best part of the day.

When we were on the boat, Bob said, "You guys feel like going to Riverview before school starts?"

Have no problem with that idea. All it takes is a few bucks and you've got a day to remember forever. I can remember the first time, the last time and all the other times I've been there. Well, I've only been there five times, but I remember every one. There's no place on earth quite like Riverview.

Six

On August 15th the Japs surrendered. The war they started on December 7th in '41 ended after Old Harry Truman dropped a couple atomic bombs on Japan. Atomic bombs are awesome. The papers say we killed 80,000 in the town of Hiroshima and another 70,000 in a town called Nagasaki. After what they did to us at Pearl Harbor, and not to mention the torturing and beheading of our captured soldiers and flyers, it serves them right. Everyone says there won't be any more wars to fight. Rationing is over except for sugar. Things are good.

We've talked about it and we're on our way. Riding the Belmont streetcar down to Western, going to Riverview. We'll be there at high noon. I'm excited and so are Bob, Mike, and Lars, for there isn't an amusement park anywhere in the world like Riverview.

I've saved some money for today and Gramps slipped me

a buck. If I run out of money I'll just leave on my own and go home.

Riverview turnstiles are on Western. We have enough free entry passes among us so we don't have to pay anything to get inside. They say the park sits on 74 acres. I don't know how big an acre is, but Riverview is big. Lane Tech high school, where Lars goes, rubs up against Riverview on the north side. The Chicago River is the west boundary.

There must be five roller coasters in the park, but the Bobs is the best. The Bobs has eleven cars, open cars, no cage over your head. For openers, you start out creeping along, climbing a track mountain to the first crest, where an overhead sign says, "Don't stand up." You can't anyway 'cause you're clamped in the car by a metal bar. When you top out on that crest, you immediately start down, almost straight down. That first drop must be half a city block if its an inch. Then you hit a curve at the bottom and its a thrill that beats all thrills. The only drawback about the Bobs is that the ride doesn't last long enough.

Thinking about what we do first, Bob says, "Let's go straight to the Bobs."

" You bet and let's get five tickets first thing," Lars says. "It's early enough that they won't make us get out and stand in line again after a ride is finished. They'll let us keep going till the tickets run out."

"Even if they don't, let's go for five." I say.

As he starts trotting ahead, Mike says, "I'm in, come on, lets go!"

All four of us run down the parkway to the Bobs ticket booth, and after buying five ride tickets each, we take our time, maneuver around so we can get the first car. I'm riding with Bob up front, Lars and Mike are right behind us. With the safety

Out of the Loop

bar closed and locked over our lap, we brace our feet against the front of the car and wait out the slow steady climb. Then at the top of the incline we throw our arms in the air as we whip down that first steep run, hearing the wheels on the track make a rumbling sound that is like no other sound on earth. And we scream. We yell our socks off, as gravity bites our butt at the bottom of the hill and we roar through the first tight curve, going at least ninety miles an hour. Seems like ninety. Has to be. *AAAAAAhhhhhhhhh!* Everybody's screaming! Then our coaster cars head into a series of curves, dips, ups and downs and into another nail biting incline and drop, to yell and scream about. What a ride!

We ride the Bobs five times without giving up our car before we move on to other things. My stomach is still going up and down as we walk away and head deeper into the park. There are so many things to do it's not hard to figure out how to spend your money. We decide to get a bottle of pop first and sit on a park bench for a while, watched the people walking by. We're not really watching people, we've got our eyes zeroing in on the passing girls. Even though it's early, there are a lot of girls in the park. Most of them are with guys, or family. Well, they're good to look at anyway.

Mike wants to wreck some bottles and win a prize.

"That booth is up ahead of us," says Lars. "Lets move on."

Before we hit the skill game we come to the electric bumper cars. We each get a car and try to knock each other around. You bump, get your neck snapped, bump and aim at anyone trying to get in your way while trying to avoid being bumped and smacked by other cars. A long trolley pole connects your car to the electric power on the ceiling. It makes a ton of sparks as you move, turn, bump and grind all around the ride area. Bob loves to maneuver his car out of the way of everyone, then sneak up behind you and whack you good.

After driving the bumper cars, we come to the booth where you toss baseballs at metal milk bottles sitting on a table. They're stacked four on the bottom, three on top of the four, then two and one on top. You get three baseballs and try to knock all the bottles off the table. If you do, you win a prize. Mike throws real well, has a hard enough fastball to knock the bottles down. He spent twenty cents on two turns but can't get the last bottle off the table, so he doesn't get a prize and is pissed.

"Damn, I'm gonna try one more," Mike says.

"Save your dough, Mike," I tell him. " They put more lead in the bottom bottles. Makes 'em impossible to knock off the table." I don't know if they do or not, but it sounds good enough to get Mike's attention, and we move off once again.

The Merry-Go-Round is a popular spot for little kids and old folks. It's big and beautiful, makes a lot of music as it circles around, but it's not a thing we are interested in. The Mill on the Floss is fine for guys with dates that want a dark place to neck. The ride gives you plenty of time for that as the boat goes through a couple of long dark tunnels. I'm not about to ride that thing with a guy. Don't want anyone to think I'm some fruit.

After watching Mike bust the bottles, we stop for a foot-long hot dog with mustard, onions and piccalilli and buy another drink. It sets me back fifteen cents but the big weiner tastes wonderful and fills the hole in my stomach. The Hades fun house is up ahead, but I like Aladdin's Castle better, and that's on the other side of the park. All the guys like Aladdin's Castle better so we'll go through it when we get over there. We spend some time at the penny arcade trying to beat the machines and buying a few baseball cards but quit before we lose too much. I don't save baseball cards, but Mike does and he has quite a collection.

Now here's another ride we can't pass by. It's the Shoot the Chutes. You get in a wide boat, ride through a tunnel, and stop in an elevator that will lift you up in the tall boat tower. When you get to the top of the tower, the guy in the back that steers the boat slips you into "the chute" and you ride it down into a lagoon. It's a steep ride and you're moving fast when you hit the water. More often than not you wind up soaked, because when you hit the lagoon, water sprays everywhere. If the guy steering is good, you really get soaked! It isn't as scary as the Bobs, but its fun. One ride is enough because it takes a good while to dry off afterwards.

When we come up to the freak show, we hang around long enough to see a few of the freaks. The sword swallower and rubber man are on the side show stage, and if you pay your dime you can see the tattooed lady, the world's tallest man, a huge fat lady, and a midget they say is the world's smallest man. I'd like to see that tattooed lady. Wonder if her knockers are tattooed. If they are, what kind of tattoos would be on 'em? When they tell everyone the show will start soon, we move off.

When we pass the cages with the black guys waiting to be dunked, Mike can't pass up the opportunity. He loves throwin baseballs. Here you have to hit the circular target with the ball. The target is only about a foot-and-a-half wide and it's about twenty-five to thirty feet away. If you hit the target, the black guy who has been taunting you gets dunked in a tank of water. The target is the trigger that releases the seat the guy is sitting on, and down he goes in the water with a big splash.

Mike buys three baseballs. There are three tanks with three sitting ducks and Mike hits all three targets. Unbelievable! He's dunked all three guys and since there are no girls or women around at the moment, the guys swear at Mike and tell him how lucky he's been with a little blue language mingled in. We're all laughing and Mike is showing off his muscles. Flexing those apple-sized biceps for the wet trio who would like to have a turn dunking him. Unbelievable! He couldn't hit all three targets again if he tried all day and he knows it! We will all be tellin this story to our folks tonight, that's for sure!

My money is running low. I want to buy some caramel corn for my sister and folks before we go, and I've got enough change left for Aladdin's Castle and maybe one more ride, but that's it.

We've been riding the Flying Turns, The Whip, and went back for one more fling on the Bobs. Couldn't resist. While we're standing outside the Castle with the huge Aladdin face on it, we catch sight of a babe with her skirt up over her head. There's a spot in the castle where people walk by an air jet that someone controls. The guy with the controls can send an air stream up under a girls skirt and people like us can see it happen on the parkway. When it happened, the girl tries like crazy to get her skirt down, but by the time she does everyone knows the color of her underpants. The girl gets a big round of applause, cheers and whistles from the guys watching. She's wearing pretty white frilly panties and is really blushing.

We decide to pass on Aladdin today, but Bob and Mike want to go back to ride the Flying Turns. Lars and I have something else in mind. We buy tickets for the parachute ride. Neither Lars nor I have ever gone on the parachutes before. The tower here goes up what seems like a half a mile or so, but it can't be that high. It is high, really high. Two people can ride on one of the four parachutes at a time and all four separate parachutes are operating today. The guys that run the ride strap us in and up we go. Up, up and away we go. The ride up is slow going, but when you hit the top you come down real fast. That's the fun part. Going up is okay too, because you can see all over the park and then some. Today, Lars and I get more for our money than we paid for. Something happens at the top of the ride. We've stopped. We're stuck. We're not going down. The view is fantastic, you can see all the way to Lake Michigan. I've never been able to see so far in all my life.

It's windy up here. We're blowing in the breeze, and both Lars and I are getting nervous.

"What's going on?" Lars asks.

"How the hell should I know," I yell, " I got no one to ask but you and you don't know shit from Shineola!"

It seems like we've been sitting up here doing nothing but observing the scenery for an hour, but it can't be that long. We peek over the side. Not both at once, one at a time. The seat tips a little when we do that. We're strapped in but it's scary when you tip the seat. There's a whole bunch of people just standing around down there on the parkway looking up. Pointing. Pointing at us. Watching us blow in the wind. Man, I have to take a leak, bad. Can't do it up here.

Out of the blue, well out on a ladder on the tower itself, a guy with a long pole appears. I'd guess he's a good fifteen to twenty feet away and still climbing higher. We yell at him for help.

He smiles, shrugs his shoulders and says, "I'll try and pull your seat over here with this pole so you can climb down the tower with me, okay?"

"Like hell!" Lars and I say the same thing at the same time and we ain't smiling.

Then the guy is gone. Gone for about minute and all of a sudden we get a jolt and we're flying down the wireway toward earth. We land where we're supposed to land, bouncing up and down like a yo-yo for more than a few seconds before we finally stop. That guy climbing the tower triggered the chute using that pole. That's how we got back down to earth.

The ride guy that unstrapped our seat says, "Sorry guys, the trigger mechanism got stuck, happens every so often."

I've got to take a leak so bad I don't wait for any more talk, but Lars is swearing and giving the guy hell. I know he about shit in his pants while we were hanging up there and now he's yelling he wants his money back. It's not going to happen. But the guy offers to let Lars go up again, free. Lars sure isn't about to take him up on his offer today or any time soon.

With my kidneys relieved and the shaking gone from my knees, I tell Lars I've had enough for one day. I'm going to get a box of caramel corn and head for home.

Bob and Mike were part of the crowd watching us swing up yonder and they really laughed it up when they saw that it was Lars and me that had been stuck.

Thinking back, the view was fantastic, but we couldn't enjoy it when we were trapped and couldn't do one thing about it. We all left then and there, and the two bozos that thought Lars and I were a lot of fun to watch, laughed practically all the way home. All in all, Lars and I were stuck for only twenty minutes, but it seemed like a lifetime.

As far as I'm concerned, the Bobs is the best. Nothing else in Riverview beats a ride on the Bobs.

****

The next big thing happening in my life is high school. I know I'm not one of the very smart kids and I'm not excited about going. The fact is, I'm a little scared. A letter came in the mail yesterday that says I'm supposed to go to room 206 on the

Out of the Loop

first day at 7:30AM. That will be where I get my class assignments, a timetable and the room numbers I'll be having class in. I'll get my locker assignment and a locker partner, too.

Seven

I awoke at 5:30 this morning. Nervous. Don't know why. Bob and Mike have told me that high school is no big deal. Well, maybe not for them, but it's my first day and I wish it was over. Those guys don't have to be at school at 7:30. They have their schedules and know where they're going. Dad made me some sandwiches before he went to work so I'm set for lunch. Mom made me eat breakfast and Gramps -- as usual -- told me what I should be doing today as he sat next to me at the kitchen table. He said do this, don't do that, make sure you listen, take notes and be polite. Don't forget your new notebook, don't be late, etcetera, etcetera, etcetera.

I, of course, said, " Yes, Grandpa."

I didn't tell him that Mom and Dad gave me the same rigmarole a couple of times in the past few days. Listening to him, Mom just smiled and went about reading the newspaper, sipping her coffee. For a guy that hasn't had a lot of schooling Gramps sure gives a lot of advice.

Foreman High School is located on Belmont Avenue just six short blocks north of where I 'm sittin, so I don't have to hurry. I can leave the house at 7:15 and be where I have to go. Before I left the house, Mom made me comb my hair again and then off I went.

Found room 206 easy enough. Went in the door and up the stairs to the second floor and here I am with room full of strange faces. I do know a couple of girls and guys, but most are strangers.

This high-school is a lot bigger building than our grammar school. It has an indoor swimming pool; big, separate girls and boys gyms, and unbelievable chaos between classes. When the class change bell goes off there is a mad rush to get to your locker and to the next class. It seems that any form of politeness or human kindness has never existed.

Right across the street from the southwest entrance of the school there's a hangout called the Sugar Bowl. Inside the Sugar Bowl there is a smoky haze from morning until the place shuts down after all the lunch periods end. You can't smoke in school, but you sure can in the Sugar Bowl. You can get a sandwich here and the greasiest, most delectable french fries ever created. A bag of fries costs fifteen cents. The fries come in a little brown bag that is covered with a grease stain the moment the fries are loaded.

Girls don't usually go near the Sugar Bowl, but they get guys to buy them fries there. You gotta watch out how you eat the fries or your shirt or pants can wind up with a grease spot that no one on earth can get out.

If you don't like the food the Foreman lunchroom is

serving, or what the Sugar Bowl has to offer, there is an old man with a three-wheel pushcart that sits on Belmont about a block away from school with the best hot dogs you ever tasted. Or you can hustle down to the hamburger joint at Belmont and Cicero next to the bank. Not having a lot of money, I'm happy eating the sandwiches that Dad makes. My locker partner brings his lunch, too. Our locker smells like cross between a Polish delicatessen and a German sausage factory. My locker partner is Leo Bonkowski. He calls me "Tepski." He says he wants his locker partner to be a brother "Polock." Not a Kraut.

Most of my grammar school friends are here at Foreman plus a whole new group of kids from other neighborhood schools in the area. It takes time to get acquainted with the faces, but we have the time.

I've got algebra, English, mechanical drawing, science, work shop, study hall, and gym. In the middle of the morning we have to go to our "home room" where attendance is taken and the teacher lets us know if there is anything special going on.

Every other week we have swimming. Guys are forced to go swimming bare ass. When girls swim they wear something called a tank suit. Guys can take ROTC and get out of gym, but I'd rather have gym. Bob is in ROTC, wears a uniform and marches. I'm not sure what the ROTC stands for. Someone said, "Rotten Old Tin Cans." I'll never tell Bob that joke.

As the days go by, the school routine becomes familiar and I'm getting comfortable with where I have to be and how to get there. It was in my second week that I showed up for a Wednesday class on Tuesday which, when I figured out my mistake, made me late for the class I was scheduled for. Embarrassing! Having to come through a door when everyone else is seated, and with the teacher taking attendance, isn't something you want to happen. Then having to admit that I thought it was Wednesday on Tuesday really made me look like a jerk and I knew everyone in the whole school would be hearing about it when the bell rang once again. All the teacher said was, "Don't let it happen again," but there were more than a few snickers floating in the air when I took my seat.

I'm getting the hang of algebra. No one at home can help me with it, but I think I'll be okay. English is a lot harder for me. Science is so-so, don't like it much, but the teacher is trying to make it interesting.

In work shop, I'm learning how to use electric tools, drills, saws, chisels, the wood lathe, and wood planes. We've learned about sandpaper and emery cloth. The day we learned how to sharpen chisels, one slid off the edge of the bench I was working at. A kid reached out to catch it without thinking, and the damn thing went right through the palm of his hand. That ended work-shop for the day. They took the kid to the hospital and he had to have an operation to tie nerves together and fix a broken bone. He said they aren't sure about whether his fingers are going to work right when the cast comes off. That was one sharp chisel and one dumb move. Teacher said it was instinct that made him do it. Could have happened to anyone.

I just finished making a hammer in shop. It was our first project. It isn't a big hammer, not a claw hammer, just a little metal job, a chunk of metal that I drilled a hole in and then cut a metal rod that fits the hole for a handle. Not much of a hammer but I got an "E" for a mark. I don't think I'm cut out for mechanical things, fixing things, making things. But, I signed up for this, so I have to try.

Out of the Loop

I'm making wooden book ends for my second shop project. If they turn out okay, I'll give them to Dad for Christmas.

There are all kinds of girls in Foreman high, a lot more than we had in grammar school. The girls tend to have cliques. The pretty ones are in one group, the brainy ones in another, the athletic girls in another. There are a lot of plain looking girls that tend to have a friend or two but don't seem to hang out in a group. Most of the popular, pretty girls that are juniors and seniors have boy friends. The guys they're dating are the personality guys, the guys that primp a lot and have the ability to talk, laugh at the right time and, in general, are good students or jocks.

It seems like athletic girls like athletic guys. Brainy girls like the smart guys. Some girls like every guy and get a reputation for it pretty quick. I like looking at girls but haven't had a date. Ever. None of us guys have had a date yet.

Mike and I have the same lunch period and since he brings his lunch, we usually grab something to drink in the lunch room and then, if it isn't raining, go outside and sit on the school steps. It's starting to get colder, but until our breath freezes we'll probably go on eating outside. We don't like being cooped up inside the school.

"You got your eye on any girl. Someone you'd like to date?" I ask Mike through a mouth full of ham, cheese and rye bread.

"No. Where would you take a girl on a date without a car?"

"Hell, you could take a streetcar downtown, go to a show, the Field Museum, or your favorite place. You know, the Historical Society. You could take her to bed."

He laughs and says, "Who told you about that. No, I don't think a streetcar date would be much fun. I'd have to talk and I'm not good talking to girls."

Dan Glaubke

Mike Bell's Mom died when he was just a couple of years old. His grandmother's been in charge of raising him. It seems as though Mike always has a slight smile on his face. You get the idea that he knows what's going on in your head even if you don't. He's in great shape and a good all-round athlete. Not a powerful guy, but he has a lot of natural ability. Really coordinated. Mike's dad is a mechanic at a service garage and it won't be long before Mike has that car he needs for dating. He told me his Dad was going to give him one when he gets a driver's licence and that's less than a year away. His dad works for a Chevy dealer.

"What's there to talk about? Girls usually do most of the talking anyway. If you go to a movie, there's nothing to talk about."

"Well, I had my eye on Nancy Someski before she started dating that brainy guy Ken, but haven't been interested in anyone other than that. You going to ask someone for a date?"

"Almost asked a girl in my algebra class, but chickened out. I was going to ask her to go to a movie. Then I found out she lives down near Hanson Park. No movies around there and I'd be spending carfare in addition to the movie show and popcorn. That would be one expensive date. Too expensive! So I'm not thinking about it any more."

" Why don't you get yourself a job? Then you could afford it."

"If I could shoot pool like you, I'd have the dough. I'd be in the pool parlor all the time."

"You're crazy. I don't always win. I'm broke right now. Got suckered last week and lost big. Can't play again until I get my allowance. You get an allowance?"

"No. When I need money I have to ask. Then I have tell what it's for. If the folks don't like my answer, no dough."

"Oh. I get two bucks a week. That's for helping my Grandma,

going to the store, keeping my room clean."

" I help my Mom all the time, do chores, do what I'm told, but I don't get an allowance. If pop cost more than a nickel, I'd die of thirst."

"Get a job."

"I'm thinking about it."

The Fall season has arrived and the colorful leaves from the big elm trees on our parkway are leaving their branches. Oakdale Avenue has huge elm trees on both sides of the street from Laramie all the way down to Cicero Avenue. In summer, if you stand in the middle of the street, it looks like you are under a never ending canopy, a beautiful arch of green. Now, tons of leaves are falling every day. There are leaves on the lawn, parkway, in the gutters and on the roof of all the homes and in the street.

Raking leaves is one of my chores. It isn't hard work, and I love burning them in the gutter on the street. The smell is fantastic. My clothes reek of leaf smoke and I think it's great. Everyone burns their leaves in the Fall. If you could see Chicago from up above, it would probably look like Chicago is burning down again when Fall rolls around.

On a Saturday, just after Halloweeen, Dad hauls the ladder out of the garage and tells me it's gutter cleaning time once again. The ladder reaches all the way to the roof. Dad holds it while I take a bucket up and pull the leaves out. I've got Dad's canvas work gloves on. The dead gutter leaves, wet from rain and saturated with dirt and grime, soak the gloves in a minute and my fingers feel like icicles. Then it's up and down the ladder, moving from spot to spot to clear the leaves. On this job, my problem is always trying to reach more than it's practical to reach, and more than once I've almost fallen off the ladder. My Dad is always bawlin me out when he sees me stretch too far. He can feel the pull on the ladder. But it's a drag goin up, comin down, goin up, comin down, over and over. Moving the ladder just a couple of feet at a time. I've got better things to do. Don't know what they are, but anything is better than this.

"We could save a lot of time if we cut that tree down Dad."

" Hey, be happy there's no tree behind the house."

"Doesn't matter much. The side gutters are filled all the way back there."

"Just be careful and watch what you're doing. Less talk and little more elbow grease and we'll be done in no time. After we're through here, you have to go grocery shopping with your mother."

"The sun will be settin before we're through."

"No, it won't. Keep on moving."

It was past noon when we finished up, and I'm tired. Must have gone up and down that ladder a hundred and fifty times. Took ten minutes to get feeling back in my hands again when I washed them in hot water. The only saving grace, Mom fixed me hot chocolate to drink while we had lunch. Then, after doing the dishes, she was ready for grocery shopping. I wasn't ready, but off we went anyway.

Grocery shopping with Mom isn't hard work but it's time consuming. Mom pulls her grocery cart, and I'm dragging my wagon along. Today we're going up to Laramie and Wellington, just a couple of blocks away. It's where we go most of the time because it is closer to home than ambling down to Cicero Avenue. There's a drug store, meat market, bakery, grocery store, cleaners and bar on the block. Cicero Avenue has all of these stores, too, and there's a tailor and Woolworth's five and ten cent store down that way if you need them. That's where we shopped when we

Out of the Loop

lived in the Swanson's two-flat. Doesn't make any difference which way we go, Mom knows all the store people and they know her.

Our pantry is small and the ice box doesn't hold a lot so Mom's purchases are somewhat meager. She has a list and she takes a lot of time deciding what to buy. The cash money for groceries comes out of the grocery envelope in her purse and dimes, nickels and pennies are held in a substantial change purse. Mom is a frugal person and she looks at all the prices of things very closely before she spends a nickel.

These trips don't go quickly for a number of reasons. First of all, Mom doesn't walk very fast and at each store and stop we make we run into neighbors. The tradesmen also like to find out what is happening in the Tepke family. There's still talk going on about rationing, ration stamps, and the war, even though the war is over and the only thing rationed now is sugar. Some things are still hard to come by. I don't run into many of my friends on these trips so I always fidget and want to keep moving, but it doesn't happen. You have to be friendly and talk, talk, talk.

As the days grow colder, shorter, I'm looking forward to the holidays. I'm looking forward to the "no school" days of Thanksgiving, Christmas and the New Year.

****

"Come on get up, get moving! Thanksgiving day is here," Gramps says, as he pulls my covers off.

"Cut it out, Grandpa."

Even if I didn't know it was Thanksgiving day, I'd know. I'm awake and I can smell the tantalizing aromas coming from the kitchen. The heavenly smell of a turkey cooking has tiptoed up the stairs to my attic room and has my mouth watering and stomach aching to be fed.

"I'm out of the bathroom. Get in there and shower up, Ben. Your Dad and Mom will be looking for your help."

"Don't you worry, Grandpa. I'll be down in the kitchen in five minutes."

Thanksgiving is one of our best family holidays. Dad doesn't go to work. Mom got up in the middle of the night and started cooking. She's a great cook and enjoys feeding those she loves. We always have a turkey with stuffing and cranberries and a bottomless pot of mashed potatoes and gravy and sweet potatoes and carrots and corn and pickles and olives and everyone eats way too much. Everyone fills a plate, eats and fills a plate again and eats way too much. Mom's made a pumpkin pie and an apple pie for dessert. She baked them yesterday. After taking care of the turkey and all the rest of the stuff, she'll be beating sugar into heavy cream so we'll have whipped cream on the pumpkin pie.

As always, the feast is wonderful and the plates of food keep passing from one end of the table to the other. No one passes up dessert, even though we have eaten way too much. In addition to Mom, Dad, Lisa, Gramps and me, Uncle Ed and Aunt Lily are with us. They're always invited.

My Aunt Pearl and Uncle Rawland, cousins Cherie and Susan would be with us, too, but they live in Wyoming and it's a bit far to come. Uncle Rawland loves to hunt. Last winter, with the war going on, they drove to our house with antelope and deer meat that Uncle Rawland shot close to where they live. The meat was frozen. Wrapped real good. Dad stored it on the kitchen windowsill outside because it was below freezing for days on end. We needed no red ration meat stamps for the meat Uncle Rawland brought. It tasted great, too!

Don't know where Uncle Rawland got the gasoline to travel to Illinois, but he got here and back okay. He doesn't own a car, just a pickup truck. He built a rear-end shelter for the pickup, where the deer, antelope meat and my cousins Cherie and Susan rode to Chicago. Even though my cousins were bundled up in heavy clothes and wrapped in blankets they nearly froze to death, because there's just no way to heat up that shelter. My cousin Susan's pet goldfish did freeze. They couldn't find anyone to leave the goldfish with back in Wyoming and had to bring it along. So it was good-bye goldfish anyway.

It must have taken us at least two-and-a-half whole hours to finish eating Mom's Thanksgiving dinner and finish talking. With everyone full and the plates empty, Mom, Lisa and Aunt Lily took the dishes away. It will take them a good hour to wash and dry all the pots, pans, dishes and silverware that we used. Probably longer than that.

While they're busy doing dishes, Dad, Gramps and Uncle Ed talk about the war, about city politics, about Truman, the political climate in Washington, about things in general. Gramps has an opinion on everything. Uncle Ed likes talking, too. Dad never talks much, but when he does, Gramps and Uncle Ed listen. More often than not, there's nothing to argue about when he puts a period on his last sentence. Dad's a smart man, reads and thinks a lot. I like to listen to the conversation for a while, but a lot of what they talk about goes over my head. It's nice to be included anyway even though I don't have a thing to say.

****

The guys I run around with aren't dating girls as yet. We have fun with the neighborhood girls, but we don't date. We go

Dan Glaubke

to any girl's home when invited and talk, play games, drink their pop and eat their pretzels and popcorn, but we just haven't started the dating or the "going steady" thing. I'm still awkward around girls, but the girls seem to like me okay.

Ricky is starting to get very friendly with a girl named Gail and she's a year older and in my class at school. Gail seems to like the attention and doesn't seem to care that he's younger. Bob has got his eyes on Nita, but he hasn't made a move to date her yet. He says he isn't interested, but we can tell he is. She's real pretty and has a great smile and laugh. A lot of guys are interested in Nita but she doesn't seem interested in anyone in particular. I don't think her mom and dad are too keen on her dating because they think she's too young to get involved with boys. Maybe when she gets to high school next year, she'll start going out. Mike, Lars and I are having a good time just looking.

Eight

The guys aren't getting together as much now that winter has set in. There's always homework to do during the week so we usually get together on Saturday afternoons after our chores are finished. The Tepke basement is a favorite spot to gather.

I leave the back-door of the basement unlocked so the guys don't have to bother knocking and get held up talking to Gramps for twenty minutes upstairs. Mom doesn't appreciate anyone tracking snow through the kitchen either, but she always treats the guys like family. More often than not, she'll bring hot chocolate down, or pop popcorn or dole out cookies when we're all here.

Dan Glaubke

We play doubles and singles in ping-pong, and give the baseball dart game a lot of action. And, of course, we read a lot of Coronet magazines. Well, maybe not read, but test the ol' eye sight on those gorgeous girls in the center spreads.

"Hey! Here's a new one. Look at the knockers!" Lars says as he turns the magazine around for all to see.

"Those are gorgeous," says Ricky, "wouldn't it be fun to play with those!"

"You're dreaming, Ricky and you'll be playin with yourself for years before you ever touch anything that resembles those. If ever." Mike tells him.

"Oh yeah. I've already had my hands on bare knockers and I'll bet none of you guys have done it."

"That's bullshit, if I ever heard it," says Lars "Where did that happen, Ricky?"

"My cousin Rosemary. She's three years older than me. My aunt and uncle came over and the folks went out with them to a restaurant. Left us at home to eat sandwiches. We played checkers and parcheesi. While we were playing she noticed that my eyes kept wandering down to her sweater. She's got real big tits and her sweater was too small for her. It kept pullin up. She kept pulling it down, and I thought those knockers were going to pop right through.

I kept lookin at 'em, not paying much attention to anything else. Then out of the blue she asked if I'd like see what they looked like. I said. 'What are you talking about?' She put her hands under them and said, 'These!' Just like that. So, I said yeah, she smiled, took her time and pulled her sweater over her head, then undid her brassiere and sat there drinking pop while I gawked at those big pink nipples staring back at me. Man, I had a hard-on a cat couldn't scratch and she just sat there looking at me, drinking her rootbeer. Then she crossed her arms under 'em. They looked like they was sittin on a pillow, pointing straight at me. I was probably drooling when she said, 'Would you like to touch them?' What do you think I said? It wasn't, 'hell no.' I got up from my chair, walked in back of her, put my arms around her, lifted them up, rubbed my fingers over her nipples. Never felt anything that soft and nice. Ever.

She never said a word, just let me do it. Then we heard the front door open. I said, 'shit' and she ran to bathroom with her sweater and brassiere under her arm. My folks came in and found me sittin at the kitchen table. Alone. When Rosemary came out of the bathroom, she smiled, said, 'So long,' and went home with her Mom and Dad. Wish she didn't live so far south. We only see each other two or three times a year. Can't wait for the next time she visits."

Was this some bullshit story? Didn't sound like it, although Ricky does tend to color things and exaggerate. Ricky Dewpinski. He's short, skinny, stands about five-five and looks like he weighs ninety-eight pounds. He's a sun bleached blonde with blue eyes, pug nose, crooked teeth and has a scar that runs from his right-eye down to the corner of his mouth. He fell on a sharp corner of a glass coffee table when he was small and it really did some damage. The scar makes him look tough, but he's about as tough as a banana. He likes hanging around with us older guys. His Dad sells insurance and he has a lot of Poles in the neighborhood he can sell to because he speaks fluent Polish. His mom's a Swede.

*****

We play dart baseball, then ping-pong, flip coins to

see who will be first up. Mike and Bob are it. They will play three games, the winner will take on Lars and then I get to play. Ricky is playing last. As the game goes on, Mike beats Bob, then Lars and it's my turn on the table. Mike and I are both pretty good and I win the first game, twenty-one to nineteen. Don't know at what point it happened, but somewhere along the line Ricky sneaked into the cold cellar. We didn't notice he was missing. We didn't know until he came out the cold cellar door half polluted.

"What in the hell have you been up to, Ricky?" I'm really ticked off and ready to beat his head in.

"I was thirsty" He's smiling and his words come back at me slurred, in a whiskey haze, followed by hiccups.

"You bastard, who told you about the booze and what am I gonna tell my Dad?"

"Hey, he's got a lot of bottles in there, he woon mish any of it."

"Damn it to hell, if he finds out we're into his stuff we won't be coming down here anymore, that's for sure. You jerk! What are ya gonna do now, you're sloshed?"

Mike says, "Let's put the little shit in a snow drift and sober him up."

And Lars follows up with, "Let's do it!"

Before Ricky can move or slur another word we've got him by his arms and legs. All four of us carry him out the basement door and into the yard where we bury him in snow. He's kicking and trying to get loose. It's cold. I take a handful of the white stuff and try to shove it down his throat. "You want something to drink you jerk, have some snow. I just hope some cat has pissed on it!" I'm livid, in a rage and screaming at him. Then Ricky starts to cry and all the struggling he did

Out of the Loop

as we dragged him through the basement and into the yard subsides. As we back off, he starts tossing his cookies. Everyone jumps to get out of the way. He's sick. Heaving. Crying. Nose is running. He's a mess.

At that moment the kitchen door opens and my Mom steps out on the porch.

She says, "What's the matter with Ricky? What are you doing out in the snow without your jackets on?

Well, there's nothing much I can do but tell the truth.

"Ricky got into the cold cellar when we weren't watching, Mom. He drank some whiskey and he's sick."

"Oh for heaven's sake. Bring him up here in the house right now." Mike, Bob, Lars, did any of you have anything to drink or is it just Ricky? Don't lie! Tell me."

Everyone says , "No Ma'am" in unison.

I look at Mom and say, "Ricky did it all on his own, you can ask him, he'll tell you, Mom!"

She says, "You boys get your jackets on and go home. Ben, get Ricky into the kitchen. Now!"

Mom cleaned Ricky up. Had him sit in a chair until he felt a little better. She made toast with butter, cinnamon and sugar on it and floated the toast in a bowl of warm milk. That's what mom makes when anyone has an upset stomach. Then she washed the vomit off Ricky's shirt and put it in the oven to dry for a while. It didn't take long for Ricky to start feeling better. Mom scolded him and said she hoped he learned a lesson.

He said, "Yes, Mrs. Tepke and I'm sorry."

"Well, put your shirt on, get your jacket on and go home!"

When he left, Mom called Mrs. Dewpinski and told her what had happened.

67

Mrs. Dewpinski thanked Mom for calling and hung up.

I learned later that Mr. Dewpinski used a strap on Ricky's butt and really let him have it. He said two hits were for stealing, two for getting drunk, two for embarrassing his mother, two for embarrassing his dad, two more so he wouldn't forget the first eight.

Ricky said, "I thought the old man was going to have a heart attack and I'd never be able to sit on my ass again, ever."

Has he learned a lesson from all the commotion he caused? I'm not so sure. He told me he has had a swig or two from his dad's booze cabinet, but never drank enough to get him drunk before. Never enough to make his old man suspicious.

Dad gave me hell for letting Ricky get into the booze and then just a few days later, he put a lock on the cold cellar door. If I ever hear Ricky bragging about getting drunk on my dad's booze, I'll clobber him good, and I can do it.

*****

Christmas is coming. I've been looking for some way to make money because I'd like to get Mom and Lisa and Gramps something. Dad is going to get the book ends that I made in shop class. I've stained the wood a Maple color and I think he will like them. He reads a lot and he'll find a place to park the book ends, I'm sure.

A new Jewel store has opened up on Diversey and Larmie. It is a big store with three or four aisles of canned goods and boxed items, a produce area, meat counter and they have all kinds of soap and other stuff to sell, too. It's a self-service store. They have carts you push around as you look for the things you need. No one takes the food off the shelf and hands it you, you do it yourself. When you fill the cart you take it to a checker who bags everything, tells you what you owe and takes your money. I walk over to the Jewel after school on Monday.

"Is the guy that runs the place around?" I ask a woman standing at a cash register?

"That would be Mr. Bush. He does run the place but he prefers to be called the store manager."

"Yeah. Sure. Do you know where he is?"

"He is probably in the storeroom at the back of the store. He's tall, has black hair, wears glasses. He has an apron on and he's wearing a red shirt. Just wait by the storeroom door. He should be out momentarily."

I only have to wait a minute. Mr. Bush comes through the storeroom door hauling a skid of can goods behind him. Walking faster than most people walk empty handed. I follow him down the center aisle until he stops, ripes open a box and begins putting cans on a shelf.

"Excuse me, Mr. Bush. I need to make some money and was wondering if you might need some help around here?"

He looks up at me from where he's kneeling and says, "Well, yes. I've been thinking about it, as a matter of fact. The store is getting real busy and Norm, our guy in charge of produce asked me if he could have some part time help. What's your name?"

"Ben. Ben Tepke."

I follow him to the produce area, where a short, stocky guy is busy putting potatoes in a bin. Mr. Bush taps him on the shoulder and says "Norm, I think I have the answer to your need for a helper. This is Ben Tepke. Ben this is Norm Jablonski, our produce manager."

Dan Glaubke

Mr. Jablonski gives me the once over and says, "He looks big enough to handle it." Then he says to me, "What time can you get here from school? On Saturday we work from 7:30 to 6:00. You get two fifteen minute breaks on Saturday and a half hour for lunch. Your job will be keeping the place neat and the bins filled. Weeding out the rotten stuff, not that we have a lot of rotten stuff, but we don't want customers to find any. Understand? You won't last five minutes if I see you loafing. When did you say you can get here after school?

"I can be here by 3:30."

"Fine! See you tomorrow." Then Mr. Jablonski turns and keeps on stacking potatoes.

As I turned to leave, Mr. Bush pats me on the back and says, "Don't be nervous Ben, you'll do fine. If you don't understand something ask. See you tomorrow."

Mr. Jablonski gives me a work out, keeps me busy every minute I'm there. I'm not an extra hand, I'm extra hands, feet, back, arms and legs. They don't need my head as long I can understand what I'm supposed to do. I fill bins, watch out for spoiled or rotten things -- potatoes and onions really stink when they're rotten, found that out. I sweep the section, I lug bushels, bags, sacks, crates, boxes and unload them, put the contents as neatly as I can in place. I polish apples, wipe off oranges and keep my backside, hands and feet moving. I bend, stoop, reach, twist, maneuver around the produce displays, always watching out for shoppers who never see me because they are intent on getting the freshest, firmest, juiciest, what-ever to take home to the family.

As the weeks head toward Christmas I collect my pay envelopes and park the money in my dresser drawer and try to figure out what I should get Mom, Lisa and Gramps for Christ-

Out of the Loop

mas. I may be too weak to shop when I find a day to do it.

The only time I see Mike or Bob is in the corridors of school. Don't see Lars or Ricky, but I've talked to Lars on the phone a few times. He's working, too. But he's got a soft job compared to mine. He works in a lawyer's office, cleaning out waste paper baskets, sweeping and mopping the floors. He has to clean toilets, too, but I'd bet that's better than dealing with rotten potatoes and onions. The lawyers knock off work around four' o clock and he's done by five-thirty or six.

With Christmas just two days away, I have a disagreement with Mr. Jablonski. The guy is really sadistic, says I'm not moving fast enough and I'm getting in the way of customers. He's leaning on me to move faster and when I do and I bump into a lady's cart. But I say " Excuse me Ma'am" as polite as possible. Jablonski saw me and reamed me out good in front of customers and everyone so I shrugged off the apron and quit.

Walked right out of the store. I thought I was doing good, but the guy's impossible and I'm not the only one that thinks so. I've heard a few of the regular guys complain about him too, but they have families to feed and have to take it. I had to lie to Gramps and say they didn't need me anymore and let me go.

Being free and with the stores open late up at six corners, I've got time to buy some presents now. Six corners is where Cicero, Milwaukee Avenue and Irving Park Road cross one another. There's a fancy Sears Roebuck store there and the Klee Brothers store where my Dad buys me clothes and shoes.

I head for Sears because it's as good a place as any to buy Mom's gift. I don't know what I'm doing, but I buy a pair of earrings for her. Then I head for Woolworth's five and ten cent store and buy a book for Lisa. Then I find a smoke shop and I buy chewing tobacco for Gramps. The guy behind the counter doesn't want to sell me the tobacco, but when I tell him its for my Grandpa, he gives in. I'm not sure he believes me. I kept telling him I hate tobacco and a chew isn't anything I want to do!

Gramps likes to go for a walk with a chew in his mouth from time to time, so I think I've got the right idea for his present. The tobacco doesn't cost me much, but it's the idea that counts, right? Right!

Since I was working, Dad, Gramps and Lisa went to the Christmas tree lot this year without me. Lisa carried extra branches home to fill in the bare spots and Gramps had the light end of the tree to carry. Dad said it took longer to buy and get the tree home this year because I wasn't around. What do you think Mom said after Dad put up the Christmas tree? She said, "That's the best Christmas tree we've ever had!" She's said that every year that I can remember.

Christmas day we opened our gifts before Aunt Lily and Uncle Ed arrived to help us celebrate. Mom liked her earrings, or so she said. I really think she did. My sister liked the book and everything else she got. Dad and Gramps gave the book ends I made a real once over and gave me some compliments on the job I did. Gramps thanked me for the tobacco and he gave me a couple bucks. Dad and Mom gave me a crystal radio set. It's neat. It has ear phones and a crystal that you play with to get various radio stations. It's the kind of radio everyone had before the radios got sophisticated like they are today.

As the day went on, it got colder and colder outside. Mom cooked a ham, made sweet potatoes, a salad and baked beans. Dad carved the ham on the dining room table. He's a neat guy and doesn't make a mess at all. I don't know how he does it. For dessert, Mom made my favorite -- a chocolate angel food cake with chocolate frosting. Melts in your mouth. It takes her a half

Out of the Loop

day to make.

When Uncle Ed and Aunt Lily get ready to go home, it's so cold out that their car won't start. Rather than run down the battery, my uncle comes back in the house and hands the car keys to me. He says, "Ben, when the weather warms up, drive the car over to the apartment, okay?"

I answered, "Okay, Uncle Ed, you bet!" Then my aunt and uncle leave to take the streetcar home. I'm not about to say no to driving the car, and it doesn't seem to bother anyone that I have never driven anything but an orange crate scooter. I know you have to shift by putting in the clutch and letting the clutch out. I've watched it done when riding with Uncle Ed. You move the gear shift with the clutch in when going from neutral to first, to second and then third. Nothing happens until the clutch is let out. I think I can drive the old car. We'll see.

Nine

1946

    We celebrate the New Year by staying up until midnight and listening to the radio. Gramps didn't wait around but the rest of us did. I don't know what the big deal is, it seems like just another day to me. Day after tomorrow, I'll be back in school, back in the grind. I'm not doing well. I've got to knuckle down and make some grades or I'll be flunking and have to take some courses over. That would be devastating. Ricky would have a great time with that. I'd never hear the end of it. Shit and two make eight, if that happens I'll leave home. Maybe Aunt Pearl will take me in. Maybe I can get a job as a cowboy out in Wyoming. No, that won't happen. I've got to study harder. I fool around too much. I'm listening to the radio too much. Got nobody to blame but myself.

Dan Glaubke

My high school days are pretty standard with fifty-five minutes per period and five minutes between classes. Gym and swim classes actually run about a half an hour of work because you are either suiting up or taking things off, getting down to nothing for a shower before you hit the pool. You can tell which girls have come from a swimming class because they wear "Babushkas" on their heads to hide the wet curls. You literally have to run if you have a class on one side of the building and the next one is on the opposite side. It's hectic, but that's how it is. I'll bet it hasn't changed since the school was built. Next semester, when I'm a sophomore, I'm going to drop shop and mechanical drawing. I'm doing okay in workshop but barely getting by in mechanical drawing. Can't keep a pencil sharp and I'm not neat. Some guys draw those lines so sharp and clean it looks like they've been printed on the paper. I'll be taking Spanish and something else in place of the two.

Bob, Lars, Mike and Ricky all go to the same church. Gethsemane Lutheran on the corner of Lamon and Oakdale. It's a just a few doors down from where Lars lives. The guys have told me that they have a club for kids called Luther League and said it would be okay for me come to club meetings.

"Come on Ben," Lars says, " One prayer ain't gonna kill you. They just start the meeting with a prayer and from then on it's pretty much fun and games."

"I'm thinking about it. You don't dance at these things do you?"

"Ben. Where you been? You don't dance in church. We never dance. It's sacrilegious. I don't know why. But it is or we'd be doing it. If we danced then you'd come along, right?"

" No! I don't dance. I've never danced. I've watched them dance in movies but it's not something I can do. You know how to dance?"

"Sure. All you do is put your arms around the girl, move your feet and try not to step on her shoes. It helps if you can move your feet to match the music beat. You're going to have to learn if you want to be invited back to the parties girls throw. Wednesday's the next meeting, you gonna come?

"What time?"

"It starts at 7:00 and ends by 9:00. Ricky will be there. You can walk over with him.

"Thought you said it was for high-school kids."

"It is, but we let the eighth graders in because they're almost in high-school."

"Okay. I'll be there."

I put on a nice sweater, combed my hair, nicked myself shaving. Not bad, but it's in the cleft of my chin. I hate it when that happens. The septic pencil stopped the blood shed but you can see where the cut is. Doesn't make any difference. Been shaving since eighth grade, when my teacher told me not to come back to school unless I got rid of the peach fuzz. Can't help it, Dad and Gramps have heavy beards, too. Why am I nervous? It's just a meeting, for Pete's sake. I don't have to impress anyone.

"Ben. Ben, Ricky's here. He says you're going to a church meeting." Mom is at the bottom of the stairs. I've got the bathroom door wide open and she can see me primping in the mirror. "Is that right, you're going to church?"

"Yes, Ma'am. Going to a Gethsemane Luther League meeting. It's some kind of club for kids and you don't have to be a Lutheran to go. Lars invited me."

"Oh. Well, Ricky's waiting so you better hurry up."

"I'm ready, Mom. I'll be right down.

As we're walking to Gethsemane, Ricky asks, "You

didn't tell your folks you're going to church?"

"It ain't church. It's in a church but it's not church. No, I forgot to tell them. I'll tell them all about it when I get home."

The meeting starts off with prayer. The guy praying is a youth minister and I thought the prayer would never end. He prayed for the sick and dying kids in Africa and Ethiopia, the kids in Germany, Japan, Poland, England, Canada and America that lost their dads in the war. Prayed for the sick and dying. Prayed, prayed, prayed. Everyone had their heads down, eyes closed, hands folded but me. I peeked. Then I lowered my head, closed my eyes and folded my hands like the rest of them. I'm not against prayer. I've prayed. Mostly when I need something fixed and I'm in dire straights. Never thought about it much until now. But you know, a lot of those prayers were answered. At least I didn't suffer all of the dire consequences I thought were about to happen. I haven't prayed like Jerry, that minister just prayed up there, haven't prayed much for other folks. I know there's a God in heaven and I've tried reading Dad's Bible, but it's hard for me to understand. A lot of the words I can't pronounce and I don't know what a lot of 'em mean.

The kids here are nice. I've known some of the neighborhood girls a long time. I know Dixie, Nita, Doris, Connie, Maddy, Gail, Joan. There are a few I don't know. Haven't met some of the guys before either. I've seen Gordy, Henry and Harry in the halls at school. They're juniors like Bob. After the prayer, I had to stand while Lars told everyone who I was. Didn't have to say anything and I was grateful for that. Then they showed a movie.

Tried to show a movie. The film kept jittering every few feet and going off the reel. Then they would turn on the lights and get the film back on the reel and try again. Then the take-up reel quit and there was film all over the floor. Bob tried to fix the thing, but he said it was shot. Bob's the most mechanically inclined guy of our group, able to tackle about any problem involving nuts and bolts. He knows how to fix bikes, tie knots, wire things and is getting familiar with his dad's car. He already knows how to change oil, tires and spark plugs. But the movie camera was beyond his help. The meeting ended up with cake and cookies and Kool-Aide and everyone standing around talking. I talked to Bob, Mike and Lars. Ricky was off in a corner talking to Gail. Before we all left for home, Ricky told me was going to walk Gail home. I walked home alone and it was snowing again.

About two new inches of snow had landed on the ground while we were at the church. I shoveled when I got home so Dad wouldn't have to do it when he got home from work. Can't really take credit for the idea of shoveling. When I came in the back door and before I could take my shoes off, Gramps let me know the snow shovel was warm and waiting for me. So I shoveled.

*****

As the days continue to come and go, Spring suddenly elbows winter out of its way on the northwest side. Rain washes the grit and grime of it off the streets, down the gutters, and out of the alleys. The neighborhood smells better. Looks better. Rain awakens the trees. Color comes back to the branches as leaves start forming. Yesterday's frozen ground yields to spikes of green as tulips think they've waited long enough to make an entrance. It won't be long before the spikes are crowned with pleasing red and yellow blossoms that are truly a sight for winter-sore eyes. The neighborhood is busy shrugging off the doldrums, people are smiling, friendly and looking forward to better days ahead.

I'm looking forward to delivering a car to my Uncle Ed's

door. I announce to Mom and Gramps that I'm going to drive Uncle Ed's car over to his apartment on Saturday. Gramps says,

"Fine, I'm coming with you!"

"That's okay with me, but you don't have to." I'm really happy he's going to ride with me because if I have any trouble, he'll know what to do.

I take the car keys out to the car and sure enough it starts on the first try. It's a prewar Dodge, starting to rust a bit, but the motor runs, the gears work, and I'm anxious to drive it.

On Saturday morning early, Gramps and I go out to the car and I start her up.

Gramps says, "What's the first thing you're going to do?"

"Well, I'm going to put in the clutch, work the gear shift into first gear, then leave out the clutch see what happens."

There isn't another car parked on our block, so if I'm careful I'm sure I can make it to the end of the street without a problem. The first thing that Gramps does is to roll down his window.   Then as I go through the motions and leave the clutch out, the car leaps about three feet and the engine dies.

"Okay," says Gramps, "what are you going to do different next time?"

"I'm gonna leave the clutch out a little slower and step on the gas pedal a little lighter."

"Okay. Do it!"

This time when I leave the clutch out the car only jumps and jerks a little bit and we start moving. Then the clutch goes in again, I shift to second and we're still moving and by the end of the block, I'm shifting into third gear.

At this point, Gramps has his head out of the window yelling, " Hey, hey! Get out of the way. We're coming through!"

Can't laugh. Can't tell him to stop it. I'm too busy anyway.

Out of the Loop

I do know where the brake is, but I'm not about to tell him to stop. In the blocks ahead, if anyone is close to crossing the street, Gramps is yelling and waving his arms. I must be traveling all of fifteen miles an hour and if Gramps wanted to hold a conversation with anyone walking down the street, it would be no problem at all.

I've been thinking about this trip for a long time. From the moment that Uncle Ed handed me the keys. I've thought out every move, every street to take, how to get where I'm going without making a left-hand turn. That's because I don't want to kill the motor in the middle of an intersection. If I do, I'm sure I'll pee in my pants and be so nervous and upset Gramps will have to call a tow truck to get me out of trouble. Or some guy that's driving too fast will clobber us. Then the cops will come and I don't have a driver's licence and they'll toss me jail. Uncle Ed will have to fix the other guy's car and the Dodge too, because the insurance company will say I shouldn't have been driving. No sir, I ain't makin any left turns today.

Driving somewhere without making a left is pretty simple. All you have to do really is to go another block, through the intersection, then turn right at the next block, and right again, and again, so that all you are doing is making right turns. Gramps didn't get it at first. When I explained what I was doing, he thought it was a pretty smart idea. Especially since I have killed the motor more than once since we started.

Uncle Ed and Aunt Lily's apartment is on the south side of Fullerton Avenue, about three blocks west of Pulaski Road. That means I have to cross Cicero Avenue, Diversey and Fullerton. These are busy streets and I don't think I want to drive on them. I do get across Cicero and Diversey okay and I keep traveling on the side streets. My shifting is starting to get smoother, and

Gramps is not hollering out the window as much. I actually went three solid blocks without killing the motor or making the car jump and jerk when I shifted. Then after crossing Fullerton, taking a right turn down an alley and coming back to Fullerton, I finally have the Dodge going east and I'm only about two blocks from Uncle Ed's door. We arrived safe and sound. No dents or scratches. I think Gramp's blood pressure will be much better when we take the streetcar home, but that drive was sure a lot of fun and I did it. I did it!

When I return the car keys, Uncle Ed asks, "Did you have any trouble Benny?"

Gramps cuts in and says, "He drove that thing like a truck driver who has been driving for years."

Wow, that really puffed up my chest.

Going home on the streetcar I said, " Thanks a lot for coming with me, Grandpa. It was fun having you along."

"Wouldn't have missed it, Ben. You did fine. I'll bet you're going to be a good driver when you save up enough to buy a car. Hope I'm still around when that happens. We could drive out to Wyoming and visit your Aunt Pearl."

"Yeah! Wouldn't that be swell."

Ten

When I met Mike in the lunchroom in school today he told me that some guy in his home room told him about a job downtown that's available. The guy wasn't interested because he has a job, but thought someone might need one.

Mike said, "You interested?"

"Sure. What kind of job is it?"

"It's a Saturday job, in a store on Michigan Avenue.

"What kind of store?"

"I don't know. All I know is that it's called John T. Shaynes and it's on the corner of Michigan and Randolph. Across the street from the public library. Since a lot of guys know about it, you better get down there if you're interested."

Went right home after school, told Mom and Gramps that I was going down to Michigan Avenue to apply for a job. Told them what Mike had said, changed to my good pants, put on a shirt and tie, shined my shoes and was out the door. This is the big time. If I can land a job here it means I'll have some money on a steady basis.

Took me an hour. Took the Diversey bus to the end of the line and transferred to an Elston streetcar. It's the way Mom always goes downtown. Got off at Dearborn Street where the streetcar turns to start back the way it came. As I walked east, I passed right by Tony's newspaper stand. Gramps friend, Tony, was there but I didn't say "Hello," didn't want to waste time jawing.

Did waste a few minutes when I reached Michigan Avenue looking at the store. It's three stories high. Has fancy '*John T. Shaynes*' lettering on all the store windows. Looks like one ritzy place. Since I don't know where to go or who to see, I ask one of the men clerks. He points to a door that leads down to the basement and says, "Ask to see Mr. Webster."

Mr. Webster is a big guy. He chews on a cigar while he talks. It isn't lit. It seems to me he just must like the tobacco taste. He asks if I've ever had a job. I tell him about the job I had before Christmas at the Jewel store. I tell him I never missed a day there. I say, I worked hard doing what I was told to do. I leave out the fact that I quit. I think he likes my looks. I try to be as polite as I can possibly be and I look him right in his eyes when I answer all the questions. Mr. Webster tells me, "We have a men's haberdashery on the main floor and women's clothes and fur coats on two and three. The third floor is junior miss, the second floor sells older women's clothes."

I can tell this is one ritzy store. Fur coats aren't cheap. I don't know one lady in the neighborhood that has a fur coat. The stuff they sell here must cost a lot of money.

Out of the Loop

Finally, Mr. Webster asks, "When can you start Ben?"

"You mean I've got the job?"

"That's what I mean, if you can start this Saturday."

"Sure I can start this Saturday. If you want to show me what I'm going to be doing, I can start right now!"

He tells me, "Saturday will be soon enough. I'll show what the job entails then. Be here by 7:30, wear a shirt and tie, neat pants and comfortable shoes. You'll be making forty cents an hour. You'll be working on the Junior Miss floor. Do you have any questions?" He doesn't give me a second to think about a question and goes on, "No! Okay, I'll see you on Saturday then, at 7:30. Don't be late."

On the way home I take inventory. I've only got one pair of shoes. I think they're pretty comfortable. I'm okay there. I've got two shirts and three pairs of pants I can wear for dress up occasions, so I'm okay in the clothes department. I don't have any long ties, just bow ties. My Dad doesn't wear long ties and that's why I don't have one. But, I'm sure a bow tie will do. It is a tie. So, there's nothing to buy for Saturday. I've got everything Webster talked about. I've got a job. I've got a job in a plush place -- John T. Shaynes on Michigan Avenue. Wow! I'll bet the folks and Gramps won't believe it. I'll be working eight-and-a-half hours on Saturday and I'll make three dollars and eighty-two cents. Streetcar fare up and back is only fourteen cents so I'll have three bucks and some left over. What a grand and glorious feeling!

On Saturday I get up at 5:30 AM. I shower as quietly as possible so that I wouldn't wake Grandpa, but as I come out of the bathroom he's standing there waiting for me.

Gramps says, "Here's a dollar. Get yourself some breakfast and lunch downtown and don't be late for that job. Pay attention, listen and learn, and if you don't understand something, ask questions, you hear?"

"Sure, Grandpa, and thanks. I appreciate your advice and the money. Thanks a lot."

Then I fly down the stairs to find Dad waiting for me in the kitchen. He made sandwiches for himself and me to take to work. He asks, " Do you have any money, Ben?"

"Yes, Dad. Gramps gave me a buck and I've got change for the streetcar."

"Okay then, you better get going."

"Yes Sir, and thanks for the lunch bag."

"Sure. You look good enough to go to a wedding, so you'll do okay. Don't be nervous. Just pay attention, listen and learn and if you don't understand something ask questions. Do that and you'll be okay."

I didn't tell him that I had just heard those same words on the floor above.

I get to the Loop in fine shape. I'm really early. The alley employee door to Shaynes isn't open yet so I spend some time in Pixley & Ehlers. It's a restaurant that sits across the alley from Shaynes on Randolph. From where I'm sitting I can see the alley door and after a while I see Mr. Webster open it. It's 7:15 and I hop off the restaurant seat, pay the cashier and arrive ready for work at 7:17.

Mr. Webster seems impressed. He shows me a place I can park my lunch bag and then has me fill out an employment form. After that he takes me up in the elevator to the third floor and tells me what the job entails.

The third floor is Junior Miss. There are 10 dressing rooms on the outside wall. Each one has curtains that can be drawn for privacy while customers try on suits and blouses, coats or furs. There is also a woman's hat area, a long counter with a couple of chairs and some mirrors. There are full length mirrors at strategic locations. The fur buyer and salesman is a Mr. Finestein. He has the only office on the floor. Other than me, he is the only man that works on the floor. Mr. Webster says that there is another section, down a long hall, where they make the fur coats. He tells me I'll never see anyone that works there because everyone uses the freight elevator in the back of the building when they come and go.

Behind the sales area is where Mr. Finestein's office is and a big room where all the items for sale hang by size and type. You go through a swinging door to get into the storage area where all these clothes and coats are kept.

My job will be to re-hang items in the right place in the store room, after the sales ladies are through showing the clothes to customers. There are hang-stands outside every dressing room. After the customer leaves, I take the clothes to a rack inside the storage area and then put each item back into the right place by size and type of garment.

I am also to relieve Ethel White, the lady that wraps packages, when she has lunch or takes a break. Ethel is the first colored person I have ever met. She isn't as tall as I am. She has a modest dress on with some kind of a garment she wears over the dress to keep it clean. She is neat, somewhat friendly. Her arms are muscular for a woman that really isn't very big. She has worked at Shaynes a few years and everyone likes her. She must be a good worker to have lasted years on the job.

The regular elevator operator is a colored girl by the name of Gwendolyn. Gwendolyn is as tall as I am, about five-eleven, and she's all arms and legs --gangly. She's a giddy girl, giggly, always smiling. She wears a neat, green uniform with a little green hat that doesn't look quite right on her head. Gwendolyn is the only one that works for Shaynes that wears a uniform. I run the elevator when she goes to lunch and Ethel runs it when Gwendolyn takes a break. Thank goodness they don't have a green uniform for me, I'd die of embarrassment. When Ethel is running the elevator, I wrap packages if there are any packages to wrap. Running the elevator isn't difficult and it's fun to do. You just turn the control handle one way or the other to go up or down. You mostly have to guess when to put the handle in neutral in order to have the elevator stop level with the floor you're at. Then you goose the control a bit up or down until no one has to step up or step down to get off. There's a lever you pull to open the floor door. You have to be polite and ask customers not to stand too close to the door when the elevator is moving and you have to tell them to watch their step getting on or off.

Before long the sales ladies arrive and I am introduced. They all seem nice. Then the store opens for business. Not much happens in the first hour, and Ethel goes over the inventory with me, shows me how suits should be put in place. She shows me how to re-hang clothes that haven't been put back right by the sales ladies. She tells me the difference between furs just in case Mr. Finestein asks me to get something for him. There's Beaver that is real soft. Persian Lamb that is sort of curly. Mink isn't as soft as Beaver, but shines more. There's a difference between stoles, jackets and full length coats. The junior miss sizes are 6, 8, 10 and 12. But not too many women are size six. Some of the size twelve's should be trying on stuff down on the second floor. That's the gospel according to Ethel. There's a special way to fold clothes that have been sold and a special way to tie the clothes box we put them in so they won't fall out. Ethel is very patient with me as she teaches me the ropes. About ten-thirty everything gets busy. We are going to have a busy day. I don't make too many mistakes. Takes time to memorize where all the sizes are located.

Out of the Loop

I think Ethel is reserving an opinion regarding Ben Tepke until I have proven that I can do the job. I haven't seen Mr. Webster since I came in this morning. I think he will ask Ethel how I'm doing or he'll ask Mr. Finestein. I have to watch my step and not waste any time. So far, I really like the job. It's easy.

At lunch time I go down to the basement and pick up my lunch, finish it off in a few minutes and go back to work. I clear all the hanging clothes as fast as I can and relieve Gwendolyn so she can eat lunch. Keeping all the clothes in the proper place and off the sales floor when the sales ladies are finished with them is a steady job all day long. Ethel backs me up when I'm on the elevator. I can pretty well keep the clothes off the floor and wrap packages, too. But Ethel only takes a few minutes for lunch anyway. I'm supposed to get a fifteen minute break in the morning and afternoon. The only break I take is to go to the bathroom.

The sales ladies have a routine that I catch on to pretty fast. When a sales lady has a customer in a new suit, a customer that quite can't make up her mind to buy, she calls on other sales ladies to help give the customer a vote of confidence. "Oh that looks so nice," says one and then another sales lady says, "That looks like it was designed just for you!" And a third comes on with, "The color is just right for you, dear!" And on and on it goes. The customer doesn't always buy the flattery, but more often than not a sale is made.

At 5:30 PM the store closes and when I finish hanging the last of the clothes up, I head for home. The Elston Avenue streetcar doesn't seem to be moving very fast as we head northwest. I'm tired, been on my feet all day, but I can't wait to tell the folks and Gramps about the job. I think I did okay.

Gramps says, "Did you make any mistakes?"

"Yes. Took some clothes off a rack that a sales lady wasn't

done with. But she grabbed me before I had gone too far. Then I took a customer's coat that was hanging on a rack and put it into the store room. No one noticed it was gone until she got ready to leave. Found it fast enough, but it was embarrassing. That's all the mistakes I know about. Might have hung some stuff in the wrong place. If I did, Ethel will tell me about it next Saturday.

Everyone treated me okay and the time sure went fast. The prices on the clothes are really expensive and fur coats cost an arm and leg. A full length mink can cost hundreds of dollars."

Mom says, " You won't find me wearing a fur coat. Even if we could afford one, I wouldn't buy it. No sir. A sweater under a heavy wool coat will keep a body just as warm."

Then my Dad asks, "What kind of men things to they sell, Ben."

"All kinds of stuff. Shirts, ties, hats, scarfs, canes, cuff links, handkerchiefs. Expensive stuff. Ethel, the colored lady I told you about, said that Mayor Kennelly buys custom made shirts with his initials on the pockets and monogramed handkerchiefs, too. She said movie stars drop in once in a while. She saw Edward G. Robinson and Bogart once. Said everyone was excited and nervous when they stopped in. It's a real classy place to work."

Everyone's happy that I have a job and that I did okay today, me included. As the weeks go by, I get better and better at running the elevator, wrapping clothes, and keeping things where they belong. Ethel is a wonderful person. She spent a lot of time teaching me how to fold suits and coats and put them in a box so they won't be all wrinkled when the customer gets home. She's not married, but she has a daughter. I guess she's divorced but it isn't a question I'm going to ask her about. The daughter's married and lives in Gary. Ethel doesn't look old enough to have a married daughter.

Out of the Loop

Mr. Webster has sent me on delivery errands a couple of times. Once, it happened just about the time the store closed. A customer called for clothes they had had altered, but didn't want them sent by parcel post. Got carfare and some overtime money. Got home real late, but I don't mind. I love riding streetcars and elevated trains.

Eleven

Everyone, except Mike and Ricky, is working on Saturdays. Lars still has a job at the Lawyer's office. Doesn't start until noon but he's finished by five. Bob's working at a garage. He's the guy that changes oil and puts air in tires. More than likely, you'll find Mike hustling at the pool hall. Ricky doesn't do much of anything other than listen to the radio and dream about his cousin Rosemary. He gets an allowance without even taking the garbage out. So we all have money for fun and games. With school over for the summer, I'm looking forward to fun and games. Passed all my subjects. Not with great grades, but I passed. So I won't be heading for Wyoming.

It's good seeing Lars more often. Since he goes to Lane

Dan Glaubke

Tech we hardly see each other during school days. He and I have grown up together. The folks rented an apartment in his dad's two-flat when I was in kindergarten and he was in first grade. He has a temper and sometimes blows a fuse for little or no reason, and we're all used it. He'll stand-up to almost anyone in an argument, whether it comes out that he's right or wrong. He tells a good story, jokes and laughs a lot. His dad's a carpenter. His mom doesn't work. She's a good cook. Makes great "Shit-a-bula." That's Swedish for meat balls, but the Swedes don't say it that way. I say it that way because I ain't a Swede and can't talk Swedish. Lars has given up trying to teach me the right way to say it. Mrs. Swanson invited the Tepke's to dinner more than a few times when we were living there. Lars and I have had a few knock down, bare knuckle run-ins as we've grown up, but we always get over whatever caused the problem and remain buddies.

The first time we really got into it -- you know, not just poking arms and shoving -- we were about eight and nine. We were coming home from school one summer day and I stopped in at the corner candy store and bought a a bottle of root beer.

"Gimme a swig!" Lars said.

"Buy your own!"

It was hot and as we turned to go down the alley toward home, Lars gave me a shove. A hard one, almost went down. Made me mad and I turned around and said, "You want a swig, here's what you get." I shook the bottle up and down, and I sprayed him good. He got it right in his face, had root beer in his eyes, on his shirt and then it started. He socked me in the mouth, split my lip. I dropped the bottle, made a fist and bloodied his nose. We grunted, gasped, punched, rolled around in the dirt and dried horseshit of the alley. We punched, shoved, pushed, hit one another until our arms were dead weights and we couldn't lift them to swing again.

"You prick. Look what you did to my shirt," Lars said as blood dripped from his nose onto his shirt and pants.

We were sitting side by side now, surveying the damage.

"Well you shouldn't have shoved me. Look what you did to my eye and lip!"

"You should have given me a swig of pop."

"Yeah. Should have. That's about all I got from the bottle. Crap!"

We were full of blood, dirt, horseshit, scrapes and bruises and got hell from our mothers that day. Lars' nose quit bleeding, my eye and lip healed up. For some strange reason, we both felt good about what happened. Had something to talk about to all the guys at school. And from that day we've been real close. Blood buddies, so to speak. Standing up for one another, lying for one another, when we've had to.

Bike riding was always fun, and many times Lars and I traveled to one of the forest preserves northwest of the city. One has a well that you can pump up water that tastes like rotten eggs. One taste convinced Lars and me that we wouldn't drink that stuff if it was the last water on earth. We'd ride along the Des Plaines River. It's a dirty river and the bike trails aren't easy to ride along, but as long as we had a few nickels and dimes in our pocket, there was nothing to complain about. If we got thirsty or hungry along the way, we would stop for a bottle of pop and Twinkies.

Had a flat tire once, all the way out in Shiller Park. Lars was moaning that we'd never get home having to walk the bikes, when some guy in a gas station saw us. Said he had a patch and would fix the flat for me. Told him I didn't have any money. Only twenty-five cents.

He said, "That's okay. Someday you'll see someone in trouble that you'll be able to help and you'll remember me fixing that flat. That'll be payback time. That day, when you help someone else in trouble, is enough of a payment for me. We're here on earth to help one another. Got that?"

Lars and I thanked the guy. Couldn't believe how lucky we were. Here's a guy that see's me walking with a flat tire, takes the time between fillin up customer's gas tanks to fix it. Free. There aren't too many guys like him around, I'll tell you that.

Another fun thing Lars and I used to do was scaling the walls of Falconer Grammar School. It's one big building, three stories high and takes up about one-third of a city block. The brick walls of the school have ledges, grooves really, that go around the entire building. The grooves accommodate hand holds and feet. Actually they will only accommodate the toes of your shoes and your fingertips. We'd climb up the brick wall until we were about six feet off the ground. Then we'd shuffle along the narrow ledges by moving one hand and a foot, and then bringing the other hand and foot along side, before we moved again. Couldn't go fast; it would take a half a day to get around the whole building. Then we'd wind up with scuffed up shoes and fingertips bleeding.

The best of all the things we did growing up were the streetcar rides and going places on the elevated. We were riding on our own when we were eight and nine years old. Going downtown. Riding to Brookfield Zoo. Lincoln Park. Going to all the museums and the aquarium. The beaches. One time we rode Grand Avenue streetcar down to Navy Pier. It was during the war. We were eleven and twelve. Wanted to see the aircraft carrier tied up there. The Navy was using the pier for training and there were sailors all over the place. We couldn't get near the carrier. We saw it though.

We had our swim trunks under our pants and we went swimming off the rocks. As we were waiting for the trunks to dry, sitting on the rocks, Lars turned to me and said, "You smell that?"

"Sure I do! And it seems like my mouth can taste it, too."

It was a chocolate smell that made your mouth water and your stomach ache because chocolate was hard to come by.

"Where's it coming from?" Lars wanted to know.

"Has to be the Baby Ruth factory. It's a few blocks west of here along the river." I'd seen it once, the big Baby Ruth lettering on the side of a building.

"Let's go down there. Maybe we can talk someone into givin us a candy bar."

"Why not. Worth giving it a try"

So we walked down Grand Avenue following the scent of chocolate. When we got close to the loading dock, there was a lot of activity. Trucks were being loaded and unloaded, idling, waiting for their spot on the loading docks. We got as close to the loading dock door as we possibly could and asked some of the truck drivers if they could get us a free candy bar.   One trucker said he'd get us some chocolate if we helped him unload the sacks of raw chocolate he had to deliver. So Lars and I climbed up on the trailer and each took the end of a bag. But, the bag wouldn't budge. It must have weighed a hundred fifty pounds. We looked at the truck driver who was laughing at us, jumped off the truck and started walking away. That's when the driver grabbed Lars and said, "Wait here for a minute fellas." Then he went inside the plant.

When he came out, he had two enormous chucks of

milk chocolate in his hands.

What a great guy! We thanked him and thanked him again and no chocolate we had ever tasted, tasted as good as what he gave us. Bet the pieces weighed a pound a piece. We wound up the day with chocolate smeared faces, hands and fingers and couldn't eat supper.

*****

Lars and I are still at it. Riding public transportation because we know how to get anywhere in Chicago and how long it will take to get there.

Today is one of those days. Lars and I are headed for Wrigley Field. He found out that we might be able to get a job working as substitute ushers at the Cubs game.

"Hope that getting up at 7:00 is worth the trip," Lars says, "We have to be there by eight-thirty. That's what I was told. Seems like it's awful early. The game doesn't start until one-thirty."

Met Lars at ten-to-eight and now we're on a Belmont Streetcar heading for Clark Street. Have to transfer there to get to Wrigley.

"What do we do when we get there, Lars?" I want to know.

"We have to go to a gate by the ticket window and tell a guy there that we want to usher. He's supposed to let us in if we're in time."

"What if we're not in time?"

"We'll give the guy a sob story and maybe he'll let us in to watch the game. That's all I care about anyway."

"Me too, this a great a idea. Who told you about it?"

"My aunt called. She said a friend that works in the Andy

Out of the Loop

Frain office told her."

The Cubs are playing a single game with Brooklyn today. We find the gate keeper without any trouble, behind the ticket window near the corner of Addison and Clark. He sends us to a big usher room underneath the grandstand area, where a man at a desk asks for our names and our Social Security Number. I have mine memorized, but Lars has to call home for his.

The next step is waiting around for something to happen. There must twenty-five or thirty kids like us waiting. Since Lars and I don't know what to do, we just stand around and try to look like we know what's going on. Finally, the Andy Frain head usher comes in, announces that they need twenty fill-in ushers for today's game. Then he starts pointing to guys in the crowd, saying, "You with the Loyola sweater, you with the St. Mels sweater, and you two with the Weber sweaters report over to your left." He keeps calling all the Catholic letter sweaters in the room. Later we find out that Andy Frain is a devout Catholic and he takes care of his own. Lars and I are lucky and we got assignments. A lot of the guys standing around didn't. The head guy tells us that fill-in ushers make two bucks for a single game and four bucks for a double header. The money's good, but seeing the game is all Lars and I care about.

We both get an Andy Frain usher hat and are assigned to handle box seats in sections of the upper deck. Lars' section is in left field. Mine is in right field. About as far as you can go in right field and still be in the ball park.

Not many of my seats are filled by game time, but I don't care. I have five people sitting in my section. A father with a little boy, two women and guy that looks like he's ten years old than Gramps. I think the women are the daughters of the old guy.

Lars has a full section, a lot of people, and he's screwed up the seating. Everything went okay until the section was about half full. Then he discovered the people sitting on the right side of the aisle should be sitting on the left side and vice-versa. When he started straightening out his mistake, some of the guys he didn't seat right gave him a hard time. In typical Lars fashion, he started giving them a hard time back. Almost got into a fight, but one of the supervising ushers showed up and got things under control. When everyone was in their proper seats, and the fussing had subsided, the supervisor moved Lars to a section further down the left field line.

Then the first guy up for Brooklyn hit a foul ball right at him. It was the first pitch of the game, and Lars caught it. I saw it all and didn't believe it. He can hardly catch a sixteen-inch softball when you lob it to him underhand, and he pulls in a hard hit genuine National League baseball, one handed, without a glove. Unbelievable! Everyone in Wrigley Field gives him a big hand and he takes off his hat, bows and holds the ball high for everyone to see. Has to give it back to the supervisor because baseballs are still in short supply due to the war. Ushers don't get to keep balls anyway. The old man sitting in my section says, "Cubs ought to sign that young fella up! That was a great catch!"

In the seventh inning we have to return the Frain hats and collect our two bucks. After putting the money away we walk back into the grandstands to watch the end of the game. The Cubs won seven to six, a thriller. The Brooklyn manager, Leo Dorocher, was pissed about something during the game and he and Charlie Grimm have words. That's always fun to watch.

Out of the Loop

The Cubs did great last year, they won the pennant but lost the World Series to Detroit. It went seven games, but we lost the last one. Right now we're 23-19 but it is still early in the season. We still have a great lineup, but we're not playing as well as we did last year when we won the pennant. Grimm has moved Cavarretta to the outfield, Stan Hack, Lennie Merullo are still around in the infield. Nicholson and Peanuts Lowery are still in the outfield. Pafko is still around, but he's been hurt and isn't playing right now. Mickey Livingston and Clyde McCullough are sharing catching duty. The infield is okay. The guys pitching -- Hank Wyse, and Claude Passeau are doing great. Borowy and Schmitz are so-so, could be better. Hope we win another pennant and the World Series this year!

On the streetcar heading for home I ask Lars, "What was all the commotion about down your way before the game started?"

"Made some mistakes seating people and a couple of wise guys started giving me trouble. I'd have gotten into it with them if the supervisor hadn't come by. I was really pissed. Then he moved me down the line to cool me off. Did you see me grab that foul ball?"

"Couldn't miss it. That was some catch. Didn't believe it was you until you turned and saw that nose stickin out from your face. Couldn't be anyone else. No one in the park could compete with that schnoz."

" Very funny. Watch your step or that nose of yours will getting bigger, too, when I bust it for you."

"Oh! Pardon me. I apologize. I'm sorry. Forgive me. Didn't mean to hurt your feelings."

"Okay, knock it off! You know what? That damn ball came straight at me like lightning and I threw up my hand to protect my face. The ball hit my hand and my fingers closed on it like a vise. Automatically. Surprised the shit out of me when I took the hand away from my face and the ball was in it. My hand still hurts. That thing must have been traveling over 100 miles an hour!"

"You going to the beach party, Lars?"

"Sure."

"You taking a date?"

"Naw. You?"

"No, but it should be fun."

Twelve

It's getting dark. North Avenue beach is thinning out a bit. There are plenty of people still in the water. Swimming. Wading. Playing. It's still hot. The sun was a burn maker today. Bob's got a burn, not a bad one but his shoulders and back are rosy. He put enough of that lotion on to keep him safe, but he still burned. Told him he smelled divine, like Jane Russell must have smelled before she rolled in the hay with Jack Beutel. He took off after me, but I'm a lot faster and he gave up.

Everyone from the Gethsemene Luther League is here. Including Jerry, the Youth Minister. He's keeping his eye on everyone to make sure we stay out of trouble. Seems like he thinks the girls are more apt to get in trouble than the guys because that's where his eyes are spending most of their time. All the guys like watching the girls in their bathing suits. Long legs and knockers and those wiggly rumps add to the fun of spending a day at the beach.

The sun being so hot makes it a real pleasure to paddle, float and be awash in the water of Lake Michigan. It's cold as usual and the waves are rolling in, but they're sort of puny today. Not the kind that we like, the kind that will knock you over is what we like. Feels great though and when you come out of the water the sun robs you of that wonderful chill in a matter of seconds and the wind dries your skin before you can get back to your blanket for a towel. When we're not in the water we toss the softball around. All the guys except Ricky. Ricky is busy talking to Gail, the girl he's been dating. Gail's a year older than Ricky, and in my class at school. She's sitting with her back against a garbage can that we used as a cooler for the pop. But the ice melted long ago. Ricky's lying down with his head on her lap and they've been talking for what seems like hours. Can't for the life of me understand what there is to talk about with a girl for more than a couple of minutes. She keeps smiling. Laughing. It's not that I'm just standing around looking at them, but every time I do look that way it seems they haven't moved. Gail's about the same height as Ricky, but doesn't have his slight build. She's got a set of knockers that must be the envy of girls twice her size. That's obviously the attraction for Ricky. Wonder if he can actually see her face with his head on her lap.

Bob, Lars, Mike and I haven't had a date as yet. Not that we haven't talked or thought about it. Just haven't done it. It's not because we're ugly or anything like that. All three of us look pretty good, but we just haven't asked any girl out.

Mike's probably the best looking of the four of us and he's very popular, always clowning around. He can juggle, do tricks with a ball, funny imitations, too. The funniest are the ones where he mimics the teachers. He loves making people laugh. I happen to think he does these things because he's trying overcome his shyness, but nobody will agree with me because he seems so extroverted. Bob's got his eye on Nita. It isn't hard to figure out that he'll be asking her out one of these days. Every so often, we spend time at Dixie's house on George Street. She has a lot of parties. The parties are like having a date except we never pair off with any girl. Dixie's mom likes having kids around. It's fine with her if we drop in unexpected. She always has pop and stuff to eat in the house. Dixie is popular with all the Luther League girls and guys.

The beach party was Bob's idea. Another good idea from Bob Banks. He's president of Luther League now. When it's dark, we'll have a fire and a weenie roast. Nothing tastes better at the beach than a fire-burned hot dog coated with onions, relish and mustard. Or the potato chips. Or the pop. We're going to roast marshmallows after the feast. At the beach, gooey, sticky, burn crusted marshmallows are one fine dessert.

The sun finally goes to bed, the moon pops up and we start a fire. The stars are beginning to wink. Little yellow-white squares are poking holes in the night sky as lights are turned on in the tall buildings behind us. A red glow to the south indicates the Loop has started to preen for attention. To the north someone is setting off fireworks, sky rockets, aerial bombs. Haven't seen or heard fireworks for a long, long time.

There's something wonderful about sitting around a fire, hearing the waves roll in, feeling the night settle in around your shoulders, feeling the sand in your toes. Talking with friends about things. You wonder how long it will last. How long you'll have these friends to talk to and get together with.

We have been singing the songs that everyone knows --

Dan Glaubke

Old Mac Donald, Jesus Loves Me, She'll Be Coming Around the Mountain, 99 Bottles of Beer On The Wall -- and all of a sudden Bob notices that Ricky and Gail are gone. They are off in the shadows, under a blanket. Bob nudges Mike and gets Lars and my attention, points toward the blanket in the moonlight. We can only guess what's happening under there, as we get up and start toward it. All the others are still singing and not paying any attention to us.

Gail sees us coming and alerts Ricky, just the moment before our hands reach out to turn the blanket over. Ricky acts like a mad man, snugging the cover up tight, swearing at us to leave him alone. And Gail's hands are moving frantically under the blanket, doing things we think might be embarrassing. We backed off for a minute before we begin again. If Ricky had been bigger, he probably would have taken a swing at someone. As it is, we leave Gail to her final adjustments, then get Ricky on the blanket and toss him in the air. We have him flying up and down, while he spews language unbecoming to any church go-ing Luther Leaguer. The four of us laugh and have a great time as we flip him in the air again and again.

Around nine o'clock we put the fire out and clean up the area where we've played and camped. We lug the leftover stuff to Jerry's car. A couple of the girls' dads, that have cars, have come down to take them home. Some of the guys are going to ride with Jerry. Bob, Mike, Lars, Ricky and I walk to the street-car.

"What were you doing under that blanket, Ricky?" Lars asks.

"Wouldn't you like to know," Ricky says, still burning.

"Yeah! We'd like to know what your fly was doing open," says Mike.

Out of the Loop

"Was not. You bastards almost got Gail caught in a bad spot though."

"I think it was you that got her into that situation, not us," Says Bob chuckling.

" Hard to get that top up once it's down in a bathing suit." Ricky says looking at each of us. Bragging is what he's doing, waiting on us to acknowledge what a great lover he is. " I almost shit."

" Well it would have served you right if you filled your pants. You shouldn't be doing that. Guess we'll have to tell Jerry what you were doing"

"Aww, come on Bob. Don't do that. Gail won't ever talk to me again."

"I won't do that, wouldn't do it. But you better watch your step, lover boy. The other girls aren't dumb and you probably ruined Gail's reputation."

"Couldn't help myself."

" Yeah, sure."

When we're only a few stops away from home Lars says, "Shit."

Bob asks "What's the matter?"

"Lost my wallet."

Mike says, "What was in it?"

"Nothing much. A buck, name and address. It was a nice wallet. Imitation leather, practically new. Got it for Christmas. Must have dropped out of my pocket when we changed clothes"

"Or when you went to take a dump." Ricky says. "That's when the whole place emptied out. Everyone thinking the end was near, that the plague had come down upon us."

"Very funny."

"If you lost it in the crapper it'll be there forever," Ricky says.

"If you have your name and address in it, someone might send it back to you," I say, trying to give Lars a little hope.

"Damn it. I'm always losing something."

"Could have been worse, if you had had more money in it," I'm feeling bad for Lars and at that very moment Mike holds up a wallet.

"And here it is, one genuine, fake leather, buffalo hide wallet. Found by one keen eyed, handsome fella in the sand when we were putting out the fire. Held safely, awaiting one stupid Swede to wake up and cry about his lost treasure. Here it is you dumb shit, take it!"

Jumping off the streetcar before it comes to a complete stop, we start going our separate ways.

"Mike! Thanks!" Lars shouts, "but you didn't have to hold on to it like you did."

"What? And have you lose it again? We would have wound up sleeping on the beach, looking for the damn thing all night long. Take it easy, see you later."

****

As usual, the warm, wonderful summer is heading toward fall faster than I want to believe. The Fourth of July has come and gone, the ball games, swim parties, Luther League meetings, working Saturday's at Shaynes -- all the yesterdays seem like a blur in my memory. Labor Day isn't laboring to arrive, it's coming at me like Superman ... faster than a speeding bullet!

****

"Ben, what church do you go to?" Ethel wants to know. It's early Saturday morning before the store has opened up. We're standing together in the wrapping room where Ethel is putting things in their place and making boxes.

"Don't go to church Ethel."

"You don't mean that."

She doesn't seem to believe what I've said.

"My Dad reads the Bible, Ethel. And something called Science and Health. It's what Christian Science people read. We don't go to church because what he's reading every week is the same thing they read on Sundays in that church. So he doesn't think it's necessary to go. That's what he told me. He says I can make up my own mind about the church thing when I get old enough. And Sunday is really the only day he's at home during a week."

"Oh, my." Ethel is biting her lip. " You should be reading your Bible and going to church, Ben. Do you believe in Jesus? God's son who came to save us, died for us on the cross?

"I believe in God. I pray. Once in a while, I pray. But I haven't gone to church. All my friends go."

"Well, you should, too. Won't cost you anything and once you give yourself to our Lord and Savior it will save your life."

Then Ethel turns away. I get the idea she doesn't want to say any more, and it seems like she is fretting about something. I can tell, that what I told her about my Dad isn't her idea of what a Sunday should be. I can tell she might be sorry she brought the subject of church up.

Ethel doesn't talk much, but when she does I can tell she likes me. She gives me advice about the job. Let's me know what's going on in the store. I'm only around on Saturdays and she wouldn't have to waste time talking to me if she didn't care about me. I've been thinking about church. The guys don't talk about it. They just go and have been going since they were old enough to walk. I like the Luther League meetings, but it isn't church. I'm not going to worry about it. Wish Ethel hadn't brought it up.

****

Como esta usted. I'm taking Spanish this semester. Could have taken Polish, German, French or Latin but everyone told me Spanish was easier and the teacher didn't flunk anyone so that's what I'm taking. And I've got geometry, a subject that's hard for me to understand. What's it's good for? No one I know has an answer to that. Geometry is worse than Spanish, I can't seem to grasp any of it. Biology is easy enough. English is okay. Thank goodness we have a gym period!

Most of the kids in Spanish class are freshmen so I'm a year older. The teacher is a Spaniard or Mexican, don't know which. Her name is Mrs. Hernandez. She talks so fast it's hard to understand her when she's speaking English. When she's saying things in Spanish, she slows down a little. You should hear Mike imitate her. He's in second year Spanish and he can talk just like her and ape her movements, too. She has her hands moving for emphasis when she's speaking Spanish and Mike has those moves down pat. Hilarious! Muy bien! I don't think he knows what he's saying when he imitates her. He just strings a bunch of Spanish words together that sound as if he was born in Mexico City or Madrid.

Bob is doing great in school. He's near the top of his class. Mike, Lars and Ricky aren't as smart as Bob, but they don't have any worries when it comes to grades. I keep my grades to myself but the folks know where I'm at. Mom won't let me listen to the radio anymore except when she and Dad are listening. That crystal set the folks gave me has crapped out, doesn't work anymore. I was getting foreign language stations mostly, anyway, so it's no great loss. I'm studying more these days. Geometery is still a puzzle. We're coming down to the wire and I think I'm going to flunk geometry. Doing okay in everything else.

Got my grades, I've passed everything. Even geometery. The geometry teacher gave me a passing grade, but wanted to see me after class. "Ben, you're not dumb. You just missed the fundamentals and I'll get you some help for next semester, okay? Someone to work with you and bring you up to speed."

"Thanks, Mrs. Polanski. I am having a terrible time and I really appreciate the passing grade. I know I don't deserve it."

"See me when school starts, first thing, Ben."

"Yes Ma'am, I will."

What's going on in my life? All along the way I've been loved and cared for in more ways than I deserve. All those I care about love me more than I deserve. I seem to come out of all the tough spots I run into okay. Mrs. Polanski doesn't owe me anything and yet I've survived her class when I was positive I was dead in the water. " Thank you, good Lord. I know it wasn't me that got me through geometry."

I've said this out loud walking down the school corridor. Said it as I passed Maddy Fletcher's locker. She was standing there, getting a book and notebook out for her next class. She smiled at me. Titled her head a bit. Looked like she was trying to figure out what I had said and who I was talking to. Boy, she's beautiful. And that smile of hers is enough to make your knees weak. Maybe I should go out for football. The guy she's dating is on the team. He's a Junior and plays end. She's a freshman. When the guy graduates, maybe I'll have a chance to take her out. That's wishful thinking, but she sure is beautiful.

Dan Glaubke

"Were you talking to me, Ben?"

"No Maddy. Talking to myself. How are you doing?"

"Just great. Isn't high-school a lot of fun?"

"Yes, it's great." I say as I hurry past her and head down the hall toward my next class.

****

At Christmas break, Mr. Webster asked if I can come in and work during the week. Said yes, I can sure use the money. The store's real busy and has a Christmas sale going on. In addition to working on the junior miss floor, I've been running errands. Took four packages to the United Parcel warehouse. It's a block south of Madison Street and a few blocks west of the Chicago River. Cabbed it there and walked back down Madison Street's Skid Row. Bums are all over the place, some sitting in the crumbling doorways, sharing bottles of cheap wine, some just staggering along, going nowhere, heads down, looking for who knows what.

Skid Row smells like piss and filthy bodies. Stale alcohol emanates from the sleezy bars that litter the broken down buildings on both sides of the street. Their door's are open even though it's cold, but the bums inside don't seem to care. They just keep on bending their elbows and draining the rot-gut. The smell along the street makes me feel light headed. Dirty. As if being on the street has pestilence penetrating my pores.

Some guy walking ahead of me dropped a cigarette and a couple of bums dove for the smoldering butt and fought over it. You have to wonder what the men on this street did before the alcohol got a hold on 'em. Skid row runs west from Canal Street, down Madison all the way to the Chicago Stadium. They say that on election days, the politicians line the bums up and trade booze for votes. Don't think it's just a rumor.

One of Grandpa's brothers was an alcoholic. Washed dishes in a restaurant in Cicero. He never married and died young.

Thirteen

1947

Spring has rolled around once again and the trees are sprouting leaves. New energy's racing through our bodies. With students racing the race for yonder class rooms, it is hazardous in the halls and an invitation for disaster. Disaster arrives in the form of knocking down a seventy year old janitor and breaking his hip. Worse yet, the janitor dies not long after the accident.

When disaster strikes in a high school it is inevitable that new rules are brought forth to lower the probability of something similar happening again. The new rules are many, aggravating and cause for revolt. Hell, I didn't even know what the new rules were when I came to school today and found kids with placards and signs blocking doorways. The kids were chanting "Strike, strike, don't go into school." Sounded fine as far as I was concerned. Someone told me that the main problem was that we could no longer wear overalls or Levis and girls couldn't wear babushkas. Since most of the guys have jobs after school, it's really nuts to say we can't wear Levis. Most jobs are dirty and you can't wear good clothes. As far as the babushka ban goes, that would be tough on the girl ego. They spend a lot of time fluffing hair and doing makeup. When their hair's a mess they feel ugly and wear babushkas.

I wandered around looking for Mike, Bob or Ricky among the strikers. I finally found Mike and Ricky near the Sugar Bowl, and Bob emerged from the crowd about the same time I did.

"Hey Mike, you going in?"

"No way. All the guys will call us 'chicken shit' if we go through those doors."

Bob thinks we should just hang around for a while and see what happens. "I'll bet they call the cops and the cops will shoo us back into school before noon."

"I'm not so sure. There are too many guys standing around out here to shoo. A lot of girls are standing around, too. Why don't we go to my house and play ping-pong. Did Nita go inside?" I want know.

"I'm pretty sure she did," Bob says. "Her dad would raise hell if he found out she ditched school."

Now that she's a freshman, Bob finally got up enough nerve to ask her out. They've had a few dates and he's nuts about her. Even though he's never said so, we know.

Out of the Loop

"I'm not gonna stand around here all day. You guys want to come over to the house, or not?"

"Mike says, "I'm in, how about you Bob?"

"Okay. Might as well."

"Ricky? You coming or you going hang out with Gail?"

"Gail isn't striking, she went to class and I'm not going to stand around here."

So the four of us go to my house for the remainder of the day. We play ping-pong and darts while fellow classmates picket the porticos of the school. Didn't have to watch Ricky. The cold cellar door is locked and I don't have a key.

Mom wanted to know what was going on. Gramps took a trip to visit Aunt Lily so I didn't have to overcome any of his objections about my striking. Mom figured if Bob was with me everything must be okay, because everyone respected Bob's judgement. She wasn't too sure about mine or Mike's. She knew Ricky would follow the leader, where ever the leader led.

It turned out that the new rules don't cover babushkas or overalls, if you can believe what it says in the Chicago Tribune. The Trib says the rules that we are objecting to cover shouting, loitering, impeding the passing of others, improving attitudes, disregarding the "Up and Down" stairway rules and a bunch of other dumb things. I can't believe it. I can't believe that the strike is still on, on day two.

So it's back to the ping-pong table. Gramps thinks we should be in school and lets us know his opinion but I told him it would be hard for us to break through the picket line and live. He didn't buy that one, but moved on and didn't bother us any more.

The strike was settled in the afternoon of day two. As far as I can tell we didn't get anything for striking with the exception of becoming the first high school in the United States to go on strike. The strike was reported in newspapers far and wide across America and on the radio. Big deal. No one interviewed me or wanted my opinion.

The Tribune had a lot of "Striker" pictures. I didn't know anyone that was photographed up close except Maddy Fletcher. Once in a while Maddy shows up at Luther League because she's a good friend of Nita and Connie. It's a nice picture, but it's too bad she didn't smile. That babe isn't meant to wear a frown but I guess a smile isn't a good thing to do when you're striking.

*****

I saw Mrs. Polanski when the semester started and she put me in touch with Harry Grumman for a geometry tutor. Wouldn't you know it. Harry goes to Gethsemane church and now everyone knows I'm a casualty when it comes to geometry. It's not that Harry told anyone. Did it myself without thinking. Someone saw us going over the text book in study hall and the someone told Mike, who told Ricky, who said," What were you and Harry doing in study hall, Ben?"

"Oh, Harry's helping me with geometry." As soon as I had said it, I knew it was a big mistake. Ricky thinks gossip makes him an "in the know" guy that has all the answers. Now it seems like someone is always asking me, "How is geometry going?"

My answer is always the same, " Just great, why are you asking?" accompanied by a cold look, a squint and a jutting chin. It usually ends the conversation then and there.

The truth is I'm still behind the eight ball when it comes to geometry. It isn't Harry's fault. He's very patient. Answers any question I throw at him, but most of the time I can't think of a question to ask. He helps me with my homework and I'm getting by, but Harry won't be taking the final for me.

Out of the Loop

Since Harry has been tutoring me regularly, we have become good friends. Harry is a very popular guy at school and he's got a lot of girlfriends. He likes to take them to Bruno's, up on Central Avenue, between Diversey and Belmont. Bruno's specializes in this new Italian food called pizza, and you can smell it baking a block away.

In Bruno's storefront window, guys are tossing balls of dough up in the air, pounding it with their fists, rolling it out flat, right before your eyes. They slop tomato sauce on the dough, heap on cheese, sprinkle it with spices and put more tomato sauce on it. Then they stick the thing in the oven using a big wooden paddle and it bakes for fifteen minutes. The oven is like an elevator that goes up, down and round and round. Some people like sausage on top the cheese. Some like these fishy little buggers called anchovies added. The result is nothing like anything I had ever tasted before, and I like it.

*****

The end is here again. It's the last day of school for the summer and I have passed everything. Not with great grades but I'll be moving on to my junior year in the fall. I would and should have flunked geometry. The final test was awful. Poor Mrs. Polanski took all those tests with her and had an automobile accident on her way home from school. It was a bad one. The newspaper said that some truck had barreled through a red light and hit her Chevy broadside. Gas leaking from the busted gas tank ignited and the car burned. So did the truck. Two fire trucks were called and traffic was a mess. They got Mrs. Polanski out before the fire started and she has a busted leg and some busted ribs and had to have some stitches in her head. The story says she'll be okay when everything heals.

Dan Glaubke

Mrs. Polanski's tragedy was a life saver for me. My test burned up in her car along with all the others and the school gave everyone a passing grade based on the last mark we got. Told everyone that I "aced" the test because of all the help I got from Harry, and no one can call me a liar. The best news is that I won't have to take geometry over again next semester.

*****

When I arrive at work on Saturday, I find out that Mr. Webster has called Ethel and told her that she should send me downstairs to his office.

"What's up? Do you know?"

She looks at me and says, "Don't worry, Ben. You're doing okay. I think you'll like what he has to say."

When I get there, Webster is chomping on his cigar and reading his newspaper. He puts the newspaper down and says, "Pull up a chair and sit down, Ben. Since school has ended, I was wondering if you would like to work full time. You've done a fine job so far and I could use your help."

What a break.

"Don't have to think much about that, Mr. Webster, sure I would. I like working here."

"Okay then, you'll be working eight to five-thirty, six days a week, except Mondays when the store opens at noon and closes at nine-thirty. I'm giving you a raise to forty-five cents an hour.

I'm trying hard not to show how excited I am, and I'm trying to figure out how much money I'll be making. I'll need a pencil and paper. It never occurred to me that I'd ever have a full time job in such a classy place.

Out of the Loop

Now my pay envelope will have twenty-one bucks in it by the end of a week. When I get back to the third floor, I go straight to the wrapping room and tell Ethel.

She looks right at me and says, "I was hoping you would take the job."

It's tough waiting for the day to end, because I can't wait to get home and tell the folks and Gramps the good news.

With me bubbling over about the job, Mom, Dad and Gramps can't help but smile. I'm jumping up and down inside, telling them what Mr. Webster and Ethel said and how I felt. What a grand and glorious feeling!

I'll have to be hurrying home after work because I'm playing softball with the guys on the Gethsemane team. I'll have to hurry home to make practice and get to the games on time.

*****

Our softball team is pretty good. We have won more games than we've lost. We are in the running to win the church league. All we have to do is keep on playing like we are playing right now.

Bob pitches, Mike plays short center, Harry's shortstop. Ricky is playing third base. Lars is catching. It's a place where he can tell the umpire how blind he is and does every so often. I'm in center field. Mr. Ryerson has me batting fourth in the cleanup spot. Mike our leadoff guy gets on base a lot. Ricky is batting behind Mike and then Harry bats. He's a good athlete, a good basketball player, too.

All the girls from Luther League are coming to our games. Our manager, Mr. Ryerson, is the father of one of the Luther League girls. He must be all of five foot, two. He is shorter than anyone on the team. But he commands respect and lets us know that if we can't make practice we won't play in the game. Before every game starts he gets us in a huddle and whispers strategy. He whispers because there is something wrong with his vocal chords.

Before the season started, all the guys on the team decided to get jackets and uniforms. We didn't want to be called the Luther Leaguers so I came up with the highbrow name: "The Gentry."

Don't know what it means exactly, something like gentlemen, I think. Anyway, all the guys thought it sounded pretty good and we are having jackets made up. Most of the parents chipped in and, now that I'll be working full-time, I'm going to buy my own. The church bought our uniforms and they really look sharp.

Being a church team, we have to be on our good behavior all the time. No swearing out loud. You never hear Bob swear, but the rest of us have to clean up our act. We don't want to embarrass Mr. Ryerson or anyone else. It's hard sometimes, though. Mr. Ryerson has let it be known that if he hears someone swear, he'll be off the team. Well, after ignoring one warning, he'll be off the team.

The church league brings some unexpected advantages. All of a sudden we are scheduled to play a few games at Rock-Ola Stadium. Night games. Under the lights. They are really warm up games to be played in advance of the Rock-Ola girls, the semipro women's softball team. The team is called the Rock-Ola Music Maids because they are sponsored by the juke box manufacturer. The stadium is located on Central Avenue, between Irving Park and Montrose, just a few miles northwest of where we live.

The stadium isn't packed for our game, but there is a crowd in addition to the Gethsemane girls who come out to cheer us on. The crowd isn't very interested in our games but there is

Out of the Loop

some polite applause at times to acknowledge a good play.

Playing under the lights is fun. But I dropped a high fly ball once when I lost the ball in the glare of the bright stadium flood lights. Mike lost one, too.

After our games we usually hang around and watch the girls play. It looks to me like some of the Music Maids are really guys. They throw harder than we do, run as fast, hit fast ball pitching we couldn't touch in a lifetime. Some of the girls don't wear makeup, some look like movie stars. One night, one of the Rock-Ola girls dove into home plate, trying to score. Hit the other team's catcher in the chest with her head and knocked her right on her backside. Then the two girls went at it. Pulling hair, swinging fists, landing some good ones while everyone watched. The benches on both sides emptied. No one got into the fight, just made sure no one was going to interfere. The ump tried his best to part them and took a shot to his midsection. If he hadn't had his chest protector in place he might have had a rib broken. It was a great brouhaha while it lasted, before the ump and a Chicago Cop got the two apart. The Music Maid wound up with a black eye and the catcher had some cuts and bruises. If that had happened in a Cubs game both players would have been tossed out. Not in Rock-Ola Stadium. Both players stayed in the game, but there were no more scuffles that night.

*****

The work week at Shaynes is always interesting. In addition to working on the junior miss floor, Mr. Webster has me running errands and delivering clothes and furs. Most of the delivery jobs take me to the north side or Evanston and Skokie. I know a lot about how to get around in Chicago and I'm learning more all the time.

Don't know that much about the south side, though. I went to the Stock Yards once. Boy, did it stink. It was really something to see once you got over the smell. Must have a million steers, pigs, sheep, calves and lambs in the place on any given day. The stock yards are right behind the International Amphitheater at 42nd and Halstead. My Dad took us to a livestock show there once. They put on a rodeo and those guys that ride the bulls are absolutely nuts. They put their lives on the line every time they come out of the gate. Those bulls weigh a ton and are mean, tough and dangerous.

Even though I don't know much about the south side, I can find my way around. Going south, all the east-west streets have numbers, and going west, the north-south streets aren't a problem. They are basically the same as on the north side. It's going east of Michigan Avenue on the south side that gives me trouble.

I had to take a fur coat to a customer that is staying up north at the Edgewater Beach Hotel today. The Sheridan bus goes right to the door. It is some posh place, I'll tell you that. They get big bands to entertain. In summer they have umbrellas and chairs on the beach where people have fancy drinks and read books and magazines without getting sun burned. People swim, too. I saw a couple wearing swim suits walk right though the hotel lobby.

Someone said that Cary Grant is staying there right now. I didn't see him, so I don't know if that's true. I do believe that it's the type of place that those big shot movie stars live in when they come to Chicago.

When I dropped off the coat, the lady tipped me dollar. That's the first time that's ever happened. I didn't know if I should take it, but she insisted. I'm not going to tell Mr. Webster about it because it might cause trouble and make him mad. Hard for me to turn down a dollar when I have to work more than two hours to earn one. So I didn't argue when the lady put it in my hand.

Once or twice, since I've been working every day, I've had to take a taxi some place because the customer was in a hurry for her duds. I feel like a big shot when I take a taxi. The Tepkes never take a taxi anywhere. Mr. Webster gives me the taxi fare in advance and I have to remember to get a receipt so he can keep the petty cash box square.

Fourteen

Sitting in the dugout of Rock-Ola Stadium, waiting our turn at bat, Harry turns to me and asks, "You ever been to Maxwell Street, Ben?"

"No, but I've heard about it."

"Hearing about it and being there aren't the same thing. Would you like to tag along with me on Sunday?"

Harry is a sharp dresser, sort of flashy. He tells me he's going to go to Maxwell Street on Sunday to buy a suit.

"That would great. What time are you going to go?"

"Thought I'd leave about ten. I'm going to go to the early service at church and I'm going to leave from there. You going to church?"

"I don't go to church."

Then I think about what I've just said. Why not go? All the guys go. I don't think they'll toss me out if I walk through the doors.

So I tell Harry, "I'll go Sunday and we can take off from there. Sure, I'll meet you in church."

Sunday came. I put on my good clothes and told the folks and Gramps, "I'm going to go to a church service at Gethsemane and then Harry and I are going to Maxwell Street. He's going to buy a suit."

Mom said, "Well, I'm not surprised about church. You've been going to all those meetings and I've thought you might get around to going to a service."

Dad told me, "It's a good idea. You know, I was baptized Lutheran. No, you don't know, but I was. You're old enough to make up your own mind about what you believe in. It's good you're going."

"Mom, why don't you go to church?"

"Well I believe in God, was baptized in the Ohio River by a Baptist minister when I was about ten or eleven. The preacher dunked me three times. It was my Mom that made sure I was baptized. She was sick and dying, but I didn't know it at the time. My Dad was a mean man, hurt my Mom more than a few times and he didn't go to church, so none of the family went."

"What do you mean? He hurt your Mom?" Never saw my Mom's Mom, my grandmother on her side. She died young and my Mom was raised by her Aunt Lizzy.

"He hit her with his fists and he would have hit me, too if my Mom hadn't kept him from it. I don't want to talk about it, think about it, remember it, so go."

This was a typical family talk. Short. But unlike most of our conversations, Gramps didn't chime in with any advice about church. Don't know why. I know why Dad doesn't go to church, but have no idea why Gramps has never gone. Gramps did say, "Don't spend any money on Maxwell Street. Most of the stuff down there is junk!"

I liked the church service. Not so much the hymns, but the sermon. Made me think I might be missing something.

After the service, Harry and I left for Maxwell street. I have heard you can get good things there cheap if you are sharp enough to know what's good and what's cheap.

We took a Belmont streetcar down to Halsted Street. Then we transferred and rode a Halsted Street streetcar to the near south side. Maxwell street is only a couple of blocks south of 12th Street.

It has a little bit of everything. In the middle of the street there are flower stalls, vegetable stands, fruit stands, junk and antique stalls. There are regular store fronts on both sides of the street. There's a fish store, live chicken store, hardware store, shoe stores and about three places you can buy clothes. There's a deli here, too. The smell of the street is a blend of cooking, produce, flowers, chicken feathers, hardware, fish and smells I've never experienced before. The place is alive with people picking at the stuff in the stalls. People trying to get around without touching each other, like there might be something contagious on the clothes of the others they're passing by. People not looking at each other, just looking at the stuff on sale. People arguing with vendors about price. You see fingers poking, hands grabbing, noses sniffing, eyes moving over merchandise everywhere you look.

Before Harry got into the buying mood he wanted to get a bite to eat. The deli had opened up, so that's where we went. We both ordered hot corned beef sandwiches with potato chips and a whole dill pickle, and I'll bet we will smell like garlic all the way home. The sandwiches are absolutely great, made with home-made Kosher rye with caraway seeds.

I think all the shop owners on this street are Jewish. They all wear those funny black beanies and half of the men you deal with here have shaggy beards.

There's a joke about a clothing store on Maxwell Street that goes something like this: A guy walks in looking for a suit. The owner says, "We got just what you want." The guy says "The color I want is blue." So the owner hollers out to a guy in the back of the store, "Hey Sam, got a guy who wants a blue suit, turn on the blue lights."

Harry must have tried on ten suits in three different stores before he found what he was looking for. Then he haggled with the salesman. The salesman called the owner over and Harry got the price down a few bucks from what the owner said he wanted. Then he bought a porkpie hat. That Harry really is sharp. I didn't buy anything, but it was fun just looking around.

None of the shops on Maxwell Street are anything like John T. Shaynes, I'll tell you that. It's like another world on this street. It sounds like, smells like, looks like no other place I've ever been in Chicago. When I need a suit, maybe I'll ask Harry to come back here with me and help me buy one.

******

Wednesday night at the Luther League meeting, Nita brought a friend with her. She's beautiful. I think she's beautiful. Nita has introduced her to everyone. Her name is Betsy, Betsy Banks. I really like her smile. She dresses very nice, has light brown hair, isn't very tall, and seems to have a nice personality.

Her eyes really threw me for a loop when I got up close enough to see them. She has different colored eyes. One eye's blue and the other's brown. I wound up looking at those eyes in a way that she caught on to right away and she smiled at me. She told everyone around her that she has Heterochromia. Don't ask me how to spell it. I'm not even sure how you say it correctly. It's some genetic quirk that she says she has to explain whenever she catches someone stare at her. Like me. She was smiling when she said it. Can't deny it, I did stare. All I know is that the eyes are beautiful no matter which eye you're looking at.

Betsy is a sophomore at Foreman High and I've never seen her before. Amazing. There aren't many girls I haven't noticed, and if I'd noticed I'd remember her, that's for sure. After the meeting ends, before she can get away, I jump in front of her and say, "Can I have your phone number?" Never asked any girl for her phone number before and now I'm acting like it's something I do every day.

She says, "Yes, you can," and starts walking away.

What's this? What's going on? "Betsy?"

"She turns, smiles and says, "Oh, you want me to give you my phone number."

"Huh?"

"You said, '*Can I*' and yes I can give it to you, if that's what you want, but you should have said, '*May I have your number*' and yes, you may. It's Belmont 5 -6521. Do you have a piece of paper and pencil to write it down or are you going to memorize it?"

Now those eyes of hers are twinkling and she's giggling.

"Tell me again and I'll memorize it."

I would like to walk her home, but she's with Nita and Nita seems like she's in a hurry to get someplace.

After I got home from work the next day, I call Betsy. Mrs. Banks answers and I tell her that I am Ben Tepke and would like to talk to Betsy, if that's okay. She seems friendly and asks me to wait a minute. Then Betsy picks up the phone and says, "So you remembered my number. I thought you would forget it by the time you got home. That was a nice meeting last night. Do you go to those meetings all the time? Nita says that everyone is very friendly and that you go the beach, have picnics, do things other than just have church meetings. She says you have been a friend of Bob for a long time."

I'm wondering if I'll get a chance to ask her for a date as she continues talking. Finally she says, "Am I talking too much? I'm sorry! What's up?"

I blurt out, "Well, I thought I'd like to take you to a movie if you'd like to go. If you have a movie you would like to see, or the Harding down in Logan Square has 'Great Expectations' playing. I've heard that its good, Montgomery Clift and Olivia DeHaviland are in it."

She says, "That sounds good, I'd really like that. Are you talking about tomorrow night?"

"I work on Saturday and don't get home until 7:00. I was thinking about Sunday afternoon."

" Oh! Well, I've got a date for tomorrow night anyway. I'll have to talk to my mom and dad and see if they will let me have two dates this weekend. I've got all my homework finished so they might say okay. Can you call back in about twenty minutes? I'd really like to go!"

I hang up the phone, but I don't move away from it or the chair I'm sitting on in the hallway. I can see the kitchen clock. and the twenty minutes seem like an hour as I wait to call again.

As Gramps passes me on his way to the kitchen he says, "Are you waiting for a call? I don't think Harry Truman is looking for any advice, and if he is he doesn't know this phone number. So, you better go on up stairs and do your homework."

"Very funny, Grandpa."

132

Out of the Loop

When I call Betsy back she tells me that it's okay with her folks, she can go on Sunday.

When I arrive at her door, I meet Betsy's Mom and Dad. They are very nice and they tell us to have a good time. We take the Diversey bus to Milwaukee Avenue and on the way talk about school and where we grew up, but we don't have a lot to talk about. When we arrive at the show, I buy the tickets and popcorn. During the show, I think about putting my arm around her, but chicken out.

After the movie we walk back to Diversey to catch the bus home. We walk past department stores, woman's shops, furniture and appliance stores. Along the way I take her hand and hold it. She seems pretty comfortable with that, doesn't say anything one way or another. I like holding her hand.

After boarding the bus on our way west, it only takes a few minutes to reach Pulaski Road. On the northwest corner of Pulaski and Diversey sits the Olson Rug Company and its unique and curious waterfall and rock garden. Unique because there isn't another man-made landmark as beautiful in Chicago and curious because it sits up against a factory that weaves carpets and rugs, seemingly without a reason for its existence.

As we ride past, we have a great view of the waterfall. Flood lights illuminate white cascading water flowing over the lips of jutting rocks and into the lagoon below. There are colored lights on the winding path and on the staircase that leads to the upper part of the falls. The bridge that crosses the water fall is a favorite place for people to stand. The path leads viewers down to the sizeable lagoon and level ground once again. Near the top of the falls sits an Indian tepee where little kids like to fantasize about how it was when the "Redskins" were on the warpath.

The effect the falls has on me is so mesmerizing that I almost ask Betsy if she'd like to get off the bus and walk around. Then good judgement intervenes and I keep quiet.

Betsy is also looking out the window and says, "I really love that place. Don't know how many times I have been there with my family, but we like it a lot."

"Me, too. I never get tired of it."

Then Betsy says, "Why don't we go there some time?"

Now, there's an invitation for another date if ever I heard one! When we arrive at Betsy's door, I say good night and don't have enough nerve to kiss her. We talk for a few minutes at her doorway, and that's it. She didn't look like she expected me to give her a kiss. I should have tried anyway.

No one would guess, but the only girls I've ever kissed are my Mom, sister and cousins. And those kind of kisses don't count. I'd like one like they do in the movies. But, it was a nice date. My first date. I really like Betsy, the girl with the eyes that don't match. So do a lot of other guys, I guess. After saying good-bye, I didn't take the bus home, I walked. No sweat. Saved the car fare.

*****

I've made my commitment to join the church. I'm going to confirmation classes on Sunday before the Sermon. I'm not going with the little kids, I'm in an adult class that meets before the first service in the basement of the church. There are only three of us attending. The other two are a married couple that have found the Lord and want to join the Gethsemene congregation. In a few weeks I will be a Lutheran, too. Didn't realize how challenging these classes would be. Haven't read or studied the Bible before. It isn't easy to read and get the meaning of, right off.

Out of the Loop

You really have to study the words. I'm trying, but I don't read very well and there's a lot of deep meaning in these words of Scripture. Now, I'm faced with confessing my sins to the Lord above, accepting Jesus Christ as my Lord and Savior, acknowledging that the Holy Spirit lives within me and not just mouthing the words, but truly believing.

I do believe!

The Bible delivers an eyewitness account of what happened to Jesus two thousand years ago. It talks about the miracles He created, miracles that people like me witnessed, saw happen, experienced standing there right beside Jesus. If it hadn't happened, wasn't true, there would be no way that Matthew, Mark, Luke, and John could have told the same stories that they created in their gospels. They wrote the gospels in their own time. Gave us the words Jesus said. All the words and thoughts expressed in the Bible were inspired by God. I don't believe for one minute that the Bible could have survived this long if it twisted the truth in any way.

Then there's Paul. He persecuted followers of Christ. But Christ shook his entire being and struck him blind, then took him, shook him up in such a forceful way that he believed and went on to preach the gospel from that day forward until he was put to death. He loved the Lord and followed the path that Jesus put him on in bringing Christ to the Gentiles of his day.

How can anyone believe there is no God when they see evidence of His miracles everywhere you look: Flowers, birds, butterflies, trees, animals, the sun and rain, stars in the heavens, everything there is to see and hear and taste, touch and smell has come from our Lord in Heaven. There would be no reason for anything without God to thank and worship and believe in. I'm no holy roller by a long shot. I've got sins to confess and I'm glad I've got Jesus on my side to grant me forgiveness. He gave His life for me on the cross and I'm glad I'm making my commitment to join His church.

******

Mom and Dad came to church the day I joined, witnessed my Baptism, watched as I took my first communion. It was a beautiful day.

******

Our softball team came in first, we were the best, hands down. Lost only one game during the season and that was a fluke. The championship trophy is sitting in the narthex of the church and has all our names engraved on it.

Fifteen

Now that I'm back in school, I don't have much free time for dating, but when I call Betsy or run into her in the hallway, she's always friendly. I've taken her to Bruno's for pizza on a Saturday night after a movie. There are a lot of Saturday nights she has dates with other guys. That's okay, but it makes me jealous. I like her, like talking to her, and I know she likes me, too.

Since Bruno's is only a few blocks from where Betsy lives, a weeknight date is okay with her folks as long as I don't keep her out late. I'm working at Shaynes after school now and I've gone right to her house without going home when I've taken her to Bruno's. I have also advanced to the "kiss good-bye" stage of our relationship. There's no heavy breathing involved, but I've done it. I've kissed a girl that knows how to kiss, and I like it.

Haven't reached the necking stage, but I have a feeling that might be possible, too, if a time and place for that kind of thing happens along.

Before the semester began, I took Betsy on a few dates during the week. Asked Mr. Webster for a day off here and there, not too often, and he didn't ask why I was asking. Heck it was only twice and weeks apart and it didn't seem to make him angry. I wanted to take her to Riverview but her folks don't think that's a proper place for Betsy to go on a date. I don't know why.

We have taken the bus to Olson Rug and walked around the waterfall. I reminded her that it was her idea, when I called and told her I'd like to take her there.

I tried to talk her into going steady once, but she said, "Ben, I like you a lot and I've even broken a couple of dates with other guys after you called. If you think that's an easy thing to do, it isn't. So you know I think a lot of you, but I'm not going to go steady with anyone. I enjoy going out with different guys. You all have different personalities and it's interesting to find out what makes you tick. I don't date every guy as many times as I've dated you lately. If I don't like a guy after the first date, that's it. But going steady isn't for me, understand?"

"Sure, I guess. What makes me tick, Betsy?"

"Well, let me see, you're nice, polite, tall, dark and handsome. Good to look at and fun to be with, okay. You say 'ain't' a lot and you know you shouldn't. You're good in sports and enjoy playing ball better than doing homework. Now you know!"

Out of the Loop

"Well, I'm glad you think I'm good to look at and I do like playing softball and basketball. You're good to look at, too and you know it."

"Well, those brown eyes of yours told me you think so from that moment you asked for my telephone number. And what was going on in your head wasn't nice when you asked."

"What? What are you talking about?'

"That's a joke, Ben. Don't be so serious."

Since Betsy and Nita are such good friends and Nita and Bob are going steady, we double date once in a while. One Sunday, after church, we went swimming at North Avenue beach. Betsy had a lot of guys giving her the once over when we were there. She's a knockout in a bathing suit. Made me jealous but made me feel like I was one lucky guy, too.

*****

"Sorry sir, that number you asked for is no longer in service."

"What? There must be some mistake. Operator, are you sure?"

"Yes sir, that number has been disconnected."

I sit there with the phone buzzing in my hand after the operator pulled the plug, wondering what has happened. Wondering if Betsy's dad forgot to pay the bill or worse yet, maybe he couldn't afford to pay the bill. Wondering if I should walk up to where she lives and knock on the door? That's not a good idea if her dad is broke. Since I know where Nita lives, I walk over to her house and ring the bell. When she comes to the door I ask, "Nita, is Mr. Banks in some kind of financial trouble? I tried to call Betsy and they said that the phone has been turned off."

Nita laughs and says, "No, Ben. There's no money problem at the Banks' house. The Banks moved to Oak Park."

"What? When?"

" A couple of weeks or so ago. I've got her phone number if you'd like to call her."

I do. In fact, after talking to Nita I go right home again and get on the phone. Betsy answers on the first ring.

"Hey, why didn't you tell me that you were moving?" I'm a bit miffed, but we aren't going steady so I can't raise a fuss about it.

She tells me, "Well, I was going to, but there are so many things that have to be done when you move, I didn't get around to it. Nita knew. Thought maybe Bob would tell you."

"No, I haven't seen Bob for a while."

"Well, moving is a lot of work. Didn't know our new phone number and I was really busy with the new high school schedule. It takes time to figure out how to get from here to there in this new neighborhood and Oak Park High School is much bigger than Foreman. We live just a few blocks east of Harlem and south of Division Street, on Forest Avenue. This house isn't easy to get to unless you have a car."

She knows I don't have a car.

Then she says, "I like Oak Park High School and I've made a lot of new friends. But I still miss the old neighborhood."

"That's no surprise, Betsy. About making new friends. You're good at that. But it's a big surprise that you've moved. I was thinking about asking you to go out. Then when I called you, the phone company told me your phone had been disconnected. I thought your Dad couldn't pay the bill."

She breaks up laughing and says her Dad will be laughing too, when she tells him that.

Out of the Loop

Then she says, "Hey, we can still go out if you can figure out how to get here. We can walk to the movie in Oak Park on Lake Street."

"How about Saturday? I'll figure out how to get to your house."

She says, "I've got a date. You can't call on Thursday and expect me to go out on Saturday, Ben. But, next Saturday would be all right. You've got a date!"

"Okay, I'll get back to you about where we're going."

How am I going to get to Oak Park without wheels? I'll call Bob. Bob can borrow his Dad's car whenever he wants. It's an old green, four door Dodge. He likes driving. He drives us guys to ball games, drives us down to the beach, to hell and gone if there's a reason. He's a very popular fella. We liked him okay before he could get the car, but now he's king of the hill. King of the road would be a better way to describe him.

One time, Bob packed seven girls from the Luther League inside the car and let six of us guys stand on the running boards and hang on for dear life when we went to a church meeting on the north side. It was great! Just like the time we hitchhiked to Lake Geneva. Wind blowing our hair, eyes watering, and feeling like we're on another great adventure. We would probably have been in trouble if some cop had spotted us, but we didn't see any cops going or coming home.

Since Bob and Nita are good friends with Betsy, I'm pretty sure he won't mind doubling with us, so I call him.

"Are you and Nita doing anything a week from Saturday?"

"No, nothing that I know about."

"Would you like to double?"

"What did you have in mind to do?"

Dan Glaubke

"Geeze, I don't know. You want to go to a movie?

He says, "Sure, lets go to the Outdoor Theatre on Harlem and Irving Park Road.

When I tell Betsy what we were going to do, she tells me she can hardly wait. I think that's BS, but I'm flattered anyway.

On Saturday, when we get to Betsy's new house, I can't believe it. It's huge. It's no bungalow, that's for sure. The lot is as big as two Chicago lots put together. Her old man must really be doing well to afford a place like this. I ring the bell and Betsy is right at the door. She's been waiting and is ready to go.

The Outdoor Theatre drive-in is really big with room for at least a hundred cars. It is still light out. We park next to a speaker spot and get it operating at a comfortable volume. Bob and I leave the girls to go to the refreshment stand. I buy a big box of popcorn and a couple of drinks for Betsy and me, Bob buys the same.

There are coming attractions and cartoons to sit through before the movie begins. As the night closes in on us and the movie finally flashes on the screen, I move a little closer to Betsy, put my arm around her, and she moves closer to me, too. Her hair smells clean and fresh against my face. She has on some wonderful perfume that has me losing my focus on the giant screen in front of the car. Her blouse has a couple of buttons open and from where I'm sitting the view is wonderful, to say the least. At the moment I don't really care about the movie. I want to hug and kiss her.

"Betsy, could you stop eating for a minute?"

"I could, but will I? No! I want to watch the movie and I know what's on your mind."

"You're a mind reader?"

"Doesn't take a lot of imagination. You're breathing hard.

Out of the Loop

If you hold me any tighter, I'll be losing my breath and it won't be from unbridled passion. It will be from the vise grip your arm has me in. Please wait. Ease up. And whisper. No don't whisper, just be quiet. If the movie gets boring, I might change my mind."

The movie is *Duel in the Sun* in Technicolor. Heavy. A lot of beautiful landscapes. The Old West is growing up. Railroads are huffing and puffing over the rails. Outlaws have their six shooters drawn and are firing twenty rounds without reloading. Jennifer Jones is an orphan that needs to learn some things. Betsy is enthralled. The movie's okay, but I'd rather be surrendering to Betsy than dueling in the shadows of the giant screen.

The end of the movie is a tear jerker and Betsy's blue and brown eyes are leaking something awful. She's sobbing and her nose is running. It's a good thing I didn't forget napkins when I bought the popcorn. When the "The End" comes rising on screen, Bob asks me something. My mind is elsewhere, watching Betsy blow her nose and tidy up her eyes. What Bob had said that I didn't hear but did acknowledge with a "Yeah!" was: "Did you put the speaker back, Ben?"

With my affirmative answer, Bob starts the car and guns off of the ramp to vie for a spot alongside the thundering herd of cars heading for the exits. I think he believes he is competing in the Indy 500. And I'm in shock. I'm in the back seat with Betsy and the speaker we've been listening to all night long. But the speaker isn't speaking any more. It's in my lap. There must be a mile of cable trailing behind us, trailing out of the broken window. The window that broke when Bob left the "gate."

Bob's great in a crisis. When he realizes what has happened, he yells at me as he continues racing for the exit, "Pull in the cable, pull in the cable you dummy, get the cable in the car!" I've been doing everything I can to fulfill his wishes. Got it all in before we made the exit, peeled out of the drive-in and headed for home.

Betsy was a bit miffed because as hard as she tried to avoid the dirty, dusty cable, a foot or two wound up nesting on her skirt. Must have had at least a hundred feet of cable in the back seat if we had an inch.

Didn't do too well as a lover boy this night. Didn't get one kiss. We took Betsy home and I walked her to the door and said, "Good-night." She said "Bye." And that was it. Then on the way home, I tried to figure out a way I could repay Bob for the havoc I had created. Even though he said, forget about it, I worried and couldn't forget about it. Shit and two makes eight! I'll bet Nita and Betsy talk a lot about tonight when they get together on the phone. I'll bet the talk isn't too favorable regarding one Ben Tepke.

*****

As time marches toward Christmas and the New Year, Mike, Bob, Ricky and I have been getting together and playing basketball after church. Lars plays once in awhile but not as often as the rest of us. Harry's a good player, but he doesn't hang around with us that often. We had a great year in softball, and we think that playing basketball in the church league is something we should do. I don't think our basketball playing is all that great, but it's fun. Mike's got a back-board and hoop on his garage roof and that's where we play "Horse" and "Two on Two" in the alley. Mike is good on long shots, Bob on lay ups, Ricky is very aggressive for a squirt and his lay ups are getting better all the time. I'm okay, can make some long ones, too, but I'm best at blocking and stealing the ball. I really like playing basketball.

Out of the Loop

*****

School is going well for a change. My schedule is better, too. I get out at 2:00 and I'm down at Shaynes by 2:45 or 3:00. When I finally told Ethel that I had joined the church she grabbed me and hugged me. Wanted to know all the details. I even told her about why my Mom doesn't go to church and about her mother being hit.

"I know all about those things," Ethel said, "Had a husband that drank and was ugly and mean and hurt me more than a few times. I finally got away from him. Took my baby and rode to Chicago on a Greyhound bus. I have a cousin here. Stayed with her until I started working and made some money. I owe her a lot."

"Where did you live before."

"Lived in Tennessee. Memphis. My Mom and Dad are both dead so I don't have any relatives down there any more."

"So, you're divorced?"

"No, I never did that. I don't want him to know where I am or anything about me. I'm doing just fine, doing what I'm doing. You should try to get your folks back to church."

"I guess, but they are pretty set in their ways."

"Well give it a try anyway. I'm so glad you found the Lord. Makes me very happy to hear it!"

Sixteen

We've done it. We have entered the Lutheran Church Basketball League. There are ten of us on the church team and some of us aren't very good, but we'll all get a chance to play and that's what counts. We have blue and gold uniforms. We practice together at Blackhawk Park. That's where we will play our home games. Three other church teams will be playing at Blackhawk, too. There are four teams that play their home games at other parks or YMCA facilities.

Dixie's dad, Mr. Algren, has volunteered to be our coach. We play on Saturday evenings. No games are scheduled before 7:00 PM so I'm not gonna be in any trouble, unless Mr. Webster sends me on a late errand somewhere. Shaynes isn't just around the corner from Blackhawk Park and if a game is going to be played somewhere else, I will have to hitch a ride.

I think I'll talk to Mr. Webster and see if he'll let me off before normal quitting time if a game is someplace that we have to travel to. He's a nice guy, but I won't ask unless I need to.

Coach Algren runs us through some basic plays. After a few practices, he puts Ricky, Bob, Mike, Harry and me on the first team. Lars is a sub, along with some guys I don't know so well named Hank, Jack, Buzz and Clarence. They are fellow church members and eligible to play. We count pretty much on Mike and Harry to make the baskets we need to win, but all of us can make a few points along the way.

The coach has Bob playing center, Ricky and Mike playing forwards. Harry and I are assigned the guard positions. The league games started in October and will end in February. As the season progresses we have won a few games and lost a few. But we're getting better, getting better playing with one another. The coach stresses defense, defense, defense. Makes no difference when we play Austin Messiah Lutheran. They have a giant of a guy playing center and a couple of other guys that can shoot from the corners that run up points, too. They really clobbered us.

"How in the hell can you guard a guy that tall? He must be six-six!" Bob is frustrated because even when we double teamed the tall Messiah guy, he scored big.

"Hey, we did the best we could. We should have stepped on the guy's shoes so he couldn't jump for those high passes," I tell him.

Mike says, "It wasn't only him, they have some good shooters, too. We just stunk tonight!"

"We're not the Harlem Globe Trotters, that's for sure,"

Out of the Loop

Ricky says.

"Next time we play those guys, we should have Ricky guard the big guy," says Harry laughing, "He's just tall enough to sink his teeth into the guy's jockstrap when the refs aren't watching. That should reduce his height real fast. I'll bet Ricky could dribble under the guy's legs without hitting his head on the guy's crotch."

"He ain't that tall, you wise ass!"

Ricky is sensitive about his height.

He isn't sensitive about much else. He keeps talking about his girlfriend Gail all the time and there's no sensitivity about what he's talking about. If she only knew.

*****

On Saturdays I always work on the third floor at Shaynes because that's the busiest day of the week. Now that the Christmas season is approaching, the company has hired two girls to work on Saturdays to model clothes and furs, especially when the store has sales. They are Pat and Shirley, and they are beautiful. I think they must be twenty-one or twenty-two. They wear one outfit for a while, then go into Mr. Finestein's office, change clothes, and walk around some more. They usually take their breaks in his office, too.

Last Saturday, Mr. Finestein grabbed me on the floor where he was talking to a customer and asked me to get a fur coat that was hanging in his office. "It's a full length mink, Ben. A full length mink with a sold ticket on it. The coat is hanging on the rack beside my desk."

In order to get to into Mr. Finestein's office you have to go into the big stockroom area first, then turn right and that's where his office is.

149

Dan Glaubke

So, I hurried into the storage area, zipped through Finestein's door without knocking and wow! Wow! There sitting in Finestein's chair with her feet up on his desk was Shirley. She swung toward me when she heard the door open and suddenly I was looking at two absolutely gorgeous knockers. Bare knockers. Not huge boobs, just beautiful with big, red nipples pointing right at me. No brassiere. She was sitting in that chair and all she had on was a pair of white lace panties.

My mouth must have dropped open a foot.

She looked at me with a smile on her face and said, "Don't you usually knock when you see a door closed?" But, she didn't move a muscle to cover up and I'm still gawking.

"I, I, I, did, didn't think about knocking and I'm, I'm sorry!"

I'm not really sorry. And you can have your Coronet Magazine. This is the real thing! The guys will never believe me when I tell them!

Shirley says, "Ben, what are you doing in here and turn around for Pete's sake!"

I turn, I turn slowly and I tell her, " I'm supposed to get a mink for Mr. Finestein. It has a sold tag and the customer's name is Riley."

A moment later, the mink comes over my shoulder and I say, "Thank you and I'm sorry."

"Sure you are!"

I think she was giggling when I left but I can't be sure.

I left the office blushing, gave Mr. Finestein the coat and went to the washroom to wait until my normal color returned to my face. That Shirley is so beautiful. Beautiful with clothes and without.

By the time I got back on the job, I thought everyone

in the store must know about what happened. Couldn't be sure, but all the ladies seemed to be looking at me sideways.

Hey, Shirley could have locked the door and she didn't have to have taken her brassiere off for heaven's sake. Will I knock the next time I have to go through that door? Probably. But I'm not positive I will.

"Ethel, did you hear about what I did?"

"What did you do?"

"I went into Mr. Finestein's office for a mink. Didn't knock and Shirley was sitting at his desk with nothing on. I mean she had her pants on, but nothing else."

"Oh, my. She does that. Those brassieres those girls wear are real snug and Shirley doesn't like being strapped so tight. You okay? You'll see a lot more than that as you grow up. Don't let it bother you, it won't bother her. But you better knock the next time."

Shirley and Pat treat me as though nothing happened and I'm happy about that. Really, nothing did happen except I got an eye full. The guys will never believe me! Maybe I should buy a camera. It's hard to get that image out of my head.

*****

We had another wonderful Thanksgiving. I ate so much it's hard going to work on Friday. When I arrive, Mr. Webster has big news.

"Shaynes is getting out of the haberdashery business, Ben. This means we will have some 'Big Sale' days ahead. When the sale ends we will have to work a couple of nights to box things up that haven't sold. What's left over will be trucked away. The two of us will be working together and I'll have a couple of 'part timers' packing things, too. One of your jobs will be making sure the 'part timers' don't walk off with things. If you see anything suspicious, you let me know, okay?"

"Right! I can do that!"

So two weeks before Christmas, on a Wednesday, I worked after school until two in the morning, boxing and packing things. None of the part-timers were a problem. You can't imagine how much stuff we had to deal with. We packed up hats, shirts, canes, ties, umbrellas, scarves and handkerchiefs. We packed all the stuff on the first floor and boxes of things in a basement storeroom. All the men's jewelry had already been taken care of before we started packing all the other stuff. When the day ended, I was really beat. But no one would have to pack a thing tomorrow. We did the whole job tonight. When I was ready to leave the store, Mr. Webster gave me some money. He said, " Take a taxi home, Ben. You don't have to come in tomorrow. You'll get paid for the overtime tonight and paid for tomorrow, too. You really worked hard and I appreciate it. Now, don't put that money in your pocket and ride the streetcar home. Take a taxi. You hear me? Are you going to be okay for school tomorrow?"

"Sure Mr. Webster, I'll be okay, and thanks for the money."

I'm tired! But, I'm not taking a taxi. I'm not wasting good money that way. I took the Elston Avenue streetcar, asked the conductor if he could remember to toss me off on Diversey. Then I sat down and fell asleep. The conductor didn't let me down. Didn't know where I was for an instant when he shook my shoulder. After stepping down off the car I had to wait for thirty minutes for the trolley bus. Stayed awake for the rest of the ride west.

As I went to my classes and tried to stay awake, things

were happening downtown at Shaynes. All the old display cases and furniture were being carted out. The painting of the first floor would happen after the store closed on Saturday night. They'd finish up on Sunday. Since the store doesn't open until noon on Monday, they will have all the new display cases and furniture in place before the doors open for business. By Tuesday, a whole new line of woman's clothes and jewelry will be in place and ready to sell. That's the plan and Mr. Webster will get the job done, one way or another, because expensive ads will be running in the Tribune. There will be a Christmas sale and the announcement that the new first floor Woman's Department is all ready to go.

*****

I've been looking forward to the Christmas break. I'm through shopping for Christmas. It's easy when you work close to State Street. Field's, Carsons, Goldblatts, The Boston Store are all within walking distance of Shaynes. Of course, I don't have enough to buy to go to all those stores.

I got my Dad a couple of bow ties at Shaynes when the haberdashery closed down. Even though the ties were on sale, I got another ten per cent off because I work there. I got my Mom a new scarf. She hates the cold weather and her other scarf is getting worn. I'm giving Lisa three bucks. She'll be delirious. I don't think she's ever had more than a dollar in her purse, ever. Got Gramps a tin of pipe tobacco. Smells sweet. Hope he likes it. Bought it at his favorite tobacco store. I spent a lot of money. Merry Christmas!

Seventeen

1948

On New Year's Eve our whole basketball team went bowling. Before Christmas, Mike made a reservation for two alleys at 11:00, and it was a good thing he did, because the place is packed. A few of the Gethsemane girls came by to watch. They are having a sleepover at the Algren house tonight. The guys all bought cigars but the thing made my eyes water. I was getting sick to my stomach. None of the guys noticed. They were all too busy puffing away on their own. It's a good thing we don't have a bowling team. Our scoring hovers at about a hundred twenty-five. Mike bowls better than the rest of us. He almost bowled two hundred. Well, a hundred eighty-eight, anyway. After bowling we all went to the Algren's house and crashed the party. We partied until four in the morning. Mrs. Algren served everyone wine highballs. Just one. She's one wonderful lady. Didn't sleep over, but might as well have. The girls didn't get a lot of sleep either.

As school resumes once again after the Christmas break and the New Year's celebration, I'm in a funk. I'm not a scholar, I like working better than I like school. I enjoy playing basketball better than chemistry, English, Spanish and all the other subjects I'm taking. I like doing things with the guys, but there's something missing. Basketball seems to be the bright spot I have to look forward to these days, but we aren't doing too good with that either. The funk has to do with missing Betsy, I think that's what it is. She was always fun to talk to and be with.

In the second round of the church basketball schedule, we lost big to Austin Messiah Lutheran once again. The big guy beat us. We played better, but that doesn't say much for losing by twenty-two points. We lost a couple of other games in the second round too, but we only lost by a few points, nothing more than seven. The season ended in March and we didn't get a trophy, but had a lot of fun. We are getting better all the time because now we know our strengths and weaknesses. Next year should be a different story.

With the basketball season behind us, Spring has sprung once again   It's warming up. The birds are chirping, bees buzzing, dogs barking, and all the girls have put away the cold weather wear that they've been wrapped up in all winter long. It's nice to see all those budding bumps and curious

Out of the Loop

curves coming to life once more, pressing against the fabric, for guys like me to notice. Luther League meetings are the big social thing I've been involved in lately, but I'm not dating anyone,

I feel like asking a girl out. There are some real good looking girls in high school and the real good looking ones seem to have steady boyfriends.

Bob and Nita are still going steady. He's a senior now, she's a sophomore. Ricky is still dating Gail and even though we don't want any details he's been telling us every move he makes. Don't have any idea if it's all BS or if his girlfriend and he are having all the fun he's talking about. I wish he'd keep his mouth shut. I told him so, but he thinks I'm jealous. I'm not jealous. He doesn't know shit from Shineola about what I'm thinking and I think he's running his girl's reputation right through the mud.

Since daylight saving time is in effect once again, it's still light out when I get home from work. So I've been going for bike rides after supper on the days we don't have softball practice. I don't go anywhere in particular. Usually. This evening I decided to visit Betsy. It's only about six miles from the house to where she lives. Didn't call her, just took off on the bike. I haven't talked to Betsy since the drive-in fiasco. Went down Diversey west to Oak Park Avenue, then south. Stuck to the sidewalks. Slow going but it's a nice warm evening. I get to Betsy's about eight and the sun is going down.

Crap! She's standing on her doorstep, talking to some guy. There's a car parked on her drive way. I'm still a half block away when he leans over and gives her a kiss. Double crap! I make a sharp U-turn and head for home,

*****

157

Dan Glaubke

We're on target for another trophy year in softball. Haven't lost one game yet and the season's half over. When school ended for the summer, my grades were the best I've had in high school. Mom gave me hug and kiss when she saw them. Gramps called Aunt Lily and Aunt Pearl. He's never done that before, called to talk about my grades. On the other hand, I think it was just an excuse to talk to Aunt Pearl. You know, an excuse to find out what was going on out there in Wyoming. Mom said, she heard him say that he's thinking of flying out there for a visit. Told me not to say anything about it. She doesn't want him to think she was eavesdropping. I told her that he practically yells when he's talking on the phone and half the neighborhood probably heard him. I'd really like to talk to him about taking a plane out west. That's exciting and no one in the whole family has flown any-where. He should do it!

*****

When I arrive home from work on Friday, Mom tells me Lars called. Mom says that he sounded strange. When I call him back, he does does sound strange.

He says, "Ben ... Harry's dead."

I can't believe what I'm hearing.

"Dead? Are you nuts? I talked to Harry yesterday. He was going to go to Bruno's with Wes and Tony for lunch. Then they were going to go to Riverview. Tony's got a new car. Traded his old one in for it. It's an Olds, ..."

"Will you shut up for a minute. Just shut up! Yeah, you're right about the three guys going to Riverview and Bob was supposed to go along, too. They never made it. Harry was with Wes and Tony, and the way I've heard it, Tony was racing with some nut down Central and the guy cut him off. So Tony lost it, lost control of his car and plowed into a trolley line post. Harry went right through the windshield, broke his neck! Bob was on the corner and saw the whole thing happen. Called me. Thinks we should get together and talk."

Everyone met at my place. Arrived after supper. Bob had to rehash all the gory details that Lars had covered pretty well. My Mom and Dad were shaken; they had met Harry and his folks at ball games. My folks remembered that Harry was the guy that got me through geometry.

Mom said, "Don't you fellows bother the Grummans now. They'll be busy with arrangements and trying to recover from the shock of losing their boy and all. Just wait until you see the obituary before asking if you can do anything."

Bob said, "I think we should walk down to the church and talk to Pastor Olson. If he hasn't heard anything about what happened, I think he would sure like know."

We all agreed with Bob, so we walked down the street to the church. We found out that Pastor Olson had been notified and was over at the Grumman house, trying to comfort them. Harry didn't have any brothers or sisters so the Grummans will be all alone with their grief tonight. I still find Harry's death hard to fathom.

There's a wake. The casket is closed but there is a picture of Harry on it, his high school graduation picture, a photo of our good looking buddy that reminds me of pizza at Bruno's, the trip to Maxwell street and a lot of hard fought ball games.

The funeral home is packed with high school kids in addition to Grumman relatives and neighbors. There must be ten girls sobbing. Harry had a lot of girl friends. I had to hurry into the men's room for a minute when I saw Harry's picture and heard the girls sobbing. Had something in my eye, didn't want anyone to notice.

At the funeral service, Pastor Olson had a lot to say about Harry, what kind of person he was, some nice things to remember about him. He said we should be happy that he is with the Lord. He told us that no one knows why these things happen and as sad as it is, we have to believe that Harry is in heaven and being taken care of. Pastor Olson said, "He's with Jesus Christ our Lord and Savior." The Grummans asked Bob to be a pall bearer. He was the only guy from our bunch that was asked, the rest were relatives, cousins and uncles. After watching Harry lowered into the ground with more words from Pastor Olson, we went back to Harry's house.

There is a ton of food that neighbors and church folks brought over and a lot of folks have come to pay respects. Mike, Ricky, Lars, and I cut out soon after we finished eating. Bob told us he will have to stick around a while longer. That Bob is one okay guy."

You think it hurt when he hit?" Lars asks.

" Probably. But not for long. The cops told the newspaper he died instantly." I don't know why I've answered the question. We were all thinking about the same thing I guess. My answer is what my mind's eye is telling me, but who knows. Only God knows.

Bob knew Wes and Tony slightly. Lars knew them too, because they went to Lane and they rode the streetcar together at times. Before Tony got a car and drove to school. It was Harry that asked Bob if he'd like to go along to Riverview. Tony died a few days after the accident, too, but Wes walked away almost without a scratch. He did have a concussion, but after two days in the hospital he is out on the street again. We ride with Bob a lot but he never does crazy things. Sure he will drive with guys standing on the running boards, but he doesn't fly when he's doing that and he doesn't drag race down a narrow street like Central ever, or really any place that I know about. You have to be careful who you ride with.

*****

A week after the funeral I decided to ride to Oak Park once again. Got there about the same time as the last time I was looking for Betsy. She wasn't on the front porch this time. She wasn't home. No one was home. And on my way home I was trapped in a downpour. Shouldn't have worn the good shirt. When I arrived home, Gramps was in the kitchen having a cup of coffee. I asked him to open the basement door for me. Sat in the basement looking at Coronet Magazines while my clothes dried.

Eighteen

We're still on top in the church softball league. We miss Harry, but we haven't lost a game. Mr. Ryerson put Buzzy in at shortstop and he's doing a good job. Harry was a better hitter, but Buzz is okay.

****

I'm doing a little bit of everything at Shaynes, running more errands these days than hanging up clothes. When Mr. Webster took two days off last week he put old Mr. Kanaras in charge of opening and closing the store. He gave me the job of answering the phone and taking care of any emergencies. Mr. Kanaras doesn't handle the phone too well. Speaks broken

Dan Glaubke

English, but he's a hard worker. When I had to go somewhere, Ethel came downstairs and took care of the phone. Then the sales ladies complained, but not to Ethel. They didn't want to hurt her feelings. My feelings they didn't care about, so they complained to me. There weren't too many emergencies. What kind of emergency does a clothing store have. Delivering clothes to the "Have to have it right now" customers is the one that happens frequently.

On the second day that Mr. Webster was gone, a customer called before lunch.

"John T. Shaynes, May I help you?"

"I hope so. This is Mrs. Rivera. I bought a suit on Saturday. It is being altered. It was supposed to be done sometime today. I need it now. Desperately. I have to have it because I'm leaving town. Flying to the west coast today."

"If you'll hold on a minute Mrs. Rivera, I'll find out if it's done."

I switched to the alteration department and Mary Cary picked up the phone. "Mary, you have something you're doing for Mrs. Rivera. She says she needs it in a hurry."

"It will be finished in about an hour."

When I told Mrs. Rivera, she said, "Will you, could you deliver it by three, please?"

"Yes, Ma'am."

"Who will deliver it? I have to tell the doorman."

"Ben Tepke, Mrs. Rivera."

She lives up north, on Sheridan Road. Took the bus. I'll be there on time, maybe five minutes late. The place is one of those big apartment buildings right on the lake. Fancy. The doorman is wearing a big red coat with brass buttons and the hat makes him look like an army general. Not one of ours, like one I've seen in National Geographic. I tell him who I am and why I'm here. He says I'm expected and to tell the elevator man to take me to the penthouse floor.

When I get off the elevator Mrs. Rivera is waiting for me, peaking around the corner of her door and tells me to come right in. The doorman must have called and said I was on the way up. She has a bathrobe on. Asks me to take a seat while she tries on the suit.

She's a big woman, probably weighs close to 200 pounds and she's inches shorter than I am. She took the box and left, for her bedroom, as I sat down on a sofa that faced a window that took up a whole wall. Outside the window Lake Michigan is beautiful, blue with dancing white caps. Birds are fluttering around and every so often they dive and fly up again. There are a few sailboats knifing through the surf with white sails billowing in the wind.

One living room wall is covered with pictures all the way to the ceiling. The ceiling is a lot higher than our bungalow ceilings. The pictures are the kind you see in the Art Institute. They aren't cardboard like those my grandma had or the Curier and Ives' prints in the basement. These are oil paintings and watercolors. People. Landscapes. One's a picture of a bowl of apples and oranges sitting on a table. I'd like to get up and take a closer look, but Mrs. Rivera said to sit down and that's what I'm doing.

There's a new Philco Television set sitting on a table in the corner. Looks new. Looks like the screen must be ten to twelve-inches. Big. The guys and I stand by the radio store on Laramie and watch television through the store window once in a while.

There isn't a peep of noise in this room, except for the

tick-tick-tock of the grandfather clock that stands near the door. No sound until Mrs. Rivera called me. "Young man I need your help. Will you come here please?"

I feel a little strange, sitting on a couch in a strange place and the lady I just met about five minutes ago is calling for help in her bedroom.

"Mrs. Rivera?"

"Ben. Please. My zipper is stuck. The zipper on the skirt of my new suit is stuck Can't get this damn zipper up or down. I'm late. Help, help, help me!" Her voice had been calm up until the last three words. These increased in volume, like turning the sound up on a radio until you break an eardrum.

In the bedroom, Mrs. Rivera is standing there blushing -- or maybe she's red from exertion. She is perspiring. The skirt is on backwards. The zipper is in front. Her slip is off her shoulders and bunched up around her waist. Her brassiere is enormous. I didn't know where I should be looking, trying to think of something to say, trying not to laugh. Here is one heavy lady with her hair all done up like some movie star standing in her bedroom in her bare feet with a skirt on backwards, a slip that sure has slipped from where it is supposed to be, with her boobs harnessed in a brassiere that looks like it could be used for a couple of parachutes at Riverview.

"Ben. Don't you dare laugh. This is serious. The zipper is stuck, its teeth are caught in my slip, and it won't go up or down. I'm late. I have to get to the airport. Help me!"

I couldn't see the zipper, but managed to get my fingers on it. Tugged and wiggled it, but my fingers keep slipping off. "Mrs. Rivera, I'm going to have to kneel down to see what I'm doing, okay?"

Out of the Loop

"Damn it, do it Ben!"

Now I'm on my knees. The slip is really caught. I'm thinking if we could get the skirt off, it might be easier to work on the zipper. There's a hazard in that thought. Something might rip if I try to pull the skirt down because her hips are so wide and if the slip slips along with the skirt, who knows what I'll be facing. Don't think I want to run the risk. On the other hand, there's no way to get the skirt up over the boobs. Need some help getting a firm grip on the zipper tab. My knees hurt and I'm as frustrated as Mrs. Rivera at the moment.

"Mrs. Rivera do you have a pliers handy?"

"A pliers? No. No. What do you need a pliers for?"

"Well, my fingers keep slipping off the zipper tab; if I had a pliers I'd have a better grip on the tab and maybe better control to get the teeth free from your slip."

"Johnson. Johnson must have a pliers. I'll call Johnson."

"Ma'am? Who's Johnson?"

"The doorman. Wait here while I call down."

Mrs. Rivera went to her night stand, picked up the phone. Johnson did have a pliers. Said he would give it to the elevator operator. With the pliers firmly in my grip, it only took a few minutes to free the zipper. I was as careful as I could be. The slip has six holes in it but the zipper looks fine. No damage that I can see.

As I say, "Done, you're free." I stand. The skirt falls on the floor. And a slip strap that's hanging loose goes over my head. As I stand, the strap tightens and pulls Mrs. Rivera into me, her face is buried in my chest, her knockers press against my stomach and one of my legs is now snuggled up between hers. Embarrassing to say the least. As I duck to get the slip strap free, my head bounces off her boobs and for an instant my nose is buried in her cleavage. Now, Mrs. Rivera is laughing.

I'm blushing, face is burning. She's laughing one of those laughs you laugh when can't stop laughing to save your soul and tears are running down her face.

When she gets under control she says, "Ben, go sit down in the living room. I have to freshen up, change and finish packing." Then she chuckles a bit more and says, "You're going to have to help me close the zipper on my suitcase and help me take my bags downstairs. You can do that can't you?"

"Yes, ma'am. I can do that."

Then as she closes the bedroom door she laughs some more.

When we get down to the curb, the doorman helps the taxi driver put the bags in the trunk, and Mrs Rivera turns to me and says. "Ben. You look like a nice person and I'm going to trust you. I don't want you to tell anyone, no one, about what happened upstairs. Understand?"

"Yes."

" I do appreciate what you did, but it's between you an me. Here's twenty dollars. Have some fun. I'll put in a good word for you at Shaynes. Promise me. Promise me you won't tell anyone at Shaynes or anyone."

"I promise, but you don't have to tip me."

"It isn't a tip. It's a thank-you from a very grateful woman."

"Driver, I'm late. Midway Airport, please hurry."

Watching the taxi go down Sheridan road, I chuckle and say, "No one would believe me if I told them Mrs. Rivera!"

Then I laugh, get on a Sheridan Road bus and head for home with a twenty dollar bill in my pocket. Twenty bucks. A fortune. How lucky can a guy get.

*****

Out of the Loop

You should have heard the family roar. I broke my promise, but Mrs. Rivera will never know. Couldn't help myself. Had to tell.

"What happened to you yesterday?" Ethel wants to know.

"Can't tell."

"Come on, I want to know!" Ethel didn't like the way I was smiling.

"You can't tell Mr. Webster, Gendolyn, any of the sales ladies. No one in this store....."

When I got to the part about Mrs. Rivera's slip strap and my nose buried in her cleavage, Ethel was losing her breath laughing so hard. She said, "Ben, Mr. Rivera is a millionaire. Owns factories all over the place. Makes stuff for hardware stores, automobile parts, nuts and bolts. It's no wonder that Mrs. Rivera wouldn't like that story going around. She's high society. I'd love to tell that story to someone, but I won't. My, oh my. Imagine. Mrs. Rivera, Mrs. Money Bags, caught in a situation with no one to turn to for help but Ben Tepke." Then she was laughing some more thinking about it.

Nineteen

On the Saturday just before Labor Day, the morning at Shaynes has been very slow and I want some fresh air. I decide to go for a walk down Michigan Avenue before having lunch. It has been two weeks since I said good-bye to Mrs. Rivera on Sheridan Road.

When the elevator stops on floor two, a man and three women get on. One of the ladies is Mrs. Rivera. I'n not about to say hello, don't want to embarrass her. I'll just slip out the door on Randolph, if she leaves through the Michigan Avenue entrance. She's seen me, too, for when she exits she tugs the gentleman's sleeve, turns toward me and says, "Henry, this is the young man that helped me out the day we flew out west. This is Ben Tepke. Ben, this is my husband."

Her husband smiles and says, "So you're Ben. Thanks for giving Margaret a hand when she needed it. I imagine it was a bit stressful for you. When Margaret is stressed everyone around her is stressed. You having lunch? It would be our pleasure, if you'd join us. How about it?"

Before I can say a word, Mrs. Rivera says, "Ben wasn't stressed Henry, he was thoughtful and quick thinking. I would have missed the plane if he hadn't come to the rescue." And looking at me she says, "Please have lunch with us Ben?"

"Sure!"

Don't want to pass up an opportunity to see where millionaires have lunch. "Have to check and see if I can take the time off. Can you wait a minute?"

When I tell Mr. Webster I've been invited to lunch by Mr. and Mrs. Rivera his mouth drops open and he can't believe it.

"Where did you meet them? Have you known them long?"

"No sir, when you were gone, had to take a suit to Mrs. Rivera, it was an emergency. That's how it happened."

"Go then! Mrs. Rivera spends a lot of money here. If she wants to take you to lunch everyday of the week it's okay with me. Go!"

When I get outside the store, there's a taxi waiting. "Let's go to The Pump Room, driver," Mr. Rivera says as we pull away from the curb.

The Pump Room is in the Ambassador East Hotel on the near north side. I've never been in a hotel other than the Edgewater Beach to deliver a coat and I've never eaten in one. It's real fancy. I feel out of place. When we entered the restaurant, Mr.

Out of the Loop

Rivera tells a guy standing there, "Will you fix the lad up with a jacket, Marvin? He wasn't expecting to have lunch here today."

"Certainly, Mr. Rivera. Will you step this way please?" Marvin says as he walks me to a little room where a number of jackets are hanging. "Try this on. It won't cost Mr. Rivera anything, but you have to wear a jacket to eat here."

When we're seated a waiter comes by and puts a napkin in my lap. I almost jumped out of my seat. When I look at the menu I can't believe it. It would take me a couple of months to earn enough to eat in this place. Mr. Rivera looks over his menu at me and asks, "Have you ever eaten oysters, Ben? They're real good here."

"No, I've never had oysters. I don't want to hurt your feelings, but I don't think I would like to try them."

"Well, we're just talking about appetizers. You like shrimp?"

"Maybe I'll have some soup, is that appetizer?"

"Well, soup is soup."

"I don't know what pate is. What escargot is. Caviar is fish eggs isn't it?"

"The Pate on the menu is liver. Escargot is snails. Yes, caviar is fish eggs and very special fish eggs that come all the way from Russia."

"I'll pass up the appetizers if that's okay with you. Lamb chops and mashed potatoes sound good, I'll have that."

"Good choice, Ben. What are you going to have Margaret?"

"A shrimp cocktail, a Caesar salad, and a glass of Chardonay will do it for me."

"Fine. I think I'll join Ben for my food order and have a beer. What would you like to drink Ben?"

Dan Glaubke

"I'll have a glass of milk, thank you."

As we wait for the food, Mr. Rivera asks me questions about where I live, what school I go to, how long I've worked at Shaynes, where we go on vacations, etcetera, etcetera. I ask him how many companies he owns. He laughs and uses his fingers as he tells me, because he doesn't want to leave one out of the conversation. Tells me where they're located, what they make, how many employees they have, etcetera, etcetera. I'm happy, because he enjoys talking, and I don't have to answer any more questions. Mrs. Rivera sips her chardonay, eats her shrimp and watches people eating around the restaurant room. I figure she's heard Henry ... Mr. Rivera... talk about his companies more than once or twice before.

The lamb chops and mashed potatoes are delicious. My Mom's a great cook, but I have to admit the food at the Pump Room might be a touch better.

While we're eating a man comes in with his wife and a kid about ten years old. The kid wants a peanut butter and jelly sandwich. When their food is served, a waiter wheels a cart to the table that has a grinder and a bowl of peanuts. He makes peanut butter right there. Spreads it on a piece of white bread, adds jelly, and the kid loves it.

After the main course, I have Baked Alaska. That's what Mrs. Rivera ordered and it's incredible. Mr. Rivera has a snifter of cognac.

When we leave, I say, "Don't know how to thank you, Mr. Rivera, that was the best."

"Listen. If you hadn't gotten Margaret out of that scrape with the zipper, we would have missed the plane. You were a life saver or should I say a wife saver. I thank you! Do you need taxi fare back to the store?"

Out of the Loop

"No. I'm going to walk. Need the exercise."

As I walked away I felt like the luckiest guy in the world.

*****

"Where did you go for lunch?" Mr. Webster wants to know.

"Pump Room."

"See any celebrities?"

"No, sir. Ate and listened to Mr. Rivera talk. Likes to talk. Food was good. Had lamb chops and mashed potatoes. Then something called Baked Alaska for dessert. Watched them make peanut butter for a peanut butter and jelly sandwich."

"Make peanut butter?"

Told Mr. Webster about the grinder and the waiter making the sandwich right at the table.

"That's some classy place. I'm going to take my wife there sometime."

*****

Labor day arrives and with it, it's back to Foreman. I have a great schedule this year. I'm through at 2:00 PM again which means I can be downtown by three. Except for losing our buddy Harry, things are good!

I've enjoyed the summer. Liked working downtown a lot more than I enjoy school work. My best class is gym. I love playing basketball and "horsing around" with the guys and the gym equipment. Swimming is okay, but I hate the chlorine smell that clings to your body after the class is over.

At the end of my junior year we got a new basketball

coach and gym teacher, Mr. Mayberry. One day, just after school began, he stood up against the gym wall watching a few of us play basketball before the period started. Then after class he called me over.

"Tepke, I've been watching you and I'd like you to come out for the team."

I'm amazed. "Heard you wanted to build a team using juniors and sophomores, didn't want any seniors trying out, Coach. What gives?"

"Yeah, I did say that, but I've changed my mind. Stay after school today and practice."

If I go out for the team I have to quit my job at Shaynes. and I'll be broke before you can finish a bag of Sugar Bowl fries. But if I make the team I'll be date bait with all the babes. That idea I like very much. "Okay coach. But I can't practice today, I've got a job. I have to tell them I won't be working anymore."

"All right, but I want you to be in the gym for practice to-morrow."

*****

Mr. Webster says he understands. He's a sports nut and he understands very well why I would want to play high school ball. He says he'll miss me and good luck. He'll mail me my money due.

I then make the rounds and say good bye to Ethel, Gwendolyn, Mr. Finestein and all the sales ladies. I think Ethel had a tear in her eye when I said good-bye. She gave me a hug. Didn't expect that. I learned a lot from her. A lot more than how to fold clothes and tie a knot. I won't forget her that's for sure.

*****

Coach Mayberry is no easy guy to get along with as he

coaches the team. He runs us ragged. We have all kinds of basics and drills to learn. All kinds of plays. I've grown. I'm six-one. Mayberry works me at forward one day, guard the next and even has me playing center when we scrimmage. Our center is six-three and talented. He can make hook shots better than most guys make easy lay ups. I'm better at guard than any other position I play and that's because I've been playing guard with the church team.

Mayberry has about twelve of us breathing hard for spots on the team. I'm pretty sure I'm up for first string guard and trying my best to impress the coach anyway and every way I can. I think I must have lost twenty pounds since I joined the team.

After practice on the day before the first game the coach tells us where we stand. I didn't make the first team. I'm sixth man, and I'm so disappointed that I take my uniform, clean and folded nicely and hand it back to the coach.

"Coach, I'm sorry, I can play more ball playing in my church league and in the park league so I'm going to leave the team."

Coach Mayberry can't believe what I've said, but he heard and says, "Get out of my sight Tepke! Leave! Now! Go play where ever you want, I don't give a damn where you play but get out of my sight!"

I seem to have struck a sensitive nerve and without another word, I leave. It seems like the sensible thing to do under the circumstances.

I go to the first game, to see how Mayberry might have used me and an odd unforeseen thing happens. Our wonderful center tears the cartilage in one knee so badly that he'll be out for the season. I feel bad. For him. For me. But, I will get to play a lot of basketball anyway. I will play for the church and I'm happy about that. I'll bet our church team will win the league championship. We still miss Harry, but we have five good guys anyway. My high school team doesn't look too good right now and I doubt that it will win a lot of games. So life is full of surprises. You have to make choices. You win some. You lose some. And life goes on!

Twenty

1949

Since I quit the Foreman basketball team, I get myself reinstated on the church team. As the season progresses, we have only lost one game out of fifteen and that was a three point heartbreaker. We get to play that team again. Mike has been making the baskets we need to win and I have made more than a few points along the way. Bob, Ricky and Lars are playing their hearts out and contributing, too. The other subs do what they can when they are in the game so we have nothing to complain about.

Ricky is still going out with Gail and she comes to all the games. Nita is always at the games. Lars and Mike don't have steady girl friends but they bring dates to the games. I

179

keep thinking that Betsy might show up because she and Nita are good friends, but that hasn't happened. I haven't taken her out since the drive-in fiasco. I haven't called her. I know she's not lacking for dates and it's hard to get to Oak Park without wheels.

Our team finishes in a dead heat with Austin Messiah, the team that beat us by three points and its the only loss we have had. In the last game of the season we played them again and this time we beat them by four. So we have a play off game for the championship. These guys aren't pushovers. Last year they beat the pants off us in both games. But we are tough competition now. The playoff should be a good game.

Win or lose we are going to have a big party at the coaches house. Dixie, the coach's daughter, has invited everyone. Guess who attends Austin Messiah? It's Betsy, and Dixie has invited her to the party, too. As we go through the warm up process before the game, I see Betsy come through the gym door. Didn't expect it.

I say, "Hi. Didn't know you would be here. Great!"

"I'm going to be at your party after the game, too! Why haven't you called? You mad about something?"

"No. Embarrassed. After that dumb thing I did at the drive-in I didn't think you would want me hanging around any more." I'm thinking, she gets better looking every time I see her.

"You're too sensitive, Ben. That was funny! Guess I was a bit upset about my skirt at the time, but I got over it. What was going through your head when you forgot to put the speaker back? No, don't tell me, I can guess."

" Thanks mind reader. What am I thinking about, now?"

She smiled, ignored the question and said, "How are you

going to play tonight?"

"I'll be sensational if you give me a kiss for every point I score."

"You're on, fella. Go get 'em," and she winked at me!

"You're kidding of course."

"No way! I'll pucker up for every point, free throws included. I'll be cheering for you!"

Talk about incentives. That's all the incentive I need. By the time the first half has ended we are six points ahead. I've scored eighteen points, blocked a few and have seven steals. The steals were responsible for eight of the eighteen. I have had six free throws and made them all. Unbelievable! I have never had more than three steals in any game I've played and my free throw average is far from perfect. I've never scored eighteen points in any game before either. All the guys and the coach are amazed.

All Betsy did when I looked at her, before heading into the locker room, was laugh.

"What's going on Ben? You think you're being scouted by the Globe Trotters?" Mike is giving me the business.

The coach says, "You're doing great Ben, keep it up."

All the guys are patting me on the back and I feel like a million bucks. The last half is nothing like the first because Austin Messiah is double teaming me. But, that's okay because it frees up Mike and the other guys. I did get six more points before the game ended and we beat Austin Messiah by thirteen. Skunked 'em!

As I take my shower, I'm looking forward to collecting twenty-four big ones from Betsy Banks.

Bob and Nita took Betsy and a few other girls to the party. I rode with Mike. Mike had a date, a girl in my class and a knock out blonde. Here name is Gloria. She's a cheer leader and very popular.

On the way to the party she tells me that she's glad I didn't stay on the varsity team. " They really aren't very good this year."

"I'm not happy they're aren't doing well. If O'Brian hadn't screwed up his knee the team would be doing great. His hook shots would have made a big difference in the win column."

Gloria then says, "You would have made a big difference, too. You played terrific tonight."

"Gloria, tonight was a fluke. I was sixth man on the Foreman team. I'm no center so I wouldn't have made much of a difference."

Mike then says, "Ben, you made a difference tonight!"

"Cut it out. I had one good game all year. You played good yourself, Between the two of us, we really had their number. All the guys played great from start to finish!"

I can't wait to find out if Betsy meant what she told me. A kiss for every point, free-throws included. What a grand and glorious feeling!

*****

Mrs. Algren put a lot of effort into the team party. There is a lot of food, drinks, cake and cookies. The cake and cookies are home made not the store bought stuff. There are Sloppy Joes, hot dogs, potato chips, potato salad, beans, olives, pickles and sour cream cucumbers. What a spread and all the guys are eating like there's no tomorrow!

In addition to great food there is mood music, dancing and everyone is happy tonight.

I've pretty well monopolized Betsy as far as dancing goes. I'm not a terrific dancer, but she really likes dancing, music and

Out of the Loop

I like the body contact.

When we aren't dancing, Betsy is talking to her girl-friends. She likes to talk and she's having a great time tonight.

I'm wondering when I will get my promised kisses. I'll do all right if Mike takes me to Oak Park. If we go to Betsy's house with Bob and Nita, the girls will talk all the way home. Can't complain. One way or another I'll get a few. Won't be counting. When the party ends, Bob tells me he will be taking Betsy home. If I want to come along I'm welcome, as long as I don't try to break a window. Didn't laugh at that one even though I know he's kidding me. On the way home, the girls do talk but I get a few words in and a few kisses, too.

When I take Betsy to the door I get a few more, but I'm not close to twenty-four. At her door she says, "I still owe you twelve. When will you be back to collect?"

"You've been counting? I think you made a mistake. You must still owe me twenty at least."

"Your mistake. It's twelve. I have been counting. Now, hold still, this it for tonight!"

"I'll collect the rest with interest. The interest rate is extremely high!"

"The interest is high here, too. When are we going out again?"

"If I say next Saturday, you'll tell me you have a date."

"No, I'm okay for next Saturday, what would you like to do?"

"We could go downtown and take in a stage show and movie at the Chicago Theater. Or we can go to Olson Rug and have them turn the waterfall on for us. That should be fun."

"The Olson waterfall on the first of February. Nice idea. I'll bring my ice skates. I'll try to think of something, you try to think of something sensible and then we'll talk about it. Call me Tuesday when you get home from work. Good night, Ben."

"Good night, Betsy. Thanks.   Oh ... I'm not working any more. Tried out for varsity at Foreman and had to quit my job to practice. I'm looking."

"Oh! Didn't know."

Twenty-One

In Church on Sunday, Bob, Mike and Lars were there. Ricky wasn't, don't know why. Asked Bob how school was going down at the pier. The University of Illinois took over Navy Pier after after the Navy pulled out.

"It's okay. I'm doing better than most. I'm getting a little tired of taking the street car. Wish I had a car. Can't use my Dads all the time and there's no good place to park down there.

"How's the sales job going Lars?" Lars is selling tools at Sears downtown.

"It's okay. Not wild about it right now."

Mike then says, "I like what I'm doing and I'm getting involved in the Union. You can learn a lot if you listen. You can make a difference in what goes on." Mike is an apprentice in the electrical union.

How you doing in school Ben?" Mike asks.

"I'm okay. I'll squeak by and graduate."

"You going to college, Ben?" Bob asks.

"No. Have to get a job. Don't know what to look for. My Dad would like me to work in the lab. You know follow in his foot steps. I'm not going to do that. Don't want to work in a dental lab. It's boring. My Dad likes it but I'm not cut out for it."

"You got any prospects since quitting that store downtown?"

"No, but I've been looking. I liked Shaynes, but you can't make much there. I'll find something."

"I've got the car today, what would you guys like to do?" Bob wants to know.

"Is Nita sick?" Lars asks.

"Hey, we're going steady, but we don't spend every minute together."

"Seems like it. You going steady with Gloria, Mike?"

"No. Just dating. I think she'd like to, but I'm not going to ask."

"You were pretty friendly with Betsy at the party, is it anything serious?" Mike wants to know.

"She likes dating guys. Has no interest in going steady."

"That was some kiss she tagged you with last night." Bob then gave a graphic description of what happened in the doorway of Betsy's house. "Thought she might have swallowed your tongue."

"Very funny. It was a great kiss. Made my knees weak."

"Made your head weak," says Lars, "Why do you keep chasing a broad that has no interest in you?"

"To tell the truth, I don't know."

*****

Out of the Loop

On Tuesday, a big winter snowfall hit Chicago and the weather report said it would be snowing off and on all week. The newspaper said that Sunday might be a nice day. I can just imagine how sloppy and cold State Street will be by Saturday. Betsy won't want to walk around in the cold with the brutal, Windy City winds blowing.

When I call her on Tuesday it's snowing hard. Big wet flakes are falling, trees and bushes are beautifully dressed in white. But it's hardly a picture perfect setting for a date that requires walking from here to there.

"Betsy, it's Ben."

"Hi. Where are we going Saturday?"

"How about sledding?"

"Ben!"

"You don't sound pleased with my suggestion and I'm sorry about that, but the paper says it will be snowing until Sunday. Let's make it after the snow melts."

"What are you talking about, Ben. I want to see you. Are you afraid of a little snow on the ground?"

"I'm not afraid of snow, Betsy. I don't have a car remember. If I reach your house without getting frost bite and we start out for only heaven knows where we might die in a snow drift. Lets make it another day, okay?"

"We don't have to go anywhere. We can stay here. Dad has fixed the basement up and there's a fireplace down there. We could make pop corn. Talk. And... (she paused for emphasis) we could have a lot of fun!

"You're talking about you, me, alone in the basement. With a fire going in the fireplace? I wouldn't need popcorn, Betsy. Are you kidding me?"

"No! I'm not kidding."

"What time?"

"Can you be here about 7:30."

"Sure! Even if I have to come by dog sled, I'll be there."

"See you then. Bye."

*****

When I get up on Saturday morning and look out the window it's snowing. It looks like a foot of the white stuff has staked a claim on the street and sidewalks and it's still coming down. Big flakes are blowing in the wind and the wind is fierce. When I arrive in the kitchen, Gramps is eating, Mom is sipping coffee and reading the paper. Dad has gone to work.

"Hi Mom, Gramps, looks like it might snow."

"Very funny!" Says Gramps, "You better have some breakfast before you test the shovel and see if it still works."

"What would like eat, Ben?" Mom says as she straightens her apron while getting out of her chair.

"Cream of Wheat, if you'll thread it with brown sugar."

"Sure. It'll take a few minutes. When you get through shoveling you'll have to go to the store, I need a few things."

"Okay. The new refrigerator really works good, doesn't it."

We've had the new refrigerator for a couple of weeks and I'm just getting used to having cold milk right in the kitchen. "What's Dad going to do with the ice box?"

"When the weather gets warmer, he said he is going to fix it up for storing some of his basement things. I don't know what, maybe paint cans, things like that. He has an idea about what to do with it. Ask him."

After eating I bundled up and shoveled. About the time

Out of the Loop

I finished, the wind had whisked snow back on the sidewalk and I shoveled it again. It was still snowing when I went to the store. As I finished helping Mom put the groceries away, I told her I was going to Betsy's house on a date and had to get ready.

"You're going out in this? To Oak Park? We're supposed to get a lot more snow this evening. Tell me you're not serious?"

"It's no big deal, Mom. I've been invited. I'll take the streetcar to the El, the El to Oak Park and walk the rest of the way. The house is only about six blocks from the Elevated Train. Not far."

"Your crazy, Ben. You'll be walking through drifts, it doesn't make sense."

"The streets will be plowed. I'll walk in the street and be careful, but I'm going to go."

"When will you be home?"

"Probably around ten-thirty or eleven. I'll be okay."

Then I went upstairs, took a shower and put on comfortable clothes. As I was combing my hair, Gramps came and stood in the bathroom doorway and said, " When you get home tonight you best shovel. It's suppose to snow all night."

"Sure Grandpa." Went downstairs, put on my heavy galoshes, coat, wool cap, gloves and left.

The clock said six as I went out the door. It's dark, snowing, wind's blowing. Blowing hard enough that you have to wince to see where you might be going. I figured a streetcar would be a safer bet to take than a trolley bus so I went down to Cicero Avenue. I was lucky enough to catch a "big red" right away, didn't have to wait a minute. Didn't take too long to get to Lake Street, but I waited twenty-five minutes for the El. Got off on Oak Park Avenue and started walking. Didn't tell Mom the truth. Betsy lives about a mile and half from the El, not that it makes a whole lot of difference. Snow's really coming down. The clock in the El station said it was seven-twenty when I started plodding through the snow. As I walk, all I'm thinking about is a warm basement, a warm fire, a warm Betsy, a warm basement sofa, a warm Betsy and passing up the popcorn. I don't want any butter on my finger tips tonight. It took me another forty-five, bone chilling minutes to reach Betsy's door. Rang the bell and waited. And waited. I was beginning to wonder if anyone was home when the door finally opened and Mr. Banks was standing there looking at me like I was someone from another world. I did have a lot of snow on me. Should have brushed it off before he opened the door.

"Ben? Is that you? What are you doing here on a night like this? What's going on?"

"I have a date with Betsy, she invited me to come over."

"When?"

"Well, we talked on Tuesday. It was Tuesday." I'm wondering if he's going to invite me in or close the door.

"It's ten after eight."

"Well I was supposed to be here at seven-thirty. I guess I should have left earlier."

"No! You shouldn't have left at all. You're walking around in a snow storm. This isn't a good night for a date. What in the world were you thinking about?"

If he had given the question much thought, he would have known what I was thinking about. Well not all I was thinking about. If he knew what I was thinking about he probably wouldn't have opened the door.

Out of the Loop

About the instant he said, " ... what were you thinking about?"
I could hear Mrs. Banks ask, "Jim, who is it?"

"It's Ben Tepke."

"What? What's he doing here?"

"You better ask Betsy what he's doing here!"

"Jim, ask him to come in, for heavens sake. And close
the door. He must be freezing!"

"Come in Ben. Take your hat, coat and boots off and
leave them in hall for a minute."

I didn't say it, but I was thinking, "For a minute? ...
For a minute?" Was he about to tell me to get out and go
home. Oh, boy, what's next.

Saw Mrs. Banks go up the stairs while I was taking my
coat off and about the time I was finished taking off the galoshes, Betsy came flying down the stairs.

"Ben. What are you doing here?"

About this time, and under the circumstances, with
pants that are damp from the snow and a shirt a bit damp from
exertion, still cold from my trek from the El, I felt like answering, "Oh, I was just out for a walk and happened to recognize your house and thought I'd stop in for a minute and
say hello. Hello. Good-bye. It was nice seeing you again."
What I said was, "Well I thought we had a date, I guess I should
have called first."

"I didn't think you'd come, Ben."

"Told you I'd be here if I had to come by dog sled."

Mrs. Banks smiled when I said it, Mr. Banks sort of
rolled his eyes and Betsy blushed. Betsy isn't a girl that blushes
easily, but she blushed and said. " I'm so sorry Ben. I should
have called and said don't come."

"Well, I best be going then."

Mrs. Banks then said, "Ben, I'm going to make some hot chocolate and after that you better get a move on because it will take you a long time to get home tonight. It's awful out there."

Never saw the basement.

Never saw the fireplace.

Never had popcorn.

Never saw Betsy alone.

Saw the kitchen.

While we were sitting there, having hot chocolate, Mr. Banks said, "Betsy tells me you're looking for a job, Ben. I thought you had one."

"I did but had to quit because I tried out for the school basketball team."

"What kind of job was it?

"I worked in a fancy, Michigan Avenue ladies clothing store. Worked in the stock room, ran the elevator, ran errands, wrapped packages."

"What time is your last class?"

"Two."

"I might have something for you in the factory. I'll check. Call me next week and I'll let you know. Call me Thursday night, okay."

"Thanks Mr. Banks. I'll call, I do need a job."

That alone made the trip to Oak Park worthwhile tonight. It was the only thing that made the trip worthwhile. When I finished the hot chocolate, I put my galoshes back on, the coat, the hat and left. It was nine-thirty. An awkward night for the Banks family. An awkward night for me. I didn't get home until midnight. When I did, I shoveled. The snow was a foot deep, two feet deep in places where the wind puffed the snow into drifts. Had no trouble going to sleep when I finally got to bed. Slept late and didn't go to church.

Twenty-Two

Mr. Banks runs the Ravenswood factory located on Ravenswood and Grace. It's two streetcar rides and about forty-five minutes from Foreman High School.

When I called him Thursday night he said "It will be the end of March before I have an opening, Ben. Can you wait until then?"

"Yes, sir. Don't have any prospects right now."

"Good. I'll be in touch."

True to his word, Mr. Banks called on April 1st. He said, " Come to the Ravenswood employment office on Monday after school. The employment office is on the second floor, across the street from the factory. When you get there ask for Mr. Richter."

"Thanks, Mr. Banks."

"You can thank me best by doing a good job."

When I get to the factory, I ask the lady behind the desk if I can see Mr. Richter. She takes my name and tells me to have a seat. Twenty minutes later I see Mr. Banks come out of an office. He passes me by without saying a word. A man he left standing in the office doorway calls my name and says to come on in. It's Mr. Richter, of course, and he's about as old as my Dad. He explains that I have to join the union and that means they take small percentage from the paycheck every month, but I'll be making $ .95 an hour to start.

"You'll be working in the factory supply room where parts are kept until needed on the factory floor or for shipping to customers. Your boss, Mr. Hartke, will explain what you do."

I have to get my picture taken for a factory badge, fill out an employment form and then Mr. Richter takes me across the street to the factory. He shows me where the time clock is located, says my badge won't be ready until Wednesday and you have to wear a badge. He shows me the men's locker room, says I can have any empty locker available. If I use one, I have to bring my own lock.

Then Mr. Richter shows me how to get to the Supply Room and I meet my boss. Mr. Hartke is about thirty-five years old and his hair is starting to turn gray. He wears glasses, has bushy brown hair and eyebrows. He's wearing a dirty blue shop apron over his overalls, has pencils and pens clipped in a high pocket in the center of the apron. He squints at me when we're introduced, as if he's not sure I'm the right guy for the job and I haven't done a thing except say, "Nice to meet you, Mr. Hartke."

Mr. Richter talked to Mr. Hartke for several minutes about the world in general and about the Cubs and the Bears and then he left. The first thing Mr. Hartke tells me is to call him 'Hank'. Then he explains what we do in the supply room and introduces me to Bill Ericksen. Bill is an old guy, in his sixties, wears glasses, shuffles his feet when he walks. He takes such small steps, I think that his legs or back must be hurting with every step. He has the same type of apron over his work clothes as Hank.

The supply room has four aisles and five long rows of tall racks containing boxes filled with nuts and bolts, knobs, metal painted plates, parts and pieces and sub assemblies. Identification numbers are printed on the boxes in such a way that it is pretty easy to find what you are looking for if you know the number of the part. At the front of each rack a sign tells you how the numbering system runs in that rack row.

The job entails filling parts orders on the requisition forms you get from various departments. On small parts like nuts or bolts all you have to do is weigh the things based on a given weight per pound. Larger items you count out. You put the things in boxes with the order on a flat bed hand cart and then Hank notifies the various departments by phone when orders are filled and someone picks up the pieces.

Since I am a part-timer, I am to work when I arrive after school until 7:00 PM. The plant has two shifts. The first shift leaves at 4:00 PM. The supply room only works one shift, which means I will be working alone from four to seven. On Saturdays I will work a full day.

When I clock out Monday through Friday night, I have to lock-up. The lock is a big padlock. He shows me where an emergency key is located in case I should have get back in the room after I've locked up. "If you don't use a locker and forget your school books in the supply room you can use the emergency key to bail them out. Just don't tell anyone where the emergency key is kept, okay?" No problem.

On Wednesday, after my last class, I flip a Belmont Street-car and ride to Lincoln Avenue, transfer and go northwest to Grace Street. I pick up my badge and time card at the employment office, cross the street to the factory and punch in.

On Friday, when Mr. Richter showed me how to get to the supply room on the second floor of the plant he walked me down a narrow aisle, next to a line of five women punch press operators, to a stairwell just beyond them. Then we walked up the stairs to the second floor and the supply room was across an aisle and just a few steps away.

Today I'm on my own. As I walk by all the women making punch press parts the younger one on the first press gives me a real jolt. As I walk by, she reaches out grabs me right by the crotch and says "Boy, would I like to fuck you!" She says it loud enough for all the women to hear. They were waiting for the babe to grab me. They think it's funny. They're all laughing.

I'm not laughing. She really took hold, held tight and I have an ache that makes me gasp long and loud. I can hardly breathe. And I'm embarrassed. Can't say a word. I just manage to get her hand off my crotch as I hop, skip and wobble to the stairwell. I will never walk that way again you can bet on that! There's got to be another stairwell someplace and I'll find it. Never saw that coming. You'd never guess any woman would do such a thing.

When I tell the guys what happened, Mike says I should have grabbed the broad by her knockers and said, "Okay Babe, where and when?" Why didn't I think of that, but it's too late now.

The supply room job is easy. When Hank goes home he leaves me a bunch of orders to fill and more often then not I finish them off in two hours after he leaves. Then I've got time to do my homework at his desk before punching out.

One Saturday, a few weeks after I started working for Hank he asks me to take a break with him in the lunch room. Makes me feel pretty good, because I know I'm doing a good job and he's warmed up to having me in his department.

He has something on his mind and asks, "Ben, how old do you think Bill Ericksen is?"

"Don't know, maybe sixty."

"Well, he's sixty-seven and at sixty-seven he isn't moving very fast and he's a little worried."

"What's he worried about?"

"Hey, I give you orders to fill and you race down the aisles and get them finished so fast no one can possibly keep up with you, including me. That makes Bill nervous because he's thinking maybe I'll replace him with another young guy. He needs this job bad. He moves as fast as he can on his bum legs. All I'm going to ask you to do, is to slow down a bit. If I need something done fast, I'll tell you about it, but s l o w d o w n, Okay?"

Hank's the boss, so I slow down and every one is happy. I even leave some orders unfilled on school days. I obviously never talk about this to anyone. Hank's a great guy and I respect him for his concern about Bill.

On a Thursday, toward the end of April, the weather turns unseasonably warm. It's hot. The stockroom, being inside the factory away from any windows has me sweating while I work. Hank and Bill were happy when their day ended. They left about twenty minutes ago. Hank told me the whole factory has a bundle of work and today we're not only filling department orders but restocking parts, pieces and subassemblies. The stock room is a mess with pallets waiting to be unloaded. When he left for the day, Hank said, "Ben the 'slow down order' has stopped for the time being. Try to get as many of these damn pallets unloaded as you can. Don't like the mess we're in. I'd like to get the aisles cleaned-up. It slows things down having to dodge and walk around the pallets. Do what you can. I know you can't get it all done. See you tomorrow."

I'm sweating. My shirt is clinging, wringing wet. I've just put about forty pounds of special screws in a bin and I'm about to move the loaded hand cart to the next location when I look up and see her standing there. Right in front of me. It's the same broad that grabbed me that first day on the job.

"Hi," she says.

I don't know what to say and I'm not only watching her face but those hands of hers.

"What are you doing here?"

"Thought I'd see how you're doing. You like working here?"

" I don't have time to talk. You're in my way. You trying to get me bounced? I need this job and I still have plenty of work to take care of before I check out, so get the hell out of my way and leave me alone."

The words came flying out of my mouth wrapped in a haze of spittle and loud enough to wake the dead.

She says, "Hey, take it easy, slow down. I came to apologize. I'm sorry, thought it was funny at the time, but I know you were embarrassed. I'm sorry. I'm not trying to get you fired. I'd like to buy you a cup of coffee. Get to know you better. That's all

there is to it. That's why I'm here. My name's Mitsie Martin. I'd
like to buy you cup of coffee someplace when you're through for
the night?"

"I don't drink coffee. Beat it! I've got work to do."

I'm wondering when all the other punch press women
are going jump out from around a corner laughing their back-
sides off.

"I'm serious, I'd like to get to know you better and I'll
buy you a Coke, sandwich, whatever you want."

"You don't have to buy me a thing," and with that I turn
my back on her, start pulling the hand cart to a new location.

She follows me for a few steps and then says, "Be a sport.
I won't bite. I've got a thirty-six Ford coupe. It's black. I'll be at
the curb on Ravenswood waiting for you. Please! I'll be at the
curb waiting."

All of that came out of her mouth in less than a second
and it ends the conversation, because she turns and leaves before
I can say another word. Doesn't matter, I don't know what I
would have said anyway. As I continue to unload pallets, re-
stock bins, the clock ticks the minutes away and I'm thinking all
kinds of things.

*She's kind of pretty. Not a knockout, but pretty. She's old.
I'll bet she's twenty-five at least. She had that stupid scarf around
her hair on the punch press line and now that that's gone she has
nice looking blonde hair. Blue eyes. Built nice, too. Shit, I'm
seventeen. What's goin on? She used the "F" word. Never
heard any girl say it before. Bad joke, if it was a joke. What in
hell does she want from me? Think I'll head out the back way.
Slip out by way of the loading dock, after I punch my time card.
That's easy enough to do. Hell, that would make me look scared.
Damn it anyhow, I'm going to call her bluff. I'll have a coke and*

see what happens.

It's time. I insert my time-card, punch, pull, stick it back in the rack. Now what? Maybe she won't be there. I wash my hands and face in the washroom. I still smell like sweat. I've been sweating plenty. More since she showed up. Took my shirt off and washed some of the body sweat off, but can't do much about the shirt. Combed my hair. Don't know why I'm fussing, this isn't a date. What am I worried about? Well, here goes nothing.

As I push the door open to exit there's no way I can miss the black Ford Coupe sitting at the curb. She's there. Waiting. The door of her Ford isn't locked. Opened it. Bent, stuck my head in. She's smiling, looking right at me. "Hop in, Ben."

I climbed in, and before I'm even settled in my seat, she's traveling. Shifting. And there's not a single tremor as the transmission glides smoothly from first to second to third.

"How do you know my name?"

"Wasn't hard to find out, Ben Tepke. I saw you punch your time card a few days ago when I was coming out of the woman's locker room. Was leaving early, didn't have my work clothes on. You never noticed. You went on your way and I looked at your card. I'm heading for that all-night diner on Lincoln Avenue. That okay with you?"

"I guess."

Can't think of much more to say and she's quiet, too, on the rest of the way to the diner. She parks on Lincoln, we get out and cross the street. Starting to get a bit cooler, but the evening's still warm. She's treating, so I order a coke and a BLT. I'm hungry and getting a bit excited. Don't know why. She hasn't talked dirty or used the "F" word since she showed up. She doesn't say much of anything until after we order. Then she tells me that she lives in a third floor flat on Waveland near Kedzie.

Out of the Loop

Not really a flat, more like a bedroom, kitchen, bathroom and closet. She's a Chicago girl, went to Hyde Park High School on the south side. Her folks still live there. She was going with a guy that was killed in Germany during the war. Thought she would be marrying him when he came home from service.

"I'm sorry what kind of outfit was he in?"

"He was in the infantry, a corporal and a medic. A real nice guy, I loved him. Went with him all during high school. When he got killed, I told my folks I would be moving out. I've worked a couple of places before I landed this job at Ravenswood. Been working here about a year and a half. The money's good and I like it. It isn't hard to do and I like the women I work with. You're a part-timer. How did you get the job? I don't think there's another part timer in the place."

I don't want to tell her that I know Mr. Banks. "Applied and I guess they needed help in the stock room. I needed the job. Hank Hartke's a good guy to work for. I like what I'm doing."

"Are you in College?"

That makes me laugh. "No, high school. I'll be graduating in June." With that answer, I thought that she would ask for the bill and take off but she didn't budge.

"What are you going to do after you graduate?"

"Don't know. Look for a better job maybe. How old are you?"

"I'm twenty-three."

We finish the food and conversation peters out about the same time. She pays the bill and we cross the street to her car. The sun has gone down, the air smells clean and fresh and I don't. My shirt had dried, but I need a shower. I don't smell foul at all, just like sweat and salt. Like Dad, when he's worked up a sweat, working around the house. It will feel good to hit the shower before going to bed.

"Would you drop me off on Belmont, Mitsie?"

"Sure. Be happy to." But, she doesn't drive straight to Belmont. She makes a left on some dark street, pulls the Ford behind a parked car and under some trees, then turns the motor off. Before I can say, "What's happening?" she reaches over, grabs me by the front of my shirt and pulls me toward her. Then she plants one big sloppy kiss on my lips and her tongue manages to get inside my mouth and flicks around. I'm thinking that it's a good thing I took one of those mints in the candy dish of the diner.

But Mitsie isn't through by a long shot. I'm panting between kisses that just keep coming and all of a sudden she takes my hand and slides it under her sweater. Her boobs are bare, no brassiere and I can't believe this is happening. It's like one of the Coronet girls has left the center spread and landed in my lap. My right hand keeps moving, from one side to the other, getting to know all there is to know about Mitsie's chest. I've dreamt about this moment, wondered what it would be like touching these things. Now I know, and don't want to stop.

As the kissing continues and my passion grows more intense, Mitsie suddenly and abruptly stops and pushes me away. Shoves me right up against the car door. Splat! As I try to catch my breath, she looks at me and blurts, "You've never done anything like this before, have you?"

"What are you talking about?"

"Listen Ben, by this time most guys I know would have had their hand up my skirt exploring the territory. You haven't made one move without my help. You've never done this before!"

She's looking at me like I must have dropped in on earth

Out of the Loop

from outer space.

I'm looking at her, looking straight into those blue eyes that look black in the darkened seat of coupe and say, "Sure, I have." Then I say, " No, I've never had my hands on bare knockers before, if that's what you mean."

"So you're a virgin?"

Can't figure out a smart comeback, so I say, "Yeah, I am."

"You act like it. I believe it! Well, we're going to have to do something about that! But not tonight. We're going to have to do something about that real soon!" She says it while starting the car and moving it back out onto the street.

When Mitsie drops me off on Belmont I walk around to her side of the car. Her window's down. She looks up at me, smiling, and I lean through the window and give her another kiss. And slide my hand under her sweater once more. She shivers as I pull away.

"Thanks for the BLT and the Coke,"

As I walk away toward the streetcar stop, she winks at me, waves, pulls away from the curb and heads home.

No one would believe me if I told them what happened tonight, and I'm not going to boast and brag about it. She's twenty-three. Don't understand why she picked me out to get friendly with, but I'm not about to complain. Thought Betsy knew how to kiss, but I think she needs a lesson or two and now I'm just the guy do it!

When I arrived home I tell Mom that I had stopped to get something to eat. Went upstairs, took a shower and hit the hay. Slept well until about daybreak, until I dreamt about Mitsie. Woke with my shorts stuck to my body and had to take another shower.

Twenty Three

A week after going to the diner, on a Thursday evening once again, Mitsie shows up in the supply room. It's about 6:30 and I'm doing homework at Hank's desk.

"Hi Ben."

"Hi Mitsie. You going to buy me another BLT and a Coke?"

"Not tonight. I want you to come home with me."

"When?"

"Tonight!"

"Tonight?"

"Yes tonight. Tonight! I'll be waiting for you on the curb."

Dan Glaubke

As she turns to leave, I say, "Can't Mitsie. Not tonight."
"What? Why?"

"I've got to get home, promised I'd help my sister out."

"Help her out next week, some other time, I want you to come home with me."

"Can't. Have to get home. Promised I'd help her study her arithmetic. She's having a test tomorrow, told my Mom I'd help her study. Should have done it last night and now I'm stuck. She's counting on my help."

Mitsie's in shock, "I can't believe this. Are you crazy."

"No I'm not crazy. You know, even if I didn't have to help Lisa, it would be hard for me to come to your place and fool around at seven thirty at night. By the time I'd get home the folks and Gramps would be all over me wondering where I've been and what I've been doing on a school night to ten or eleven. Hell, last week when I went to the diner with you and all the rest, I didn't get home until a quarter to ten and everyone was upset then. Mom usually fixes me something to eat when I get home from work. I had to lie and say I was so hungry I stopped at a diner for something. Wasn't a total lie. Nevertheless, everyone was wondering what happened and I had to talk fast."

Mitsie says, "Well, I'll be damned. Arithmetic. I've never been turned down for an arithmetic lesson before. Okay champ, but its your loss, we could have had a ball."

Before she could turn to leave, I got out of my chair, took her by the hand and said, "Follow me for a minute?" I've found a nook at the end of aisle one in the supply room where two people can stand and not be seen by anyone passing by the door way. I lead Mitsie back there, pull her her toward me, give her kiss. This time I'm the aggressive one and I've got a hand under her sweater before kiss number two hits her lips. Once again,

208

no brassiere and she doesn't mind me exploring one bit. Between kisses she says, "Better slow down champ. Are you sure you can't pass on the arithmetic problems tonight? What can I do to get you to come up to my place? What I've got in mind shouldn't take too long! Come on, Ben."

"If we get to your place, I won't want to leave, Mitsie. I just can't do it tonight."

After another kiss among the nuts and bolts, Mitsie says, "Enough. I've had it. I'm going and that's all you get tonight!" With that she took my hand away, pulled her sweater down and said, "Have a good time with your sister and her arithmetic problems you sucker!"

She's miffed and doesn't waste any time leaving and doesn't look back. Boy, I'm having a hard time adjusting to what's happening to me. Most guys my age dream about this kind of thing but it never happens. If this is a dream, don't wake me up!

It's time for me to clock out. I pack up my homework, lock the supply room door and head for home. Boy, that broad really kisses good and feels nice. I know it isn't right doing this. It's sinful, but I don't want to think about sin at the moment. I can't help it. Nothing like this ever happened to me before and probably never will again.

*****

With the money I'm making I can take a date to Bruno's, the movie show, hell I can take a date to a real restaurant if I want to. Not the Ambassador East, but someplace nice. Things are good. Since Betsy moved to Oak Park, I'm not seeing her much at all. Oak Park is a long way to go for a date and she has other boy friends. Guys with cars. Hard to compete with guys that have cars. We still talk on the telephone once in a while and I can tell she still likes me, but things have cooled off. After my high scoring basketball game, Betsy told Nita about our "kiss for every point" deal. Nita told Bob. Bob told all the guys. From that moment on, I've been peppered with disparaging remarks and fun filled ridicule. They all want to know if I collected, how was it, did I get more than we bargained for and stuff like that. It gets boring real quick as far as I'm concerned, but they won't let up. It's really embarrassing since they know I really poured in some big points. I guess this might be the reason I'm not taking Betsy on dates where any of the guys will be. They'll make jokes. Betsy will laugh. I'll turn red and won't be laughing.

My senior prom is coming up and I don't know who to ask. I finally talk to a couple of girls I would like to date, but they both say they have dates. It figures. I'm more than a little slow when it comes to girls and dates and proms and everything female. Maybe I should ask Mitsie. Wouldn't that be a gas.

Enter Ben Tepke with a twenty-three year old date in a ravishing, shocking, breathtaking formal that leaves nothing to anyone's imagination. Guys turn away from their dates, leave them hanging and try to maneuver Ben away from his girl. Ben takes on the thundering hoard of guys in his class in a clash that rips his tuxedo to shreds as he battles to protect his girlfriend from the villainous, lecherous, lustful seniors that are relentless in their onslaught as they try to subdue him. Yeah. Right. If I ask Mitsie, and she accepts, I'll be the talk of the whole school and then they might not even let us in.

Didn't know if Betsy would be interested in the prom, but I'm desperate. I don't want to miss it, so I finally call and ask her. I figure that she's my last alternative.

She says, "I'd love to be your date Ben. How are we going to get there? You still don't have a car as yet, do you? My folks will want to know who will be driving. Bob and

Out of the Loop

Nita aren't going are they?"

"No, I already asked Bob about it. He took Nita to the junior prom and that's it as far as it goes regarding his tux rental for this year. I'm going to talk to Mike about doubling. I'll let you know what he says, okay? Mike's a good driver. I've gone a lot of places with him and he knows what he's doing behind the wheel. He has a car. He's been dating Gloria Paterson"

Gloria is in my class, Mike graduated in February and is working. "We can have a good time with those two, Mike's a lot of fun to be around and his girlfriend Gloria is nice. Is that okay with you?"

"I know Gloria, she's fun. Mike's nice. We'll have a good time with those two."

Betsy's excited about the dance because she likes big social affairs. Since she transferred to Oak Park she doesn't get to the old neighborhood too often so she's looking forward to the prom.

Mike likes the idea of doubling. He thinks that it's better than going alone. Gloria's a big talker and will have someone to talk to other than him. He knows that Betsy likes to talk, too.

"Here's what we'll do. We go to the dance, then head for Sally's for a bite to eat after. The dance doesn't end until eleven or eleven-thirty. We should be at Sally's for a couple of hours at least. Then it's one or two in the morning. By the time we get the girls home it's going to be three or four o'clock. Then we go home, sleep for a couple of hours, change, take the tux back and then go to the beach with the girls. Everybody is going to head for North Avenue beach if it isn't raining or too cold."

"Sounds okay to me and thanks Mike. I owe you one."

Twenty Four

On Prom night, before Mike picks me up, I take a long hot shower, shave, and put on the tux. The shoes aren't too comfortable, but I think I can get through the night with them okay. My Mom thinks I'm one handsome fella, Gramps tells me I look like I'm about to get married. Tells me he's never had a tuxedo on for any occasion. Dad's working. Lisa thinks I look like a movie star. She loves me so much that if I looked like Boris Karloff or Bella Lugosi, she would think I looked like Cary Grant. I feel conspicuous, embarrassed, out of place in the 'monkey suit'. But it's only for one night. And every guy going will look like me, so what's to worry about.

At the appointed time, Mike rings the front door bell and he really does look like a movie star. He carries himself like John Wayne even though he's just few inches taller than James Cagney. He does great imitations of both those guys.

When we're about a block away from the bungalow, I remembered the corsage I bought for Betsy. It's still in the refrigerator, so we have to turn around. I'm happy I remembered it now, and not when we arrived in Oak Park.

For some reason I take it for granted that Betsy will know what will be happening at the Prom and after. Kids do the same things year after year. It's the dance, Sally's restaurant, the beach, Lake Geneva or some other thing.

Then I get thrown a road block I didn't expect.

After picking up Gloria, after her dad took a dozen pictures of her with Mike, we go to Oak Park to get Betsy. I ring the bell and when Betsy answers the door she's crying. She has on a knockout blue strapless dress and is crying. She looks beautiful, but it sure makes a guy nervous to see his date cry and I'm wondering what in hell is going on. Then her dad appears in the doorway.

Without even a, "Hello Ben," Mr. Banks proceeds to tell me that he wants Betsy home by midnight. "Do you understand, midnight. Can you do that, Ben?"

What's there to say to a question like that? Especially, when this is the man that has fixed me up with a steady income. I look up at him and say, "Sure, Mr. Banks, no problem."

This seems to increase the amount of water escaping from

Out of the Loop

Betsy's beautiful blue and brown eyes as we leave the house and head for the prom. It takes a while for Betsy to compose herself and then she says that she's sorry; sorry to spoil this special evening for me.

I tell her, "Hey, it's only a dance, we are going to have a great time."

She says she doesn't know why there's a midnight curfew in effect. I think it might be the dress she has on. Sure gives a guy ideas. It doesn't matter because after the dance, I think I know what I'm going to do.

The prom is great, there's a good band playing and Betsy is having a good time, but she's sort of sad, too. She's talking to all of her friends. We dance most of the dances and the time goes pretty quick. It feels nice having that body of hers close to mine as we dance. But, I have to admit, the shoes hurt and I'm pretty happy when it's time to leave to get Betsy home.

Don't know how Mike did it, but we reached Betsy's door at five minutes to twelve. Gloria tells Betsy she's sorry that she has to leave and I can see that Betsy's eyes are getting watery once again. But she's home.

After dropping Betsy off at the door with a short and sweet good night kiss, I ask Mike for a favor. I ask him to drop me off on Addison and Harlem before he goes on to Sally's. He asks if I'm crazy. "Are you nuts, Ben? What are you going to do on Addison and Harlem in a tux at midnight?"

I say, " I'm not crazy. I'm the odd guy out tonight without a date and I'm not going to hang around with you and Gloria and spoil it for you. I'm going for a bus ride. I'm all right. I won't be going to the beach unless I call you, okay?"

With that Mike shakes his head, then drops me off on Addison and Harlem. Both Mike and Gloria think I'm nuts. I may be. I'll find out soon enough. I think Gloria was happy that I was bailing out so that she would have Mike all to herself.

Nobody is riding the Addison bus tonight in a tux but me. There are only a couple of late riders and they look at me with a look that seems to say, "He's nuts. The kid is nuts."

I'll soon find out if I'm nuts or not. When I get off at Kedsie, I walk north to Waveland.

My subconscious says, "Where are you going now Ben?"

I'm going up three flights of stairs. I'm going to ring the bell when I get there. I hope I'm not shot when I wake up Mitsie and she answers the door.

It's a Friday night and I've never seen Mitsie on a Friday night. I've never been to her flat before, but I memorized her address when I gave some thought to doing what I'm doing now. And here I am. I have no idea what is about to happen, and I'm one nervous guy in a tuxedo.

As I climb the back stairs, I try not to make any noise but the leather rented shoes stepping on the hardwood stairs and landings find it hard to cooperate. Finally, I'm at the door. It must be one or one-thirty in the morning by this time. Should I ring the bell or knock? Or should I turn around and leave? I'm not as brave at the moment as I was when I thought up this dandy idea. Well, here goes. I ring the bell. I cringe. It sounds loud enough to wake the whole neighborhood. Nothing happens for what seems like five minutes and I'm about to head down the stairs when the back door opens. It opens just a crack and a small sleepy voice that I don't recognize says, "Who's there?"

I answer in voice not much louder than a whisper, "It's Ben."

I hope she doesn't say Ben who? I hope I have the right house, the right floor, the right door.

Out of the Loop

Mitsie finally says in a stronger, louder, clear and bolder tone "What in the hell are you doing here? You're wearing a tux! Oh, this is your prom night isn't it? Are you nuts?"

"Most of the folks I've seen tonight think I'm nuts. Hope I'm not. Can I come in?"

She slowly opens the door wide and says, "I shouldn't be doing this."

The kitchen isn't very big, has white walls, a small table with two chairs under the only window. There's a refrigerator, stove and a small sink. A simple room divider, about waist high, separates the kitchen from the bedroom. I can see her bed, there's an indentation in her pillow that her head has made. There's a small reading light on a night stand next to the bed.

Mitsie is in a white bathrobe, she smells like she just took a shower. Her hair still looks damp. The night light in the kitchen makes her look real sexy standing there in the semidarkness, leaning against her refrigerator.

She says, "And here you are. Handsome Ben Tepke in a tux without a date at one-thirty on a Saturday morning. What am I, the booby prize? Did your date say, 'go to hell' when you tried to put her on the grass? What's happening?"

I then tell Mitsie the sad tale of having to get my date home by midnight. I tell her about the prom, briefly. I tell her that she was the first thing I thought of when I knew my prom night was a bust. I then say, "If you want me to go, I'll go, but I don't want to go."

"Well" she says, "I knew this would happen sometime and it's my fault. I've been promoting it ever since you were hired at the factory, but you know all about that. You didn't take me up on the offer I made the other day and just because your date fizzled out tonight is no reason to be here. You really should

217

go." She isn't smiling. She's just looking at me with arms crossed, waiting for me to say something.

"I know I made you mad the other day. Messed up. I haven't given you any reason to put up with me now. But, I'll tell you this. My knees are shaking in these rented shoes. I'm shaking all over! My feet hurt something awful. I hate this tux. I wanted to see you and here I am. It's my idea, not yours. I'm not begging. If you want to go back to bed, go! But let me sit at your kitchen table for a while if that's okay? Then I'll head out. Just don't tell me to beat it right this minute, okay?"

I've said it, looking right at her, looking into her eyes with some hope she'll let me stay. Even in the dim light she can tell it took some doing on my part to get this far tonight.

After a few moments, in a slow deliberate movement, Mitsie unbuttons the button holding her robe closed, loosens the robe's sash and shrugs the robe off on the floor. She stands there in the night light as bare as all those Coronet Magazine girls. She looks absolutely, goose pimple beautiful. She's as well proportioned a babe as any babe I've ever seen in the movies. She can tell that I think she's beautiful because she can see it in my eyes. Plus my mouth is wide open and my knee's are shaking so much my whole body must look like I've got some kind of malady. Okay, I admit it. I'm scared. Don't really know what to do or how to proceed and she knows it.

As a smile lights up her face and dimples her cheeks, she holds out a hand and says, "Come with me."

At my age, I've read a few dirty books. I've heard a lot of words that describe what goes on when you're making out with a girl, but there are no adequate words to describe how Mitsie treated me tonight. She taught me things. Showed me things, not things to see, but to experience and feel and remember.

Out of the Loop

She stroked, coaxed, guided, kissed, and gently, powerfully, lovingly nudged, petted and poured out her heart and body for me in a way that I can only describe as magical, breath taking. Exhilarating. Like the Bobs at Riverview when you go over that first big incline and zip down and hit that curve at ninety miles an hour. Best of all this ride wasn't over in two minutes. That's how I felt. We didn't talk much. We merged and melted. In the heat of the night and in the heat of her bed we romped and glistened with sweat. We continued to merge and melt and sweat until dawn's early light.

Exhausted. Finally. I turn on my side and look at her lying beside me and say, "Mitsie ... thanks for the BLT and the Coke."

When her giggling stops, she gives me a kiss, sits up looks down at me and says, "I've got to hand it to you Ben, you really learn fast. That was very enjoyable, but this is it Benny, we end it here. I had a good time, you had a good time, but this is it. And this is why: I met a guy at the Arragon Ball Room and he's going to propose pretty soon. In fact, if you had been an hour earlier I would have had to introduce you. Thank goodness, you didn't arrive an hour earlier. I don't how I'd ever be able to explain it. Anyway, we've had six dates so far.

"And you're not going to believe this, knowing me as you do, but I haven't let him do a thing. Yet. We've been necking, of course, but that's all. I haven't even let him squeeze my boobs."

Then after a small pause, she said. "Well, that's a lie. He got that far tonight. But that's as far as I've let him go. Not that he hasn't tried to get a lot closer. I've been one frustrated broad lately, trying to keep him frustrated, too. You've made me very happy stopping by tonight, I'll give you that much.

"But, the time is coming when it will be hard for me to put Jake off. Hopefully, he'll pop the question soon. I'm sure he's in love with me and I've fallen for him, too. He's a wonderful person, has a good job. He's in the accounting department at Sears down on Hoyne Avenue.

"You're wondering why I ever wanted to get involved with you, right? Well, I liked your looks. You're cute. You're handsome. Black hair, brown eyes, dimple, nice smile, cleft chin. I really like your looks. Thought you were a college boy. You look older than you are. The day I grabbed your pants at the factory it felt good and it surprised me. Told all the girls you really had something there.

"So, your being so young, me being older, I thought I could pretty well control the situation, take advantage of you. It didn't quite work out the way I thought. How did your sister make out with her arithmetic test? No, don't tell me. Anyway, I wasn't looking to you for love, just plain ol' sex. I'm one horny broad, or haven't you noticed?

"I thought you had been around, you've got that look. It sure didn't turn out that way. I was really looking forward to getting involved with all that youthful, pent up energy guys your age have.

"Then when I found out you didn't have a clue about sex, you were a challenge. I still wanted you. Wanted to bring you up to speed. Wanted to teach you the ropes, teach you all I know and have a great time doing it. That's sinful of course, but as horny as I am couldn't help myself. But this is it. No more. You okay with what I'm telling you?"

"No, you're telling me that this is the beginning and the end in one fell swoop. If you really mean no more, I'm not happy about it. It hurts. I sure would like to do this again some-

time. It was fantastic. I never dreamed it would be like this.
You're terrific! But, I won't cause you any trouble, if you mean
it.   Hell, I don't want to leave and I feel great, but if you say
that's it, that's it!   You have to get to work and I've got to get on
a bus, go home and take the tux back. A lot of people are going
to be laughing at me at five in the morning, I'll tell you that. I
hope your guy is the best there is Mitsie because ... well, I hope
he is and you won't be sorry." I'm thinking, maybe the guy
she's dating won't last and I'll get another chance.

  Mitsie makes me take a fast shower. We take a shower
together. Oh, man what a delicious sensation that is. Our wet
soapy bodies mingling under the shower head, tingling as the
cool water cascades over us. I don't want the shower to end.
But, Mitsie turns the water off, helps me get the tux back on and
that's it. It's over.   We talked for a few minutes more. I give her
one last kiss, hug her one last time and I'm out the door. I fly
down the three flights of stairs, two at a time, and head for
home. No one would believe me if I told them what happened
to me tonight. It's a sin and I'm not going to boast or brag
about it. But, I won't forget it either.

  On the bus ride home, people do stare and wonder what
I've been up to and I'm thinking, *"Lord, I know I've sinned
and forgive me, but ... and I know there are no 'buts' when it
comes to sinning, but..."*   I'm thinking, *"I don't hate myself
and should, but..."* and I continue to get a warm feeling when
my mind drifts back to climbing those three flights of steps
and what happened after. Sinful? Yes! Unhappy about what
I did? Not at the moment! I'm so wrapped up in my thoughts,
my guilt, the pleasure of it all, that I go past Cicero Avenue
two stops and have to walk back to catch a streetcar south for
home.

Twenty Five

As I arrive home, my Dad is coming out of the front door on his way to work.

"Hello Ben," he says smiling, "a little late getting home, aren't you?"

"No, Dad. Everyone comes home late on prom night and you know it."

"What were you doing all this time?"

There's no way I'm about to tell the folks about Mitsie anytime soon. Never, really, so I say "Well, after the dance we went to Sally's. That was about midnight. Sally's stays open all night. Had something to eat and talked. Left Sally's about three. Then we took the girls home and talked some more, among other things.

"What other things?"

"Come on Dad. Did some necking, that's all. Then Mike and I talked a while and here I am. We're going down to the beach at North Avenue today after I dump the tux."

"Are you taking Betsy to the beach?"

"No, can't ask Mike to be going all over picking up my girl friends. She's moved to Oak Park, you know. Most of the kids at the beach will be from my class, so she understands and she's okay with it."

"Well the next time you go someplace on a date you might be able to drive yourself."

"What? What do you mean?"

"I bought a car. That's what I mean. It's a Merc, a four-door sedan with automatic drive, whitewall tires, the whole she-bang. It's easy to drive, rides like a dream. I've been taking driving lessons. I've got my license. I pick the car up Monday. Then we'll get you some lessons and a license. If you're a good guy, I might, just might, let you take the Merc on a date now and then."

I can't believe it. I never thought in a million years that Dad would learn to drive or buy a car. This is just great! I've never seen him so excited. I'm excited, too!

"Wow, you did it Dad, you really did it?"

"Yes, I did. Now, I've got to go. Got to keep the pay-check coming so I can pay for this thing and the gas it takes to run it. Be quiet when you go in the house. Don't wake Mom or your grandfather."

Mom was still asleep, but Gramps is up. I tell him the

same story I told Dad. He shakes his head and says, "I never stayed out all night when I was growing up. Of course, I never went to high school. But, nobody I knew would ever let a daughter stay out all night when I was growing up. I never let your aunts stay out all night, that's for sure. It's a different world today. I'm not sure it's a better one, either."

"Maybe you're right Grandpa, but, I did have a nice time."

After taking off the tux and showering again, I call Mike and ask if I can go to the beach with him minus a date.

He says, "Sure. Gloria asked a couple of girlfriends to come along. Girls that didn't go to the prom. So, you can join the party. What did you do last night? Did you get laid?"

I'm on the phone that sits in the hall between the dining room and the kitchen so I can't very well say, "No, I didn't get laid" because Gramps is having breakfast and Mom is looking right at me, waiting to ask if I want eggs, Wheaties or Cream of Wheat. I answer, "No. I'll talk to you later. Will you pick me up or where do you want to meet?'

"I'll see you at the Tux store at ten okay? We'll pick up the girls after that."

*****

On the way to pick up Gloria and her friends, Mike says, "You got laid didn't you?"

"No, I didn't get laid. I rode the Addison bus to Cicero, took the Cicero Avenue Streetcar south to 26th, the end of the line. Then rode it back north and went home. On the way back, at twenty-second, where the Western Electric plant is, a lot of the Western workers got on the car. They asked me where the party was. That Western Electric plant is huge. All in all, it was a nice ride. The tux never got wrinkled. I enjoyed every minute of it. You should try it sometime. There's no ride better than riding a streetcar in a tux."

With that Mike says, "You got laid!"

I'm doing my best trying not to smile. I just turn my head so he can't see my face and stopped talking.

*****

North Avenue Beach is a wonderful place for a swim, sun tan and small talk. Today, it's great place to take a nap. I'm so tired. Really tired. I feel like I've been up all night doing calisthenics. That's not too far from the truth. After forty winks and then some, Lake Michigan is cold, refreshing and fun. Gloria's friends are nice. Gloria told them I had to get my date home by midnight. They wonder what I did after leaving Bud and Gloria on a street corner in a tux after midnight. My story doesn't vary and the girls think I'm pretty strange, I can tell. Well, if I hadn't had a place to go, I probably would have wound up taking an "all night" streetcar ride.

Gloria will have this story circulating far and wide, I'm afraid. I just hope it doesn't get back to home or to Betsy. I don't want to explain my fantasy story to the folks and don't want to humiliate Betsy. I've become a man of mystery who says he likes to ride streetcars in a tuxedo.

It's a beautiful day in Chicago, as the guy on the National Farm and Home hour program always says on WLS. The sun is hot, the water cold, the wind brisk and the waves high. There are high school kids everywhere. Guys with steady girl friends are on or under blankets. Guys like me are playing catch, swimming or just making conversation.

Gloria's two friends seem to be interested in talking to me, but I'm not too interested in talking to them. I don't have much to talk about. The girls are nice, but I seem to be having trouble concentrating. My thoughts are continually drifting

226

back to what happened last night. My head is filled with details, remembering things about Mitsie's flat. About Mitsie. Remembering how the night progressed. Not only remembering the wonderful romp; I keep hearing the sounds of the night in my head and the conversation, too. Remembering that this encounter was a once in a lifetime thing, that won't happen again. And I don't want to think about that. I'm not proud of what happened. It was sinful. I've already asked the Lord to forgive me. It's not easy asking for forgiveness when I feel so good about what happened. I know you're not supposed to give in to sinful ways. At seventeen you aren't supposed to be thinking about a night in bed with a twenty-three year old woman. I have been thinking about it though. Started thinking about it the moment Mitsie invited me to her place and I couldn't go. What's done is done and there's no taking it back even if I wanted to.

*****

Graduation day is pretty much just another day in my life. I don't have a speech to make, or a gold tassel on my hat, or tears in my eyes or profound things to say to my classmates. I just walk up on the stage, get my diploma and that's pretty much it. My Dad is proud. He only went as far as eighth grade and he thinks I have a great future.

My Mom is proud. She went to high school and secretarial school and now her boy is a high school graduate. Don't know how far Grandpa got in school, but he's proud of me, too. After returning the cap and gown, I clean out my locker and I go to work.

Working full time at the factory is okay, the money is good, but I don't think it's something that I will want to do with the rest of my life. I haven't seen or talked to Mitsie. Thought she might be waiting at the curb for me one of these days in spite of what she told me, but no dice as yet. She's one hot number and I miss her. I'm abiding by what she told me. She said that's it and that's it!

On June 25th, President Truman gave General Mac Arthur the go ahead to get involved with a war in a place called Korea. It's somewhere near Japan or China. In July we are in it up to our necks and the newspapers say that my draft board will soon be knocking at my door. I am registered and they are drafting guys.

Lars has been talking about volunteering for the service. He says we are going to go anyway, why not join up now and get it over with. I've already done a little checking about the navy. Thought I'd rather go into the navy than the army, but the navy only has three year enlistments. The army has a two year hitch. I don't think I want to enlist for three years but maybe Lars is right and we should join up.

*****

Now that I can borrow Dad's Merc my dating game has improved a lot. I've been taking Betsy out and a couple of other girls. I've dated Dixie, the coach's daughter and a girl named Margie Evans. Margie's a girl I danced the Charleston with at the Senior Night Show. Senior night is the last act of high school, so to speak. It's like a vaudeville show that seniors put on. Margie's a tall, natural, redhead with a great personality and like Betsy, she has a lot of boyfriends. I've taken Betsy to the Will Rogers on Belmont near Central across the street from Goldblatts department store. It's new, nice, has a balcony that I collected all the kisses that Betsy owed me and then some. Took her bowling at Manor Bowl and back to Bruno's for pizza. She likes visiting the old neighborhood and looking in all the store windows. She always runs into friends of hers and acquaintances of her mom and dad when we bum around Belmont and Central. There isn't anything serious going on between us. We just enjoy being with each other. We talk about all sorts of things. She likes to talk about the vacations she has taken with her folks. They have been all over the country. Florida, California. She's flown but her Dad prefers driving vacations. I'm a little jealous, but now that Dad has a car maybe we can take a trip or two.

The dates with Dixie and Margie are just that. Dates. We are good friends and have fun. We are comfortable with one another.

Bob, Mike, Lars and I have gone to Riverview with dates a few times. The girls usually stand around while we ride the Bobs. They will ride the Blue Streak which is okay, but it's nothing like the Bobs. The Mill on the Floss is something we all enjoy. Once Betsy got the big air treatment when we went through Alladin's Castle and her skirt flew up. I was a few steps behind her and enjoyed the view. Nice legs. Have seen them on the beach but never with her skirt up around her neck. She wears frilly blue panties. Had never seen those either. Everyone including Betsy laughed after she finally got her skirt back in place.

No one rides the Parachutes. Everyone has heard about Lars and me being hung up at the top and don't want to experience anything like that.

We've driven to Lake Geneva in Wisconsin for a day on the beach. We've taken the mail boat ride, too. We all chipped in and rented a motor boat for a couple of hours one time. Bob ran the thing. He's really good at driving anything. If you put him at the controls of an airplane, I think he'd be doing loops in twenty minutes.

Dan Glaubke

After a day on the beach, we usually wind up having something to eat in one of the Lake Geneva restaurants before we head for home. Lake Geneva is a long way from where we live, about a two hour drive over two lane highways that are really crowded all summer long.

My boss Hank likes me well enough that he'll let me take a day or two off when things are slow. I don't abuse the privilege. The money is too good. It's an easy job and I like it okay, but there isn't much of chance to better yourself. Sure, I've had a small raise now and then but I know there isn't any future here. I'm not doing anything about it though, just coasting along. And the months are flying by. Labor Day, Thanksgiving, Christmas and the New Year has come and gone.

We welcomed in 1950 with the war in Korea getting hotter all the time.

I've seen Mitsie in the factory lunch room and have even had a cup of coffee and a private conversation with her. Her guy Jake finally popped the question at Christmas time. Took her to a fancy place for dinner. It was the Chez Paree, east of Michigan Avenue on Fairbanks, north of the Loop. They have a floor show featuring sexy dancers called the Adorables. You can dance in addition to eating dinner. Jake and Mitsie like to dance. That's how they met and still go two-stepping and jitterbugging at the Arragon and Melody Mill.

Mitsie said that on the night they became engaged Jake had their waiter bring the ring with the dessert. He brought the ring box to the table on a silver tray and said "For you Miss, from one of your admirers."

When she opened the box Jake proposed.

I asked to see the ring, but Mitsie doesn't wear it to work. She says it has a square-cut diamond and a couple of baguettes. I don't have any idea what a square-cut diamond is or what baguettes are, but it sounds pretty impressive. They haven't set a wedding date as yet but she said it will be soon. Her mom and dad like Jake fine which makes everything good. She's excited and everything is wonderful in her life I didn't ask her how her sex life was, but I have a vivid imagination.

*****

Since prom night, I've prayed, asked the Lord to forgive me. Not once. Many times. Don't understand why our fooling around doesn't bother Mitsie. If I let my mind wander, I have do ask for forgiveness over and over again.

Twenty Six

Spring is in full bloom. Dixie is having another party at her house. The only difference with this one, she has invited everyone to bring dates. So it is pretty much a Luther League party plus their guests. She's been going steady with Chuck, a cousin of Lars, another Swede. He's a junior at Augustana College in Rock Island. With the party a couple of weeks away, I call Betsy. With my luck she's probably busy.

"Hi Betsy, it's Ben."

"Hi Ben, how are things?"

"Great. Dixie's having a party and I called because I need a date."

"Oh, well I have something I need to talk to you about."

"You need to ... oh, I don't like the sound of that, what's up?"

"Well, it's like this. I've only been dating two guys for the past three months. You and Jack Thomas from school. I'll be going to the U of I next fall and so will Jack.

"I've decided to go steady with him. Having a boy friend that I can travel to school with and come home with on breaks is important to me. We'll be going through the same freshman things when we get there and can help one another out.

"I know, I've said that I didn't want to go steady, but Jack is a sweetheart and we're going to the prom together. Jack's been driving me to school and we've been seeing each other almost everyday since school started."

"Oh."

"Gee Ben, I do like you a lot and its been fun dating, but I hope you understand. We can still be friends. Don't be mad."

"I'm not mad, Betsy. It does hurt a bit, can't kid you about that. I'll get over it. Hope your dad lets you stay out after midnight on prom night. Just so your boobs don't get wet from crying."

"Ben! Ben Tepke! My boobs didn't get wet on your prom night. What are you talking about?"

"I'm sorry. That was supposed to be a joke. Bad joke I guess. But, you were upset and I do remember that you cried a lot when I picked you up that night."

"I was upset. I don't have any idea why my dad insisted I be home by twelve. I think he must have had a bad day at work. I thought I ruined your special night. The senior prom is something special. Did you really ride the streetcar all night that night? After you dropped me off at home? We never talked about what you did after taking me home. Nita said that Gloria told her that you rode a streetcar all night. Is that true?"

" Yes. Rode the Cicero Avenue streetcar all the way to the end of the line and back. And this is the end of the line for us, isn't it? Well, maybe I'll go out and ride the streetcar all night tonight, too. You of all people should know how much I enjoy riding streetcars and trolley buses. Well, I guess that does it. Have a good summer and I hope you like the U of I. Bye, Betsy."

"So long, Ben take care of yourself. And don't go for a streetcar ride, tonight. I feel bad enough having to say good bye on the phone, but I think it's better this way."

"Sure. Take care."

Well, that's that. Now I'll have to find another girlfriend to take to the party.

*****

Things are going good at work and I haven't been dating much, but all things considered, I'm enjoying myself. Bob's still going to the University of Illinois down at the Pier, but he's going to transfer to Augustana next semester. He's working at the garage full time, but he's a full fledged mechanic now and making good money. He'll need it when he goes away to school. The reason he wants to go to Augustana is because Nita is going to go there. I think he wants to protect his interest. They are going steady but I'll bet he doesn't want a bunch of other college boys breathing hard and asking her out. She's beautiful, getting prettier all the time. Mike is putting in time on a big building project downtown. He's a full fledged electrician and likes the work. He and Gloria have parted company. No hard feelings, but she will be going to Stanford University in California.

Lars is still with Sears but he's seriously thinking about being a carpenter. Doesn't like selling. He's dating but doesn't have any steady girlfriend. Ricky is planning to go to college somewhere after he graduates and for the summer is helping his dad. He doesn't speak Polish, but he's been running around, delivering polices and collecting premiums. He still dates Gail, but he says that he's going to dump her when he goes away to school.

When we get together now, we've been going to the bowling alley or a tavern on Cicero where we have a couple of beers and talk. Lars is convinced we should all join the army and get it over with. Nobody agrees with him, but I've been thinking about it.

*****

At the end of June, I'm on a crowded streetcar heading home from work. As it approaches Cicero and Belmont, about a block away, it comes to a screeching halt. The motorman informs everyone that there is an accident on the tracks up ahead and we won't be moving for a while. The night is hot and humid. So is the streetcar. I'm hot, dirty, sweat caked, and looking foreword to a cool shower and a change of clothes. I decide not to wait for the tracks to clear. I get off the streetcar and I'm going to walk the six long blocks remaining before my stop. I leave the crowd of disgruntled passengers bemoaning their fate and start to amble home.

The accident is at the corner. A car turned left and another coming from the opposite direction slammed into it. At least that is what it looks like to me. As I elbow my way through the gaper block on the corner, I see her. Maddy. Beautiful Maddy

Out of the Loop

Fletcher. One of the girl's I've known since grammar school. She was a year behind me at Foreman. In Nita and Betsy's class. She didn't know I was alive in high school. But, I knew her. Cheerleader, popular with girls and guys alike. And beautiful. Long brown hair, green eyes, and a smile that other girls would die for. I also remember that she has great legs and a beautiful body to match her wonderful personality.

The last time I saw her she was going steady with one of the guys on the football team.

"Hey! Maddy! Hello! Over here!" I shout above the crowd to get her attention. I thought I'd say hi, how are you, what's going on in your life? Why not. Nothing is going on in mine.

She heard me, looked around and our eyes met. At first it was a look that said, do I know you? But recognition followed quickly. "Hi Ben, how are you?" Her reply is warm and friendly.

Over the dozen heads between us I holler, "I'm fine and what are you doing these days?"

Maddy then moves toward me to close up the distance between us and says, "I'm working at the Garfield Park Hospital, in the maternity ward. What are you up to?"

"Working in a factory. Do you have time for a cup of coffee or a bite to eat?"

"As a matter of fact I do."

That was the beginning of an unbelievable evening for me.

There's a small restaurant on the corner and a booth is waiting for us. I learn she's planning to go to North Central College in Naperville in the Fall.

"What's keeping you busy these days, Ben?"

"It's my job and I'm doing okay. You remember Betsy, right? Betsy Banks? Well, her dad got me a job at the factory that

237

he manages. I've been working there since my senior year. I like it and they treat me good. I work in the supply area."

I asked her about her steady boyfriend.

"Paul and I decided to go our separate ways. I still think a lot of him and he still likes me but we aren't going together anymore. He's at the University of Wisconsin, doing great up there. Working in Madison. He says when he finishes college he's going to live in Wisconsin. He likes to hunt and fish and thinks Wisconsin is wonderful. He has another girlfriend and I'm happy for him. He's a popular guy."

We ate, talked, talked some more, and all of a sudden I realized that it was almost ten. We had been sitting in the restaurant for almost three hours. It seemed like twenty minutes to me but it had been three hours since the accident. After I pay the bill, I walk Maddy home. When we arrive at her door, I ask if she would like to go dancing.

"Don't you have a girlfriend, Ben?"

"Well, I'm working on it. Go dancing with me on Saturday night and I'll be a step closer. I'll try to dazzle you with my footwork, charm you with witty stories, mesmerize you with clever tales of my past. Then if I find that you aren't bored to death, I'll ask you out again. Are you doing anything Saturday night?"

After a slight pause, Maddy smiled, looked right at me and said, "Yes I am doing something Saturday night." Then after another short pause she followed up with, "I'm going dancing Saturday night with a tall, dark, handsome guy I ran into tonight by accident!"

On Saturday night, I pick her up promptly at seven. She always did look good to me, but on this Saturday night she looks spectacular. She is wearing a blue knit dress, blue hose, blue high heel shoes and smells like heaven, fresh and clean with a

Out of the Loop

hint of some fragrance. On the way to the Melody Mill, she asks all kinds of questions. She seemed interested in everything I had to say the night of the accident, tonight she's the same beautiful girl hanging on my every word.

The Melody Mill is big. The band plays both fast and slow music, tries to please everyone. I don't like the fast music, because I don't know how to jitterbug, but Maddy doesn't seem to mind. I really don't dance all that well, but I've got this beautiful body pressed close to mine and I just keep shuffling along with the music and try not to step on her feet. Seems to work and I'm having a great time. She is really fun to be with.

After the dance, we head for Sally's and have a sandwich. Then I talk her into having a dish of ice cream. She's so easy to talk to, good to look at, and nice, I don't want the night to end.

She lost her mother at age twelve and still misses her. She has a younger sister that she feels responsible for. She said that her dad has raised her and her sister by phone. They have to call him at his office before going anywhere, if he doesn't know about it in advance. She said she should have called him from the restaurant the night we met and had dinner, but she forgot.

Her dad, like mine works all the time. The strange thing about me dating Maddy is that her dad is a Dentist. My Dad makes false teeth and her dad pulls the real ones out. I know that Doc Fletcher and my Dad don't do any business together because my Dad has never talked about him. My Dad tells me funny stories about the dentists he works for all the time.

Maddy thinks she'll like college but her Dad will only pay for two years of school and insists that's enough. Then she plans to get a job somewhere.

When we arrive at her house, after leaving the restaurant,

it's late. Very late. I don't want our first kiss to be one sitting in an automobile, I want her close when I kiss her, want to see her face before and after I make the move to put my mouth against hers and thank her for the wonderful evening. I know I'll get a kiss. There isn't any doubt in my mind. I know because of the way she talks to me, listens, looks at me, smiles and by the way she let me hold her when we danced.

I take her hand, help her out of the car and I walk her to the door. When we reach the front steps, she turns to say good night and I put my arms around her, pull her gently toward me and I kiss her. It isn't like kissing Mom or my sister. It isn't like kissing Betsy or Mitsie. It's a new experience. Discovery. Lips exploring lips, tasting, touching, then pressing a bit harder as if both Maddy and I are testing, trying to tell each other something not knowing if there's an answer. Wanting an answer, but not wanting an answer that is disapproving in any way shape or form. The kiss make me feel like every blood cell in my body has come to life for the first time. Electric. Produces a feeling that trickles from my lips downward, lingering, sensitive, warming my being from head to toe.

We kiss and kiss again and then Maddy backs off, looks me in the eyes, gives me a hug, whispers "Thanks." and she's gone. She disappears before I can stop her. Her dad has left the front door open and she doesn't need a key to get in and she's gone.

I stand there on the steps for minutes wondering how I let her get away so fast. I didn't want the night to end. I wanted another kiss. And another. I thought that she should have stayed with me longer. Thought that I shouldn't have left her get away. Both Mitsie and Betsy have said that I'm a little slow when it comes to knowing how to handle girls. I wish that wasn't so, but

Out of the Loop

I guess it is. I shouldn't have let her get away.

When I walk away from the house I tell myself that I'm through being slow. This isn't going to be a one date affair if I can help it. I don't think she's the type of girl that hands out kisses like the ones I just got to every guy she dates. I think I've fallen in love.

******

Over the next few weeks Maddy and I have a lot of dates. We've gone to Melody Mill again. We've gone to the Olson Rug waterfalls. We've gone downtown and walked around Michigan Avenue. We've gone out to eat. We've had pizza at Bruno's. We've double dated with Bob and Nita. We've gone to the Shedd Aquarium and the Field Museum. We've gone to church together. I'm nuts about her. I've taken her home and my Mom, Dad and Gramps are nuts about her, too!

We talk. We walk. We ride streetcars and buses when I don't have Dad's car to use. We'd rather not work and just be together alone but that's not possible. I love her, I've told her that I love her. She's said that she loves me. I've never felt this way before.

Having experienced what it feels like to get involved physically with someone, I find myself wanting more of Maddy than earth shaking kisses. My hands want to explore the inviting places that I know exist behind the whisps of material she wears and my hands seem uncontrollable, seem to have a will of their own when our lips have merged on many occasions. Maddy is quick. Quick to head my hands off at the pass. She knows how I feel. Knows that if she gives in we would be heading for trouble that would ruin our relationship eventually.

Dan Glaubke

"Ben, it's a sin. I don't want you mad at me. Don't want to hurt your feelings, but stop it! I don't want to lose respect for myself. Or you. You have me feeling like I'd like to give in and I don't want to be tempted or constantly pushing you away, Please, please understand and stop."

Even though I know how she feels there are times when my hands seem to forget what she's said. Thank the Good Lord, she's patient and doesn't give in.

I now have a big problem. One I haven't given too much thought to before Maddy. It's the job I have. It's a dead end. I know I can't cut it in college. I'm not a good student and don't want to waste my folks money. What would I major in anyway?

I have no idea what it is I want do with my life, but know I'm not going to work for the Ravenswood Company forever. I'm frustrated. How am I going to keep Maddy interested in me if I'm a factory worker with little prospect for getting ahead and making real money.

In a few days Maddy will be going off to North Central College. Way out in Naperville. She says she loves me, but how am I going compete with those college guys. She'll be hard pressed to say no to a bunch of good looking guys that keep pressing her for dates. Got to think of something, start doing something about the future or I'm going to lose her.

Twenty-Seven

The day arrives for Maddy to leave home and start school in Naperville. I borrow Dad's car, and help her on her way. Doc Fletcher wants to give me money for gas, but it's my treat even though I'm filled with dread. Maddy has clothes, boxes of things, luggage, a lot of stuff. Thought I might have to rent a trailer or make two trips as I load the car. Marion, her pretty sister, is sitting on her bed, watching as I make trips back and forth. She's one happy girl, for she won't have to share the space in the little bedroom, or the bathroom, or listen to the advice of her concerned sister in the days ahead. Since their mother died, Maddy has tried to keep Marion from falling from the straight and narrow, making the mistakes all of us make as we grow and stumble along, tripping over the bumps in life's road. Maddy has said that they love each other, play tricks on one another, tell each other most of all there is to tell. She will miss her.

The drive to Naperville is sad for me, exciting for Maddy. It's a whole new life adventure for her. She'll meet new people, learn new things. Experience new things. It's awkward for me. As I carry things up to her dorm room, she's busy putting everything in its place. The place is chaotic, like an ant hill, as her new room mates and the other girls stuff drawers, hang clothes, move furniture, and park 'this and that' in their confined dormitory space. There are a lot of good looking guys hanging around. I figure they are checking out the new girls and getting reacquainted with those they met last semester.

I'm jealous. Could act hateful at any given moment. Shit and two makes eight, I don't want Maddy here, a place where I can't see her every day. She knows what I'm thinking. She can sense I'm having a bad time.

"I've got to go, Maddy."

"I know. " she says and adds, "You can get out here weekends. It's not like I'm in California or Alaska or that far away."

"You might as well be. You're going to have homework and social things to do on weekends. You can't have me waiting for you on the corner for those times when you ain't -- aren't -- busy. Who's going to be correcting my English now that your a college girl in Naperville and I'm still in the city? Shit! Pardon me. I'm going a little nuts. You'll be fine. I'll get over this. I love you, kid."

Maddy then reaches up, puts her arms around my neck, pulls my face down to hers and gives me a big kiss. She does it like no one else is around. When she lets me go, she says, "I love you Ben and that's not going to change because I'm a college girl. Got that?" She's teary, too.

"Yeah, I got that. I'll be okay. I'm just jealous and can't kick the feeling right now. I'm okay, just let me know how things go and when I can see you again. Promise me a call when you've got things under control."

Maddy walks me back to the car, gives me another kiss, and I head for home. Sad day for me. Hope I didn't spoil it for her. I've never felt this way before. I liked Betsy a lot. Can't deny that. But Betsy didn't love me. I was a date, pure and simple. This is different. Sure, I'm eighteen and too young to be thinking about marriage. But, I'm thinking about it. I'm thinking that Maddy is the someone I'd like to spend the rest of my life with. I know my Dad is nuts about my Mom and my Mom is nuts about my Dad. You can see it when they look at one another. You can sense it the way they talk to one another. You can understand how much he loves her when you see him give Mom a playful pat on her backside when she walks by him sitting on a kitchen chair. And she giggles. Then turns around, bends over and gives him a hug and kiss. That's how I think my life would be with Maddy.

As the weeks go on, I'm surprised that our relationship doesn't change at all with the exception that she is in Naperville and we don't see one another that often anymore. We talk on the phone a lot. She's doing well with her classes, she thinks. When I do get to see her, it's as if we haven't been apart long. I'm very much in love and so is she. I'm one lucky guy.

Since I've got a lot more time on my hands now that Maddy is in school, I'm getting together with Lars, Mike and Ricky a lot. Ricky is going to Wright Junior College for the time being. He'd like to go to Notre Dame, but that's not going to happen. We go bowling or to a tavern on Laramie and Barry for the most part. The guy that owns the bar lets us drink beer even though we aren't twenty-one as yet. He knows we aren't legal and won't complain, he says, if we stay sober and don't act up. We don't drink enough to get drunk. We have a couple beers, eat pretzels and play darts or the pin ball machine. He's got a shuffle board, which we keep busy, playing against the other locals once in a while for a beer.

The bar we go to on Cicero Avenue is so dark, the bartender can't tell if we are ten or ninety-two. We order, and up come the mugs. He uses a flashlight to count money and make change. The juke box supplies most of the illumination for the place and the music is so loud you have to shout at the guy sitting next to you to be heard.

Work, play, Maddy, work, play, work, play, Maddy, work play, work play, work play, Maddy. Time marches on and I still don't know what it is that will get me out of this rut I'm in and on to better things.

The only important thing in my life these days are the trips to Naperville, seeing Maddy. Making sure she knows how much I love and miss her. She's doing very well in college. Guys are trying to cut me out, but she tells me about that. She likes college life, the work and social aspects but she is still "Ben's girl" and doesn't care who knows it.

Lars is still after me about joining the army. He says we are going to be drafted anyway, why not join and get it over with so we can start living a normal life.

"Can you think of any way you are going to get out of being drafted?" He tells me.

"Yeah," I say, "I'm illiterate, can't read or write."

"That ain't gonna do it! They will ask you to sign the

draft papers with an 'X' and then some selective service guy will witness your 'X' and you'll be in."

"I'll think of something."

"No, you won't. Let's join and get it over with!"

*****

Maddy isn't so sure that joining the army is a good idea. She understands my thinking, but still isn't sure that it's the best way to solve the problem of my future employment.

She says, "Why don't you wait a couple of weeks and see how you feel about it, that won't hurt. Why, you could enroll here at North Central and I could help you with the homework and things. It's not that hard Ben."

If my high school experience is any criteria for being a success in college, I have no chance at all.

"No Maddy, that won't work. But I'll wait a couple of weeks before signing up and think about it. That's all I can promise."

At home once again, I call up Lars and explain that I've promised Maddy that I'll wait a couple of weeks before taking the step.

Lars says, "You're a goof ball Ben. You think Maddy is going to marry a supply room boy or wait around until you come up with some magic that makes you a millionaire? She's in college now. She'll meet some classy guy that's going to be a doctor or lawyer, marry him and live happily ever after. She's a knock out. You're a bum. So let's go. Why wait until she breaks your heart when we can be off doing something that gets us out of Chicago. Have you ever been outside of Chicago?"

"Been to Lake Geneva, the Dells, Baraboo and Devils

Lake in Wisconsin once. My Uncle Ed and Aunt Lily took me to Devils Lake. That was a great trip. Camped out, climbed rocks. Took a ferry ride on the way home. But that's it. Where have you been?"

"I've been to my cousin's farm a few times. It's down in Southern Illinois. I haven't really been anywhere. No where! That's what makes going into the service such a good deal. We'll be seeing something, going places that neither one of us have ever been before. We might wind up in Alaska, Japan, Germany, California, who know where. Places we probably never would be able to afford to go. It will be a great adventure! Come on Ben."

"You're probably right. About Maddy and seeing the world, but Lars I really love this girl. I promised her I'd think about signing up for two weeks before I make a decision. If you can't wait, go ahead without me, okay?"

"I'll wait, but we're wasting time."

Lars has some good points. I probably should sign on now and do Maddy a favor. The two weeks come and go and I tell Maddy that I've made up my mind.

"Lars, I'm in, lets do it."

Mom, Dad and Gramps are okay with the decision. Lars and I go to the local recruiting office, sign some papers and get a date to report downtown.

I quit working. Hank says he'll miss me and to take care of myself. He saw a lot of action in World War II, but won't talk about it. Old man Ericksen told me that Hank went into Normandy on D-Day and was in the thick of things in France and Germany. He was wounded in his left leg and still walks with a slight limp.

I haven't had a chance to see Maddy much, but, the night before Lars and I leave for our induction and destinations

Out of the Loop

unknown I take Maddy to the Melody Mill once more.

The music is wonderful tonight. I don't know when I'll have another opportunity to hold her this close, take in the nice, fresh, clean smell of her. I love to touch her hair, feel her head on my shoulder. Everything is perfect.

People say it's a small world and tonight of all nights a strange thing happens. As Maddy and I are dancing to 'Sentimental Journey' I see a woman's left hand sort of waving my way on the crowded dance floor. Not an overt waving, like the waving of a flag -- wiggling fingers that I can't help but notice. There's a big diamond on the third finger of the hand.

When the couple turn as the music plays, I see the woman's face. It's Mitsie and her husband. She isn't making any move to say hello or recognize me. She's just smiling that smile of hers, making me believe that all is well in her life and that she's happy. I smile back and subtly give her a thumb's up and she winks back. I don't think I'll ever see her again, but I'm feeling good about seeing her tonight anyway.

Saying good-bye to Maddy at her dorm isn't easy. Couldn't talk long because she had to get inside before they locked the doors for the night, I can't remember much of what we said. I just wanted to keep hearing her voice and keep looking at her, holding her. I want to remember how beautiful she is. The sparkling eyes. The smile that lights up my heart when she looks at me. And how her mouth feels against mine when we kiss. She says she loves me and I love her, but who knows what the next two years will be like. I really can't expect her to be sitting around waiting, even though she says she will.

When I left the house the next morning, Mom shed a tear or two, Dad and Lisa seem to be okay. Gramps said his piece last night as we sat together in his room. Said "We shouldn't care if the Koreans want to kill each other. Maybe you'll wind up in Germany, not that you could visit where I came from, but that would be a better place than Korea."

My Grandpa came from a town in Germany called Stolp, located in an area that was given to Poland after World War II. He said, " Maybe you won't leave the United States. There are a lot of Army Camps here. Just listen, learn, ask questions when you don't understand things. And drop me a postcard now and then."

"Gramps, they won't be sending me overseas for quite a while, if ever, because you have to go through basic training first. That takes time. I'll write, I promise."

When I left, I kissed Mom and Lisa good-bye, shook Dad's and Grandpa's hands and walked away from the house down Oakdale Avenue with mixed emotions. This is a big step. I've never been away from home on my own before. I sure hope this turns out okay. I do know that I won't be in charge of my life anymore. I'll belong to the army where you say, "Yes Sir! No Sir!" Never, "I'll think about it, Sir!, or how about tomorrow, Sir!" Well, like Lars said, in no time at all we'd be drafted anyway.

*****

I met Lars on Belmont Avenue and the two of us took the streetcar and El downtown to be sworn in. For some reason the familiar clang, clang, clang, of the old red street car clangor fill me with thoughts of times past and I wonder about what tomorrow will bring. Lars and I don't talk much on the way downtown. In spite all of his bravado, I think he's a bit apprehensive, too.

At the induction center we raise our right hand, vow to serve with honor and help protect our country. We are given physicals and told to come back later that day for a trip to Fort

Out of the Loop

Leonard Wood in Missouri. So Missouri is the first stop on our great adventure. Doesn't seem like an exotic destination to me, but there's nothing I can do about it. There's no place to go while we wait, so Lars and I walk around the Loop and down Michigan Avenue, knowing it will be sometime before we see these sights again. I thought about dropping into Shaynes and saying hello to Mr. Webster and Ethel, but I know Lars will be bored with that so we just keep roaming around for awhile.

"You want to walk down to the Baby Ruth factory?" Says Lars.

"Sure, we can wait around for our favorite truck driver and get another hunk of chocolate."

"We've had some good times, haven't we?"

"We're going to have some more, but they won't be around here."

"Who in the hell is Leonard Wood?"

"Got me."

When we report back at the appointed time, we have already "lost" a few heads. Some of the guys sworn in with us in the morning haven't shown up again for the train ride west. Then we walk to the train station and board the train.

As we ride west we see farms, factories, rivers, streams, small towns. Trucks and cars going places. I have always enjoyed sight seeing and this has been great so far.

Twenty Eight

When we arrive in St. Louis, we get off the train and have dinner in a special area of the train station. Then we board another train for the ride to Fort Leonard Wood. It is late at night when we arrive. We have to wait a while by the rail-siding and then trucks arrive to haul us to a barracks area. The Fort hasn't been in use since the end of World War II. It reopened a few weeks ago.

Our barracks is a strange environment. I gave up a room of my own, in a nice comfortable home, for a room filled with forty guys, double bunks, and not one bit of privacy. We now shit, shower and shave without any privacy at all. The barracks has a huge shower room, eight toilets without any stalls and a line up of ten sinks you have to wait in line to use.

At night guys snore, talk and mumble in their sleep, toss and turn, pass gas and you wonder how long it will take to learn to live like this. I've got a thousand things going on in my head, not knowing what will happen next. I think about what I'm going to do when I get out and that's two years away. I think about Maddy. Will she wait, will we get married, if so where are we going to live. There are a lot of things to think about but not many answers.

We were told not to bring any extra clothes when we signed up, just shaving gear, toothbrush, and toothpaste, so it is a little disturbing that we haven't been given a uniform or any clothes since we arrived four days ago.

Everyone keeps wondering where the officers and non-coms are. Wondering why we aren't doing things. We sit on our bunks, talking, reading, taking naps, writing letters home or playing cards, but that's it. The only army uniforms we see are those we see in the mess hall. We found the mess hall easy enough, so we all are eating pretty good.

Five days after we arrive, a sergeant finally shows up and starts calling out our names. He says, "Where in the hell have you guys been?" It isn't us that have made a mistake. It's the army. Someone forgot where they put us. The processing phase of army life now begins. We get clothes. Finally. We are supposed to send what we had on home. Most of us just toss what we have worn in the garbage bins. Why subject the folks back home with clothes that smell like someone has died in them.

We receive our dog tags with our serial number. Lars and I are one number apart. There are more papers and documents to fill out. We have to "police" the area, police meaning we pick up paper and cigarette butts off the ground surrounding the barracks.

Out of the Loop

There are KP chores to handle now. We have to keep the barracks and latrines clean. The army finds many ways to keep everyone busy.

One night I decide to go to a movie with a couple of other guys. Lars doesn't want to go. The movie is about a half mile from the barracks on a main post road. While we're walking on the road's shoulder I get hit by a car. Some "turkey" swerves his car into the gravel and I hear it churning behind me as the headlights cast ominous shadows ahead. I know what's about to happen and can't get out of harms way. Luckily, I just get side swiped and knocked down. But my elbow caught the windshield, as the car whipped by, and it feels as if my arm is broken. To make matters worse the car doesn't stop. My buddies help me up and ask if I'm able to walk. The answer's yes, but the arm is killing me. They ask if I want to go back to the barracks. Said no, lets keep going toward the show.

When we get there, a car with a broken windshield is parked along side an MP jeep but no one is in it. An MP is standing there. I tell him that the guy who owns the car ran me over a hundred yards down the road. My barrack buddies are telling him what happened, too.

Now listen to this: The MP says, "What do you guys expect me to do? The guy that owns that car is my Company Commander. You think I'm going to arrest my Company Commander? He's a major! I'm just one the troops. Sorry, about the arm and I'll take you to the post hospital if that's what you want. But that's it. Understand? That's all I can do for you."

I understand. "Okay, but that son-of-a-bitch should be put in jail!" My two comrades go to the movies and the MP gives me a ride to the medics. At the hospital, they take my name, serial number, x-ray my arm and tell me to wait. For a few minutes the

MP waits, too, then disappears. After a half hour of waiting, a doctor arrives with the MP right behind him.

"Private, your arm has had a bad bruise but nothing is broken. I'm going to put it in a sling. Don't want you to use it for a couple of days. I'm giving you a cold pack for the elbow area. The swelling should subside shortly. This bottle contains some all purpose pills ... aspirins ... if you can't sleep take a couple with water."

Then the doctor looks at the MP and says, "Corporal, drive Tepke back to his barracks."

In the morning, when we fall out for revelry, Lars' name is called along with mine. We are told that we're shipping out. No one else in our barracks is called, just Private Swanson and Private Tepke. After breakfast we report to the office with our duffel bags. Seems like something isn't Kosher, but in the army you do what you are told to do.

Lars looks at me and says, "What's going on?"

"I think it has something to do with me being hit last night."

"No. The army can't do anything that fast."

"A major is pretty high up, he probably can arrange anything. They had my serial number. Took it at the hospital. Yours is only a number away. We're both regular army. The Major probably figured we both joined together. Our records must indicate some connection."

When we report, they have our records, a jeep is waiting and we are driven to a rail head where a couple hundred guys are boarding a train. We are told to get on board, too. One Ben Tepke, duffle bag, sore arm and buddy Lars get on a train and we haven't a clue to where it is we're going. We are off on another adventure.

I have lived on the northwest side of Chicago all my life;

escaped being hit by a car in a city with a jillion automobiles. I am in the army less than two weeks and hit by a car on an army post that has a couple of civilian cars. The man who hit me is the post's top cop. I can't press charges and somehow, the major has had Lars and me cut on orders to leave Leonard Wood the morning after he hit me. We're gone before I can think of anything I can possibly do about it.

Twenty Nine

The train ride is interesting. I pulled KP chores on part of the trip which meant I could sit by the open door in the cook car with feet hanging over the car's side while peeling potatoes. I could see America's little towns, villages and farm land close up as we traveled down the track. It would be great to visit some of these places some day and see what small town living is like. There are some landscapes that we are passing that look like the Currier and Ives prints that are hanging on our basement walls at home.

At the rate we're moving it will take forever to get any place. Our train is being side-tracked to give priority treatment to freight and passenger trains along the way.

Dan Glaubke

The swelling in my arm is long gone. We've been riding for two days now and there's nothing that looks like an army post on the horizon.

Along the way we hear a rumor that we are headed for a place called Camp Pickett. It's in Virginia. I was a terrible student, but I remember that Pickett was a Southern General during the Civil War.

When we finally arrive we find out that we have been placed in a reactivated National Guard unit from the state of Connecticut. Camp Pickett has been reactivated, too.

Lars and I are hauled off to the Regimental Headquarters Company, of the 102nd Infantry Regiment, of the 43rd Infantry Division. Our barracks complex is old and antiquated, but the exteriors have been freshly painted, the plumbing works, and we have a place to sleep. We have a place to sleep after bringing cots, mattresses, sheets, blankets, pillows and pillow cases from trucks parked along the street.

Our top sergeant looks and acts like he can and will kill with his bare hands if necessary. His name is Baxter. He's short, wide, muscular, and old. I think he's a dead ringer for the movie star, William Bendix but a William Bendix with a mustache, He has a voice that is loud, irritating; but it gets and keeps your attention when he talks. He tells us we will be going through basic training when the company has a full compliment of men and until then we will be doing calisthenics, we will be policing the area, we will be doing KP, we will be cleaning the barracks, latrines, windows, and whatever else he feels needs cleaning. He doesn't say, "Is that clear!" It is clear.

Baxter doesn't waste time. He calls out names, makes assignments. Some of us don't get a specific thing to do, but are told to get busy cleaning barrack windows, making our bunks, hanging up our uniforms and getting our foot lockers in order. It feels like we are in the army now. Finally!

As the days go on we get an M-1 rifle. We find out how to field strip it, clean it, put it back together. There is a basic routine to becoming a soldier. You get up at 5:30 AM, shower, stand reveille, make your bed, eat breakfast, do calisthenics, march off to class or the rifle range, eat lunch, police the area and are busy until it's time eat once again. We learn how to march, crawl with a full field pack and rifle. We get hand-to-hand combat training, run the obstacle courses, and learn what to do and not to do to coexist in the regimented environment in which we live. At day's end we shine our boots, clean our rifle, and make sure our foot locker and hanging clothes are neat and tidy.

We continue to live in an atmosphere without privacy. We shower and shave, poop and piddle, sleep, snore and suffer much with a bunch of strangers of every conceivable family background. I am eighteen years old. One of our "men" is a fifteen year old boy that lied about his age to get into the service. He chews tobacco like an eighty year old man that can't live without tobacco juice running down his chin. It takes the army about three weeks to figure out that our friend is too young to be doing this stuff and he's gone.

The draftees in our outfit include guys that have been teachers, factory hands, farmers, salesmen, construction workers, truck drivers, guys of all shapes, sizes, ages and stages. Most of the drafted guys are twenty-one to twenty-three. The noncoms are all from the Connecticut National Guard. Most of the guard guys are older, and many are vets of World War II. Some of these guys are really old.

We don't see much of our company commander, Captain Hundley. He usually stands revelry and disappears. The sergeants run the show and we are slowly becoming soldiers. As we go through basic training we are learning what a regimental headquarters company is all about. It's a lot different than a rifle company. We have two-hundred and sixty guys in the company. When basic training is over we will be put in various platoons.

The company is comprised of six platoons and a very large motor pool.

The headquarters' platoon is comprised of noncoms and soldiers that work for the brass that run the regiment. Our regimental commander is a colonel and the officers under him at regiment tend to be majors and captains. Running a regiment is a big job. The soldiers assigned to this platoon are made up of guys who can type the general orders, file paper, make signs and take care of the maps and officer stuff.

The other platoons in the company support the regimental commander and his staff officers. Our platoon leaders are first and second lieutenants.

We have a security platoon that has the job of guarding the regimental headquarters. You don't want the regimental commander and his officers to be vulnerable in combat situations. These guys are like Military Police at the regimental level.

The communication platoon is the biggest platoon we have. This platoon has radio operators and guys who string communications lines, put up antennas, and maintain radio equipment. You have to be able to communicate with the infantry rifle companies that make up the regiment and the communications platoon has the guys that makes it possible.

There is an antitank and mine platoon that is supposed to blow up enemy tanks and mines that we run across during combat.

The Intelligence and Reconnaissance platoon operates in front of the infantry rifle companies in time of combat. These soldiers help locate enemy forces. They help determine the size and strength of the enemy that the regiment has to deal with. These guys, obviously, have a very dangerous job when bullets are flying. It is said they sometimes are caught in the middle of things and have to watch out for bullets coming in two directions.

The Counterfire platoon has some fancy hardware and antennas that enable them to tell the range of incoming enemy fire and help locate where the shooting is coming from. I got along in arithmetic and algebra, but geometry is the key to understanding what these guys do. Never did figure out what geometry was all about. In combat this platoon has an important job. All the platoons are important.

The motor pool has trucks, jeeps, trailers, and tent equipment to maintain. So we have mechanics and drivers in this platoon that spend their time tightening nuts and bolts, changing oil, greasing axles, changing tires and washing a sizeable fleet. The fleet has to be in readiness at all times in order to move the brain trust of the regiment and all its various parts.

*****

The day arrives when we have to pick a platoon.

"Lars, what platoon are you going to shoot for?"

"Commo. Not the wire crew. I want to learn radio, Morse Code, sit on my ass, stay warm and tidy. Commo guys don't pull guard duty and you don't have to crawl through the crap the other platoons are faced with. How about you, Ben?"

" Think I'll go for I&R. Intelligence and Reconnaissance sounds like fun. I like Flynn, the platoon sergeant. Treats everyone fair. Saw a lot of action in World War II."

Dan Glaubke

"Sounds like a lot of work and you'll freeze your ass off in winter. I'll take Commo."

I go into I&R.

Army life changes once again We have to learn about our platoon's specialty. Lars is confined to a classroom with headphones. Listening and learning Morse Code, learning the fine points of being a responsible radio man. It isn't long before he's dubbed "Swede." and his "dits and dahs" of Morse start dancing off the "J-38" key the army uses to send and recieve code. He gets the hang of it fast and in a short time is one of the better operators.

The ins and outs of I&R are much different than Commo. We're in the classroom one day and out doing field work the next. Seems like there's something new to learn everyday of the week.

Christmas is coming. We have gone a long time without any free-time or a pass. There's been a lot of bitching and complaining. Not a thing we can do about it other than bitch. It takes some Senator's son to bring us some relief. He's in a rifle company and has written his old man about the evil things happening in Camp Pickett. It starts a Congressional investigation. Our Division Commander shows up on the cover of Time Magazine. He's a two-star general and he tells *Time* that the reason he's been holding us hostage is that the Division will soon be going to Korea. He wants everyone to know what they are doing when we get there. Makes sense to me, but no one has asked my opinion.

Christmas arrives with a bang. Some guy in the barracks across the street brought a Bazooka Rocket dud back to the barracks from the rocket range. Someone else billeted there smuggled booze into camp coming back from a pass, and anumber of guys get looped

This is what I've been told happened.

Out of the Loop

As the guys got drunk, the guy that had the rocket dud took it out of its hiding place and started tossing it around. They played catch with this rocket range misfire. When someone missed a catch, the rocket hit the floor and it went off. The missile didn't have a live war head, but packed plenty of explosive, rocket propulsion power. That rocket flew all over the barracks, ricocheting off the walls, setting things on fire, killing and maiming as it went. The barracks almost burned to the ground before fire equipment reached the scene. Luckily, a majority of the guys got out okay, and helped evacuate the wounded.

Young guys drinking can make some dumb moves. This was a fatal mistake that we all learned a lesson from.

*****

A couple of weeks after Christmas I get a two day pass. Not enough time to go anywhere, but I decide to head for Richmond anyway. It isn't far from Pickett and a change of scenery will be a good thing.

Got here late in the afternoon, went to the Richmond Hotel which is right in the middle of downtown. It's a lot older than our barracks, and in about the same shape, but it's only for one night. The room is clean enough. I've never stayed in a hotel room before so I can't judge whether this is a good place or isn't. The outside of the hotel reminds me of the Hotel Elinor on Cicero Avenue back home. The one thing that's great about this room is privacy. I really like the privacy and that is what I miss most about my room back home.

Since, I have no idea about what to do, I ask a guy in the hotel for help. He tells me that the Museum of the Confederacy is a place a lot of people visit when they come to Richmond. After getting directions, that's where I go. The place is sort of moldy, has old uniforms, confederate money, muskets, rifles, a lot of old paintings. It cost me a quarter to get in. Didn't stay long, but I did look around. Got my quarter's worth.

After leaving, I saw a trolley bus and decided I'd take a ride. Thought I'd go to the end of the line and back again. The front of the bus is real crowded but the back is empty. I maneuver to the back, sit down on the rear bench seat. The bus starts, then stops. People are looking at me in a strange way. Can't figure out what's wrong. Then the bus driver gets out of his seat, comes back to where I'm sitting and says, "You have to change your seat soldier or git off my bus!"

"What? Why should I do that?"

"Tell you why. That's a colored seat you're sitting on."

" Looks the same as all the others and it's empty, so what's the big deal?"

"You must be a Yankee."

"From Chicago, don't know if that makes me a Yankee." I really don't like this guy or his attitude or what's going on. I'm embarrassed and don't know why.

He says, "Well I've never been to Chicago but in Richmond we don't let the colored ride up front or the white folks ride in the back of the bus. Get it? So get up, move to the front or get off the bus!"

Before I leave I yell, "The Bible says love thy neighbor and it doesn't say anything about white, black, red, yellow or anything at all about any color that I know of. And a lot of the men that ride in the back of your bus have made it possible for you to drive it. A lot of men of color have died in wars to keep this country free so that you could sit in that seat you're sitting on. So, I'd rather walk than ride with you."

Out of the Loop

My thoughts drift back to Ethel and Gwendolyn, the two women I worked with at Shaynes. They were wonderful. Kind, generous and giving. They helped me out a lot more than I ever helped them. I hope they never, ever come this way. The South lost the war, slaves were set free, but a lot of Southerners must still be carrying a grudge. It doesn't make any sense to me.

I didn't see any more of Richmond. I went back to my hotel room, had a good night's sleep, a big breakfast and went back to camp.

Thirty

I'm enjoying I&R training. We don't march a lot, don't pull guard-duty like the rifle companies. We usually travel in our jeeps. Our platoon has eleven jeeps that we are responsible for. We have map reading and map making classes. Observation classes. We have radio classes because we need to know how to communicate over radio and wire setups. We'll never be as good as the Commo guys, but we learn code. I'm too slow, but I'll keep working at it. We have camouflage and night training programs.

Still do calisthenics, police the area, shine the barrack windows, clean what needs cleaning. and learn a lot about our fellow GI's.

No one here is perfect. We all have flaws. Some guys are tough, some are soft. Some smart, some dumb, some illiterate. But, we all wear the same uniform and are trying to do the best we can to learn what's required. A lot of the guys had to give up good jobs when they were drafted. They worry about getting the jobs back. They worry about the guys taking their place, passing them up on the promotion track. There's not a thing they can do other than worry. Some of these guys had just been married when they were drafted. That leads to another type of worry. Most guys don't talk a lot about personal problems but that doesn't mean they don't have them.

With rumors going around that we will be going on maneuvers in North Carolina, the platoon leader of Security Platoon thought it would be a good idea to test the results of the training his men had received. Lt. Osmanski has been with our company a short time. He was a rifle company platoon leader in Korea before he was assigned here. He's one combat hardened SOB who loves to tell tales about the fire fights he's been in. His idea of testing includes our I&R platoon. He has talked our platoon leader, Lt. McReidy, into having a night problem that will test the ability of both platoons by pitting one against the other.

" Men listen to me." Lt. Osmanski says as both platoons sit in the mess hall, "We are going to have a night problem the day after tomorrow. My Security Platoon will set up a command post and a perimeter of defense somewhere in the wooded area north of here. I'll be playing the Regimental Commander and our command post will be a tent located in the middle of my platoon's defense perimeter. I&R's job will be to crack that perimeter and capture me. If any Security guy spots and challenges an I&R guy, the I&R guy has to surrender. If any of you I&R guys can get through our defenses, he has permission to put me down and take me prisoner and then the exercise will be over. The problem will run from dark to dawn. If I&R hasn't cracked the perimeter by daybreak, the exercise is over. We'll be digging in and setting up tomorrow during the day. Any questions?"

Sergeant Flynn asks. "What do you mean by *'putting you down'* Sir?"

"I mean you can get rough. You guys won't get near me so I have nothing to worry about. You can hit me. Got that?" Lt. Osmanski is smiling as he says it.

"Great Incentive, Sir and we welcome the opportunity." Sgt. Flynn is smiling, too.

For some unknown reason, Lt. McReidy was suddenly called away from the post for the remainder of the month and this meant that Sgt. Flynn would be in charge of the "Osmanski Exercise." That's what we're calling it.

Back in our barracks, Flynn called the platoon together and said, "Guys. Osmanski doesn't think we have much of a chance, but we're going to give him a run for his money. I've got an idea how we're going to handle this and we'll talk about it before we leave here tomorrow night.

The next day we did what we do everyday, the normal routine but when the sun was setting, Flynn called us together again. He had maps of the area that he handed out to all of the squad leaders. He then put one up on an easel and said, "Osmanski won't ever hear what I'm about to say because none of you are going to tell him. If any of you are so inclined, please leave." No one budged. "Okay, I've already done a little recon work and we know where Security is setting up. I had a little talk with our cook, Sgt. DeMarco. His crew took lunch and dinner to the Security

271

troops and has let it slip that Osmanski's command tent is in this area." Then Flynn points to the map and says, " The tent's here! This will save us a lot of time. And we won't be running into each other. If the tent is where DeMarco says it is, I'm betting that Security will be concentrating its defense in a 270° arc that will leave us a 90° window practically unguarded. I say that because the ground to the north falls away sharply behind the command post and this stream runs wide and deep for hundreds of yards. I'm guessing that Osmanski won't have a heavy concentration of his guys back here because he'll think we won't want to get wet.

"Okay, squad leaders here's what we're going to do. Dick Slocam, your squad will set up here to the west. Parson, I want you to come in from the south. The east will be covered by Regenmeiser. I'm going to be working with Marv Wokart's squad to the north. Osmanski will have someone here near the road, reporting back when our Jeeps leave the road at point 'A' but that's okay. I want 'O' to believe we will be working as a platoon rather than squads. At this point it won't look like we know where he is. We'll all park together about here.

After midnight, all drivers will start your Jeeps, keep the lights on and start moving up and down roads 'C' and 'D' and 'E'. I want you to travel back and forth -- individually-- don't bunch up. You'll never be near the command post but the Security guys will hear you see your lights. They'll wonder what's going on. I want them confused. You're going to be doing that until day break. We're literally going to drive the enemy nuts. They won't come after you for a while, because that would weaken their defence. It will also tend to make the troops lose there edge. Our Jeep movement will make everyone alert to begin with but after a while they'll relax. We won't start moving toward our objective until two.

Out of the Loop

Then at four Slocam will shoot a flare. That's our signal to move. Security will be looking west, watching the flare. Wokart's squad and I will ford the stream and be in position by the time the flare ignites.

"Wokart and Percy will hit the guards at the tent door, Tepke and I will go into the tent and hit Osmanski. Tepke will hit him low and I'll hit him high. It would be nice if all squads infiltrate in time to see it, but the objective is to put "O" on his "A.S.S". and that is what we are going to do."

The game went off just as Flynn outlined. When the flare ignited, there was only one guard at the tent door to take care of. Lt. Osmanski was flattened by two wet, black faced guys he never saw coming until his coffee went flying and he was going down. Flynn gave him a bloody lip and knocked out a tooth. A number of I&R guys had slipped through the perimeter and were there to watch "O" take the hit.

At the critique, Lt. Osmanski said," You I&R guys were lucky, sneaky and I have to admit pretty good. Didn't think you had it in you to wade through water. Never entered my mind. Flynn you have a great right, but wish you hadn't busted my tooth. Tepke, did you play football?"

"No sir. Grew up in Chicago. Northwest side."

"Well it was a good tackle."

The Security guys liked the idea of Osmanski being clobbered as much as our I&R platoon, but they had a lot of extra field work on account of it.

*****

With rumors flying about the 43rd going to Korea as a unit, the Division left Camp Pickett for maneuverers in Southern

Pines, North Carolina. It's a big war game involving the whole division against an aggressor force and lasts a full week. There is air support for our division and new jets are in the air having dog fights with old propeller fighter planes. Fun to watch. We aren't shooting real bullets but the maneuvers are being monitored by referees that can knock you out of the action. When you get into situations where there are aggressor troops to deal with, umpires can stop the action and say things like, "You're dead, you, and you have been wounded. You with the runny nose, drive the truck back and tell your Commanding Officer that you lost a guy and left three wounded on the road."

One day, my I&R squad goes on a patrol mission with some medical umpires. These umpires hand out fake wounds that require first-aid, or a major operation in a field hospital, as if you got hurt in an actual combat situation. As we maneuver behind "enemy" lines, I'm declared "wounded," in need of an operation. I've never flown before, but on this day I'm strapped on a litter, placed and locked into a basket on the outside of a helicopter and flown to the army field hospital. On the Riverview parachute ride I went up and came down. On this thing, I've gone up and we're zooming over the tree tops faster than a ride on the Bobs and I'm trying hard not to pee in my pants.

When we arrive at the hospital, the helicopter comes down with a lot fewer bumps than the Riverview parachute ride and if I wasn't strapped so tight on the liter, I would bend over and kiss the ground.

The liter is rushed into a hospital tent, and except for my shorts, nurses stripped off all my duds. They put me on a operating table and I have a two-hour operation. A group of doctors use colored ink pens for scalpels on me.

The doctors don't joke or act like they're having a great

274

Out of the Loop

time. They're serious and when I try to make conversation they tell me to shut up or they will give me a real dose of anesthetic. So I close my mouth and go to sleep.

Thankfully they don't take me back to the platoon on the helicopter. The helicopter ride took about twenty minutes in the air. The jeep ride back, takes over an hour. And now I have multicolored ink marks all over my body. They tell me the marks will be there for a week, even if I shower twice a day.

All the guys in the platoon say that I have lucked out and they would have liked to have had the helicopter ride. It's a load of BS!

*****

Every day is more of the same as we progress with our training. We are becoming more proficient at all of the things we are learning and passes are becoming more plentiful. One day we are told an important visitor will be reviewing the division. The visitor: General Dwight D. Eisenhower.

It's a cold morning and we have to put on our dress uniforms and wear the " horse blanket" overcoat we have been issued. Then with our M-1 rifles on our shoulders we are marched to the Camp's air strip -- about five miles from our barracks -- where we have to wait a couple of hours for Ike to arrive.

While we're waiting the weather turns warm. Not warm, hot! And we are stuck wearing this unbearably hot overcoat as we wait. It isn't long before a few guys keel over from the heat and have to be carted off. We are "at ease" but there is no ease and guys are busy bitching under their breath as we sweat and time creeps along with no Ike in sight.

Finally, his airplane makes a perfect landing on the air strip that's about a mile from where we stand. Ike emerges from

Dan Glaubke

the plane, gets into a special jeep that has a stabilizer bar. The bar allows Ike to hold on as he stands to reviews the troops at twenty-five to thirty miles per hour. The review takes all of ten minutes. Then he mounts a platform that has a microphone and loud speakers and gives us a pep talk.

The pep talk moves pretty fast, too as he tells us that we should report any officer or noncom that makes life too easy for us. When we get in combat we need to be tough and know what we are doing. So complain if life gets too easy. I'd guess the speech lasted about five minutes. Then Ike got back on his plane and flew away.

*****

Life sure wasn't easy today. We had to march the five miles back to the barracks and endure the sweat, overcoat and miserable hot weather with a left... left... left, right left. No Ike, nothing was too easy to complain about on this day.

*****

Since we are in the midst of the Korean War a number of the guys from our regiment, who have gone through basic training and advanced training, are being transferred to Korea. Today, I found that I am among them.

How did I get picked? Did they pull my name out of a hat? Toss darts at the regimental manifest? Play eenie, meenie, minee, moe at reveille? I'd like to know, not that it matters or that I can do anything about it. I do know one thing. I have a five day furlough before heading to the west coast and the Far East. It actually amounts to three days because it will take a day to get home and a day to get back to Camp Pickett.

Well, I asked for it. I'm in the army now and going to war.

Thirty One

Furlough papers in hand, I head for the Greyhound bus station and ride to Washington D.C. In Washington, I get a plane to Midway Airport in Chicago. Another first. I've never flown inside of an airplane before. A different experience than the helicopter. Makes you a little nervous when the plane dips, shakes and quivers over the miles, but all I'm thinking about is seeing Maddy.

Dad picks me up at the airport and we talk. He wants to know what the past weeks of basic training and I& R training were like. I've written about everything but he wants to hear it. Hear my stories, impression, how I'm feeling about going overseas.

"I really don't know anything about Korea, Dad. I think I'm ready to go there, we've done a lot of work getting ready for it. I think I'll be okay."

I know he's worried. Mom and Gramps are worried. Hell, when it comes right down to it, I'm not happy about what's going on, but there isn't anything I can do about it. I'll go, try to keep my head down, wits about me, follow orders. Not much else I can do.

Then I talk to Mom. I talk to her and Lisa in the kitchen. Lisa isn't saying much, but Mom wants to know motherly things. Do I have enough warm things, enough socks, etcetera, etcetera.

"Mom, they give us more than enough to wear. You'd be surprised how heavy my duffle bag is. Heavy enough to get a hernia if you lift it wrong. Heck the army gives us four hours of basic training on how to lift a duffle bag. "

Got her laughing with that.

"It's cold in that country. We've been reading the paper and they say it really gets cold there."

"Well, I'm sure they have ear muffs, scarfs, long underwear waiting. Don't worry, I'll be fine."

Then when I finally get ready for bed, Gramps came into my room for a talk. He's worried, wants to know the same things the folks have been asking me about. How can you head off the worry? I just answer the questions as best I can and try to act like it's no big deal going there.

"Ben, what will they have you doing there?"

"I don't know Grandpa. Not everyone goes into combat. But, that's what I've been training for. I've been in training since last October. That's what, four months. I'm in good shape. I do everything asked of me and like you've always told me, I ask questions, keep my eyes and ears open. I'm doing fine so far."

Dad is riding to work on the streetcar for the time being.

Out of the Loop

I have the car to use. The wheels I need to see my girl. Three days isn't much when faced with the reality that soon you will be overseas and in combat. Maddy cut classes and has a big homework load. Makes no difference, she makes time for us to be together.

We talk a lot. About the only place I can find to park, talk and kiss her, is in a cemetery. That doesn't last long because someone called the cops and I have to move on. When I tell the cop I'm about to ship to Korea he says, "Well, I won't bother you for another ten minutes, but find some other place to park, okay?"

Seems like I just got off the plane, and my time is up. At the dorm door I look at Maddy and say "So long kid, I love you! I'll be back before you know it."

"Ben, be careful. I love you, too! Oh, please be careful."

I saw Mike and Ricky. Said good bye. Bob and Nita are at school in Rock Island. Mom, Dad, Lisa and Gramps took me back to Midway. Dad drove. We went past Palmer where the plane went down, past the Western Electric plant and Joe Poolala's gas station. Past a lot of store fronts and places I'd seen a hundred times when riding the streetcar south.

I can see the folks from my window seat and they can see me. We wave, then the plane is no longer at the gate. I got back to Pickett around seven, cleaned out the foot locker and packed my hanging stuff in my duffle. Turned in my rifle. Changed into fatigues and shined the boots real good. I'm going to be riding to the coast in fatigues. The I&R guys aren't saying much. I'm the only one going from I&R. Only a few guys from the company are going.

The only thing left to do tonight is to say so-long to Lars. I meander over to his barracks. He's on his cot reading.

"Hey Ben, how was the trip home and back?"

"Great. Flying is easy and you get to Midway fast. Took me almost as much time to get to DC as it did to get to Chicago. It was sort of bumpy going, pretty smooth coming back. At any rate, it's a lot better flying inside a plane than on the outside."

"The next time I get a furlough I'm going to fly home. You see anyone I know?"

"Sure. Saw Mike, and Ricky. Didn't do much, talked mostly. They're okay. Spent more time with Maddy."

"You get any?"

"Damn it, Lars! She doesn't put out and I didn't try. She's not some bozo you screw around with. Knock it off!"

"Hey, okay. Don't get mad. I'm kidding. How do your folks feel about you going over?"

"They're okay with it. They know I don't have any choice. My Dad told me a funny thing. I got drafted last week. He went down to the draft board and told them I wasn't going to go. Said the fella he talked to was real uppity. Said I had to go or I'd be going to jail. Then my Dad said, "Well then you better send that induction notice on to Camp Pickett in Virginia, if your serious." The guy didn't understand. Dad said he practically had to draw the guy a picture. That's a hoot isn't it?"

"Yeah. What time are you taking off tomorrow?"

"They're taking us to the rail head bright and early. Seven."

"Geeze, if I had known this was going to happen I don't know if I would have twisted your arm like I did to join up. Can't understand why I'm not going, too. We should be going together."

"Listen Lars, you'll be over there in a month or so. The whole Division will be going. By that time I'll have everything under control, all the hot spots located and I'll take you on a tour.

Out of the Loop

We'll have a ball. Don't sweat it. When you gotta go, you gotta go! That's all there is to it. I'll probably have a sleeve full of stripes before you even get on the boat to go."

"Yeah, but I'm gonna miss your smiling face. Be careful over there. Don't volunteer for anything except KP. That will keep you safe enough if the food doesn't kill you."

"Yeah. Gotta go. Have to turn in, get some sleep. Won't be seeing you tomorrow."

"Bye, Ben. Write when you get there?"

"Sure."

That was almost as bad as saying good-bye to Maddy and the folks.

ThirtyTwo

Train left at eight-fifteen. On the way to the coast we see farms, orchards, forests, hills, rivers, streams, lakes, cities, towns, mountains, deserts -- our country is a kaleidoscope of constantly changing scenery. Every hour produces something different and beautiful to see. Wish I had a camera. Wish Maddy was with me to see it.

When I get home again I'm going to buy a car and travel. I'm going to travel with Maddy and hopefully a car full of kids. Our kids, mine and Maddy's. What a beautiful, country God gave us to live in.

Didn't stay long on the coast. Flew to Japan and then on to Korea.

Dan Glaubke

I've been placed in a Reconnaissance Company of the U.S. 2nd Division. I figure my I&R training put me here. On my first day spent an hour listening to a lecture about Korea, why we're here, what we're up against. Spent a week learning about what our Recon Company does, what things I'll be doing as an observer, what to be aware of when we're out on a mission, etcetera, etcetera.

Now, nine days after getting here, I'm going on a mission. "Okay guys, gather around." Lt. Crosby tells us as he lays a map on the hood of his Jeep.

There are nine of us, including the Lieutenant.

"Listen up. We're right here." He says it as he points to the map, " Sparks saw some activity in this area. It's where 'A' Company is supposed to deploy and if the enemy is there the fighting is going to be heavy. For you guys that don't know, Sparks is our head in the clouds, flies our small observation plane. What he saw wasn't much but that's why we're going out there. We have to find out if he's wrong or if he's right, confirm how many bad guys we're looking at. Hopefully, it was his imagination playing tricks and he didn't see anything. 'A' Company is on the road behind us. They've started moving out and we're late getting started."

Then Crosby put an "X" on the map and said, "We'll drive beyond this bend in the road. Park about here. It's five miles away from the point that Sparks made his observation. Then we'll move in this area and follow the general direction of the road. There's better cover doing it this way and we'll have to be alert, because better cover doesn't mean shit here. If we draw fire we'll back off a little, see if we can determine what the bastards have in place and then get the hell out of there as fast as we can and let 'A' Company do their job. That's the mission. Any questions?"

Sergeant Wynne piped up then and said, "Sir, I think it would be better to park the Jeeps before that bend in the road. Beyond the bend, there are hills and the high ground is an ideal spot to deploy for an ambush."

"I know that Sergeant, but Sparks didn't see a soul in that area. We need to get further up the road before we put boots on the ground. Okay? Mount up and lets get going. We're late."

"This is it." I say to myself, getting in the back seat of the second Jeep. Then we moved out and down the road. It's a cold day. Really cold. As cold as any day I can remember growing up. Like one of those days before Christmas when I walked with Dad down to Cicero Avenue to buy a tree.

Lt. Crosby, is in the first Jeep along with his driver and radio man. I'm riding with two combat-tested men. Sgt. Wynne is in the third Jeep, he's a combat-hardened vet of World-War II. The two guys riding with him are like me, new to Korea. As we creep along, Lt. Crosby keeps checking his map and suddenly the bend in the road is just up ahead. At that moment, Crosby signals the Jeeps to stop and cut engines. We sit there for a minute, listening. You can sense that Crosby isn't keen about driving around the bend, he knows Wynne is right about the danger of the terrain, but Sparks said it was clean. Crosby signals the Jeeps to start up again and move out once more. His lead Jeep didn't travel more than a hundred yards beyond the bend when it happened.

Lt. Crosby, and the men with him are no more. One deafening explosion has completely obliterated the Jeep and men in it. There's machine gun fire now and mortars exploding.

*****

285

Dan Glaubke

When the Jeep in front blew, Ben's reaction was quick and instinctive. He stood straight up in the back seat, turned to leap to safety and in midair was hit by a shell that made him flip, produced an aerial somersault. He landed on his butt, sitting straight up in a ditch minus his right arm. He knew he was hit bad, blood was everywhere. He didn't know his arm was gone, but it didn't matter. As he sat there in a daze, in shock, he started to mumble... "I believe in God the Father ... All Mighty ... Maker of Heaven ... and Earth ... and in Jesus ... Christ His ... only Son. ... Our Lord..."

Thirty Three

Ben was buried in Mt. Olive Cemetery. In addition to his Dad, Mom, Grandfather, aunts, uncles, cousins, and a few neighbors; Bob, Nita, Mike and Ricky were there. And Maddy.

Maddy was numb. Not understanding. Not wanting to understand. Numb. Not responding to any comforting and concern. Vacant. It was as her heart, mind, body and soul had closed down, waiting, wanting something, anything to cling to, that would tell her, "It wasn't true." Telling her that Ben wasn't in that box, he couldn't be. Her tears had dried up long ago. Long days ago. Sometime after Mom Tepke had called with the words she had refused to believe.

Less than a month ago, Ben had been home and said his good-byes. Less than a month ago, Ben had kissed her, held her, told her how much he loved her.

After Ben was put to rest, Alfred Tepke took all that were gathered to a restaurant. He said he didn't want his home filled with unhappiness and gloom. There was much unhappiness and gloom stalking those that mourned anyway and the words spoken by Pastor Olson at the grave site didn't do much to comfort loved ones or soften the mood of the day.

Ben was no hero. At nineteen years of age he was just one of 54,000 other young Americans who were to die in Korea. Who knows what might have been if these men had lived. Who knows what would have happened in Ben's life. Would he have married Maddy and lived happily ever after? Would he have gone to college or found a meaningful job. There are no easy answers to these questions. No answers at all.

After the funeral, Ben's Dad went back to working long hours wondering why he had lost his son. His Mom did much of the same routines a wife goes through doing her daily housekeeping chores. Only many times during the day, some tears flowed now as she passed reminders of her lost son that still lingered in the house. A few months after Ben was killed, his grandfather passed away. Then Ben's Dad sold the family bungalow on the northwest side and moved out of Chicago into the western suburbs. It helped old family memories dim somewhat.

Epilogue

Lars and the 43rd Division never went to Korea. They went to Germany. The unit was the last of the World War II occupation troops and one of the first divisions of the NATO command in Europe. Lars met and married a German girl from Augsburg, Germany, while stationed there. He served his two years plus a three month extension and was honorably discharged. He was offered a commission to reenlist, having attained the rank of master sergeant, but gracefully declined. Then he followed in his father's footsteps and became a successful carpenter contractor and eventually bought a home in the north shore suburbs of Chicago. He worked hard and long hours to support his wife and six kids.

Bob and Nita graduated from Augustana College, married and had four children, two boys and two girls. Using all his mechanical skills and business abilities, Bob became the president of a manufacturing company in Ohio.

Ricky never married. Never graduated from college. Works with his dad selling insurance and does very well. He still lives with his folks.

Mike became more and more entrenched in his electrical union and wound up its president. He married and had two children and continues to live on the northwest side.

Betsy married an airline pilot she met in the airport on her way to Florida in her junior year. She was on spring break, and there he was. One handsome guy in a tailored uniform with an unforgettable smile. He was fascinated by her eyes and everything else about her, too. After Betsy graduated from the U of I, they tied the knot, moved to Tampa and had one daughter.

Two years after Ben was buried, almost to the day, Maddy married a man that she had met in church, a young minister destined to have his own church in a small town in Iowa. Two years after her marriage she gave birth to a baby boy.

The boy was named Ben.

Out of the Loop

About the author

Dan Glaubke grew up on the northwest side of Chicago. After high school he joined the U.S. Army during the Korean War.

He graduated from U.S. Army Intelligence School, Ft. Riley, Kansas, served overseas in Germany for sixteen months and was honorably discharged in January of 1953.

His professional life includes being a copywriter for The Buchen Company, and Fensholt Incorporated, both business-to- business advertising agencies.

He served as Creative Director, President and Chief Executive Officer of Fensholt from 1974 to 1995. "*Out of the Loop*" is his first novel. Dan's been happily married for 53 years and resides with his wife Bonnie in Huntley, Illinois. They were Blessed with three wonderful children (who are happily married) and have six beautiful grandchildren.